D1736224

Greek Antiquity
in Schiller's *Wallenstein*

University of North Carolina Studies in the Germanic Languages and Literatures

Initiated by RICHARD JENTE (1949–1952), *established by* F. E. COENEN (1952–1968), *continued by* SIEGFRIED MEWS (1968–1980)

ALICE A. KUZNIAR and RICHARD H. LAWSON, Editors

Publication Committee: Department of Germanic Languages

For other volumes in the "Studies" see pages 153–54.

Number One Hundred and Four
University of
North Carolina
Studies in the
Germanic Languages
and Literatures

Greek Antiquity
in Schiller's *Wallenstein*

by Gisela N. Berns

The University of North Carolina Press
Chapel Hill and London 1985

Library of Congress Cataloging in Publication Data

Berns, Gisela N.
  Greek antiquity in Schiller's Wallenstein
  (University of North Carolina studies in the Germanic
  languages and literatures; no. 104)
  Bibliography: p.
  Includes index.
  1. Schiller, Friedrich, 1759–1805. Wallenstein.
2. Schiller, Friedrich, 1759–1805—Knowledge—Literature.
3. Greek literature—History and criticism. I. Schiller,
Friedrich, 1759–1805. Wallenstein. II. Title.
III. Series.
PT2468.W8B47   1985   832'.6   85-1112

ISBN 0-8078-8105-8

To Laurence and Anna,
my family

and to America,
my new country

Contents

Acknowledgments

I wish to express my warmest thanks to Kathryn Kinzer, librarian at St. John's College, Annapolis, Maryland, whose cheerful and dauntless efforts provided me with Schiller literature from libraries all over the country. Without her help, this book would have been much more difficult to complete.

To Mera Flaumenhaft, George Anastaplo, Harvey Lomax, and Laurence Berns, who took the trouble of reading the manuscript and giving me many valuable suggestions ranging from matters of style to matters of substance, I offer my heartfelt thanks.

I would like to thank Leslie Lewis, my student and typist, for her dedication and precision in carrying out a difficult and unfamiliar task.

My thanks also to the Schillerarchiv in Marbach am Neckar, Germany, for its hospitality during the summers of 1979 and 1982.

For the genuine encouragement and constructive criticism I received from Richard Lawson and Alice Kuzniar, my editors, and from Helmut Koopmann and Wolfgang Paulsen, my official readers, I am deeply grateful.

To Hertha Hartmann whose exacting questions guided my first reading of Schiller's *Wallenstein* I owe more than I can easily put into words. She gave me a sense not only of what it means to read but also of what it means to be a teacher. My life has been the richer for her example.

St. John's College   Gisela N. Berns
Annapolis, Maryland

Greek Antiquity
in Schiller's *Wallenstein*

Introduction

Von jeher war Poesie die höchste Angelegenheit meiner Seele,
und ich trennte mich eine Zeit lang bloß von ihr, um reicher und
würdiger zu ihr zurückzukehren. In der Poesie endigen alle Bahnen
des menschlichen Geistes und desto schlimmer für ihn, wenn er sie
nicht bis zu diesem Ziele zu führen den Mut hat.
  Die höchste Philosophie endigt in einer poetischen Idee, so die
höchste Moralität, die höchste Politik. Der dichterische Geist ist es,
der allen Dreien das Ideal vorzeichnet, welchem sich anzunähern
ihre höchste Vollkommenheit ist.

(Schiller to C. v. Schimmelmann, 1795)

In his *Briefe über die aesthetische Erziehung des Menschen* Schiller
sketches out a history of mankind from a state of nature to a state of
civilization where the progress of the species towards a fulfillment of
human nature depends on the fragmentation of nature in the individual. This view of history is complemented, however, by Schiller's
hope that the totality of our nature destroyed by art in the process of
civilization might be restored by a higher art.[1]
  In his *Über naive und sentimentalische Dichtung*, a discussion of poetry as *one* representative form of art, Schiller distinguishes between
two types of poetry expressive of two states of mankind: naive poetry as expression of a union, sentimental poetry as expression of a
separation between man and nature. In the first state, still being
nature, the poet imitates reality and thus preserves nature. In the
second state, now seeking nature, the poet presents the ideal and
thus avenges nature. Both types of poetry, in different ways, show a
perfection of art: naive poetry in fulfilling a finite goal, sentimental
poetry in striving for an infinite goal.[2]
  Schiller's poetic ideal to "give mankind its fullest expression possible" implies a union of naive and sentimental poetry, the one providing individuality, the other ideality. In the first version of *Über
naive und sentimentalische Dichtung* Schiller considers the possibility
and the degree of such a union in one and the same work of art "the
most important question in all philosophy of art." Under the regulative assumption of the presentability of the ideal, he sees it as the

greatest challenge for the modern poet to "individualize the ideal" and to "idealize the individual." The fulfillment of this ideal, of the "union of the old poetic character with the modern," Schiller envisions as the "highest peak of all art."[3] Encompassing naive and sentimental poetry and thus transcending the division between man being nature and man seeking nature, this ideal form of poetry seems to correspond to that higher art which, in his *Über die aesthetische Erziehung des Menschen*, was expected to restore the lost totality of human nature.

As Schiller, only in a footnote, remarks:

> Das Gegenteil der naiven Empfindung ist nämlich der reflektierende Verstand, und die sentimentalische Stimmung ist das Resultat des Bestrebens, *auch unter den Bedingungen der Reflexion* die naive Empfindung, dem Inhalt nach, wieder herzustellen. Dies würde durch das erfüllte Ideal geschehen, in welchem die Kunst der Natur wieder begegnet.[4]

The widening of "sentimental," from a mere constituent of to an equivalent with "ideal," puts into question the status of either term with respect to Schiller's poetic goals.

Together with his earliest reference to *Wallenstein*, Schiller complains about the damaging effect of critical philosophy on his creative powers. At the same time, however, he expects the resulting poetic self-consciousness to lead to a new and higher naturalness of the creative process.[5] Considering *Über naive und sentimentalische Dichtung* "as it were a bridge to poetic production," Schiller claims a special closeness to this work, both for its thought and for its application to himself.[6] In the absence of further explanation, this claim points most directly to Schiller's understanding of himself as a sentimental poet. But whether "sentimental," in this case, is meant in contradistinction to or inclusive of "naive" remains unclear.

At work on his *Über die aesthetische Erziehung des Menschen*, on *Über naive und sentimentalische Dichtung*, and on his plan for *Wallenstein*, Schiller comments on his entering a "completely unknown and never tried path."[7] In similar terms, the *Prolog* to *Wallenstein* announces:

> Die neue Ära, die der Kunst Thaliens
> Auf dieser Bühne heut beginnt, macht auch
> Den Dichter kühn, die alte Bahn verlassend,
> Euch aus des Bürgerlebens engem Kreis
> Auf einen höhern Schauplatz zu versetzen,
> Nicht unwert des erhabenen Moments
> Der Zeit, in dem wir strebend uns bewegen.[8]

This statement points toward the great historical subject matter of the *Wallenstein* trilogy. At the same time, however, it initiates the *Prolog's* dominant theme which concerns the relationship between history and art:

> Und jetzt an des Jahrhunderts ernstem Ende,
> Wo selbst die Wirklichkeit zur Dichtung wird,
> Wo wir den Kampf gewaltiger Naturen
> Um ein bedeutend Ziel vor Augen sehn,
> Und um der Menschheit große Gegenstände,
> Um Herrschaft und um Freiheit wird gerungen,
> Jetzt darf die Kunst auf ihrer Schattenbühne
> Auch höhern Flug versuchen, ja sie muß,
> Soll nicht des Lebens Bühne sie beschämen.[9]

In this higher flight, leaving the old path, the poet takes his cue from the "stage of life" for the "shadow stage of art."

In the ninth letter *Über die aesthetische Erziehung des Menschen*, Schiller advises the artist to take the material for his work from the present, but the form from a nobler time. Due to the difficulties inherent in taking the material for a poetic work directly from the present, the *Prolog* refers back to that "far-off stage of war," which up to Schiller's own time had shaped the political scene in Europe.[10] By linking the present to the past Schiller highlights the historical moment with reflections of human nature caught in permanent patterns of life throughout history. Yet, for the "higher scene of action" to justify the poet's higher flight, it has to match the quality of the historical moment. To present "reality" in such a way that it becomes "poetry," art cannot simply rely on historical material. Understanding poetic figures as symbolic beings which, through historical representations, express the truth of nature,[11] Schiller transcends the narrow limits of historical existence. In compliance with his own advice to the artist he takes the material for his *Wallenstein* from modern history, but the form from his experience with a "better age." Guided by his notion of the poets as avengers of nature, Schiller likens the artist to Agamemnon's son:

> Der Künstler ist zwar der Sohn seiner Zeit, aber schlimm für ihn, wenn er zugleich ihr Zögling oder gar noch ihr Günstling ist. Eine wohltätige Gottheit reiße den Säugling beizeiten von seiner Mutter Brust, nähre ihn mit der Milch eines bessern Alters, und lasse ihn unter fernem griechischen Himmel zur Mündigkeit reifen. Wenn er dann Mann geworden ist, so kehre er, eine fremde Gestalt, in sein Jahrhundert zurück; aber nicht, um es mit seiner

Erscheinung zu erfreuen, sondern furchtbar wie Agamemnons
Sohn, um es zu reinigen.

A contemporary and citizen of more than one world, the artist is
supposed to look on Greek works of art as his models in his effort to
restore the lost dignity of mankind.[12] Though convinced about this
function of Greek art, Schiller in the end suggests that the artist,
true to the "absolute unchanging unity of his being," take the form
for his work "from beyond all time." This qualification, which leaves
the distinction between naive and sentimental behind, seems to support Schiller's hope for a fulfillment of the ideal through a reunion of
art with nature. In his modern striving for the presentation of the
ideal, Schiller is willing to avail himself of the imitation of nature in
Greek works of art and thus to point to the restoration of naive sentiment (as far as content is concerned)[13] even under the conditions of
reflection.

As he formulates the matter in the first version of *Über naive und
sentimentalische Dichtung*:

> Nun entsteht natürlicherweise die Frage (die wichtigste, die
> überhaupt in einer Philosophie der Kunst kann aufgeworfen wer-
> den), ob und in wie fern in demselben Kunstwerke Individualität
> mit Idealität zu vereinigen sei—ob sich also (welches auf eins hin-
> ausläuft) eine Coalition des alten Dichtercharakters mit dem mo-
> dernen gedenken lasse, welche, wenn sie wirklich statt fände, als
> der höchste Gipfel aller Kunst zu betrachten sein würde. Sachver-
> ständige behaupten, daß dieses, in Rücksicht auf bildende Kunst,
> von den Antiken gewissermaßen geleistet sei, indem hier wirklich
> das Individuum ideal sei und das Ideal in einem Individuum *er-
> scheine*. So viel ist indessen gewiß, daß in der Poesie dieser Gipfel
> noch keineswegs erreicht ist; denn hier fehlt noch sehr viel daran,
> daß das vollkommenste Werk, der Form nach, es auch dem In-
> halte nach sei, daß es nicht bloß ein wahres und schönes *Ganze*,
> sondern auch das möglichst *reichste* Ganze sei. Es sei dies aber
> nun erreichbar und erreicht oder nicht, so ist es wenigstens die
> Aufgabe auch in der Dichtkunst, das Ideale zu individualisieren
> und das Individuelle zu idealisieren. Der moderne Dichter *muß*
> sich diese Aufgabe machen, wenn er sich überall nur ein höchstes
> und letztes Ziel seines Strebens gedenken soll.[14]

Seen from this vantage point Schiller's remark about the essay's ap-
plicability to himself might mean a great deal more than is at first
apparent. Alerted to this possibility one might also want to recon-

sider Schiller's statement that none of his old plays has as much purpose and form as *Wallenstein*.[15]

Shortly before the planning stage of *Wallenstein* Schiller vows: "Gelingt es mir die Gunst des Dichtergottes wieder zu gewinnen, so hoffe ich die Spolien, die ich im Reiche der Philosophie und Geschichte zu machen mich beeifert habe, in seinem Tempel aufzuhängen, und mich seinem Dienst auf immerdar zu widmen."[16] Applied to *Wallenstein*, the first major poetic work after years of historical and philosophical studies, this vow of Schiller's allows for more than one reading. "Hanging up the spoils from philosophy and history in the temple of the god of poetry" might mean to forsake philosophy and history for the sake of poetry. Yet when Schiller remarks, "Von jeher war Poesie die höchste Angelegenheit meiner Seele, und ich trennte mich eine Zeit lang bloß von ihr, um reicher und würdiger zu ihr zurückzukehren,"[17] he seems to value history and philosophy as means towards a higher form of poetry. Compared with the role of history, however, the role of philosophy in *Wallenstein* appears to be somewhat tenuous. While Schiller's *Geschichte des dreißigjährigen Krieges* establishes the historical background for the *Wallenstein* trilogy, Schiller's philosophical writings contribute to it only insofar as they raise the specific question about the relationship between ancient and modern poetry in the context of the general question about the relationship between historical and poetic truth. As Hebbel's "Schiller in seinen aesthetischen Aufsätzen" claims: "Unter den Richtern der Form bist Du der erste, der einz'ge, / Der das Gesetz, das er gibt, gleich schon im Geben erfüllt."[18] Whether this statement applies only within the philosophical writings or is valid for Schiller's dramatic work as well Hebbel does not specify. Reminiscent of Schiller's own formulation about knowing too well what he wanted and what he ought to do than to make his business any easier,[19] the law Hebbel alludes to might very well apply to the modern poet's task outlined in *Über die aesthetische Erziehung des Menschen* and *Über naive und sentimentalische Dichtung*.

Intent on initiating a reform of the drama, Schiller suggests that the "introduction of symbolic devices" would "displace the common imitation of nature" and thus "provide air and light for art."[20] In his essay *Über das Pathetische* he explains: "Selbst an wirklichen Begebenheiten historischer Personen ist nicht die Existenz, sondern das durch die Existenz kund gewordene Vermögen das Poetische."[21] Using the historical existence of Wallenstein as the basis for his individualization of the ideal and idealization of the individual, Schiller, in the *Prolog* to *Wallenstein*, outlines his poetic proposal:

Von der Parteien Gunst und Haß verwirrt
Schwankt sein Charakterbild in der Geschichte,
Doch euren Augen soll ihn jetzt die Kunst,
Auch eurem Herzen, menschlich näher bringen.
Denn jedes Äußerste führt *sie*, die alles
Begrenzt und bindet, zur Natur zurück.[22]

This notion of the power of art to extend the potency of human nature to its limits, and to define its limits within the framework of nature as a whole, uses "nature" in the sense of the footnote from *Über naive und sentimentalische Dichtung*: art and nature are expected to meet again in the ideal. The means to fulfill the ideal, in specific terms the means to approach the heightened "purpose" and "form" of *Wallenstein*, seem to be none other than the symbolic devices expected to provide air and light for art.

In their pursuit of an ideal form of poetry that would "give mankind its fullest expression possible," Schiller and Goethe, in 1797, discuss the relationship between epic and dramatic poetry. Considering epic and dramatic poetry, in analogy to naive and sentimental poetry, as complementary art forms, both Goethe and Schiller become deeply involved in a discussion of Homer and Greek tragedy.

Given his understanding of naive poetry as imitation and therefore preservation of nature, Schiller is confident that "die Wahrheit lebt in der Täuschung fort, und aus dem Nachbilde wird das Urbild wieder hergestellt werden."[23] Striving for a higher art that would restore the totality of human nature destroyed by art in the process of civilization, Schiller explores the possibility of a fusion of naive and sentimental poetry. Far from imitating either Homer or Greek tragedy, he integrates aspects of both into his modern historical drama about Wallenstein. In accordance with Schiller's understanding of epic and dramatic poetry as complementary art forms, *Wallenstein* echoes both Homer's *Iliad* and Euripides's *Iphigenia in Aulis*, the dramatization of the pregnant moment before the action portrayed in the *Iliad*. Though parallels in the constellations of characters and plots might simply be a result of the theme of War and Peace common to those works, echoes in *Wallenstein* from both Johann Heinrich Voß's translation of the *Iliad* and Schiller's own translation of *Iphigenia in Aulis* invite a more careful comparison. However questionable they may at first appear, remarks of Schiller's about "living in Homer" and "using Euripides" for the formation of his own dramatic style[24] should alert one to the possibility that Schiller's integration of Greek epic and dramatic poetry into his own modern historical drama might essentially connect with his understanding of the relationship between naive and sentimental poetry. Thus *imitation of nature* (in the form of Homeric and Euripidean plots and characters interwoven with the story of the historical Wallenstein) would emerge as an integral part of Schiller's *presentation of the ideal*.

In accordance with the structure of *Wallenstein* and the nature of its three plays, I shall consider Schiller's dramatic poem first in the light of Homer's *Iliad*, then in the light of Euripides's *Iphigenia in Aulis*, and finally in the light of Schiller's own philosophical writings. The comparison between Schiller's *Wallenstein* and both Homer's *Iliad* and Euripides's *Iphigenia in Aulis* follows Schiller's understanding of the complementary nature of epic and dramatic poetry. The application of Schiller's aesthetic theories to his own poetic practice follows his understanding of the complementary nature of naive and sentimental poetry. The poetic affinity between epic and naive as well as between dramatic and sentimental poetry points, finally, to the problematic unity of time and timelessness, one of the dominant themes of Schiller's *Wallenstein*.

Part I. Homer

Unter demselben Blau, über dem nämlichen Grün
Wandeln die nahen und wandeln vereint die fernen Geschlechter,
Und die Sonne Homers, siehe! sie lächelt auch uns.

(Schiller, "Elegie")

I. *History of the Thirty Years' War* and *The Iliad*

The central books of Schiller's *Geschichte des dreißigjährigen Krieges* present the story of the rise and fall of Wallenstein in the service of the Emperor. Framed by an account of the causes and consequences of the war, the story focuses on the confrontation between Wallenstein, the imperial general defending Catholicism, and Gustavus Adolphus, the Swedish king fighting for Protestantism. Still in the planning stage of his historical work, Schiller speculates:

> . . . die Geschichte der Menschheit gehört als unentbehrliche Episode in die Geschichte der Reformation, und diese ist mit dem dreißigjährigen Krieg unzertrennlich verbunden. Es kommt also bloß auf den ordnenden Geist des Dichters an, in einem Heldengedicht, das von der Schlacht bei Leipzig bis zur Schlacht bei Lützen geht, die ganze Geschichte der Menschheit ganz und ungezwungen, und zwar mit weit mehr Interesse zu behandeln, als wenn dies der Hauptstoff gewesen wäre.[1]

As if in answer to this challenge, Schiller's presentation of the rise and fall of Wallenstein, even in his historical account, reminds one time and again of Homer's *Iliad*, the first and foremost epic poem in the Western tradition. Earlier on, while considering an epic poem about Frederick II, Schiller had deliberated:

> Die Haupthandlung müßte wo möglich sehr einfach und wenig verwickelt sein, daß das Ganze immer leicht zu übersehen bliebe, wenn auch die Episoden noch so reichhaltig wären. Ich würde darum immer sein ganzes Leben, und sein Jahrhundert darin anschauen lassen; es gibt hier kein besseres Muster als die Iliade. Homer z.B. macht eine charakteristische Enumeration der alliierten Griechen und der trojanischen Bundesvölker. Wie interessant müßte es sein, die europäischen Hauptnationen, ihr Nationalgepräge, ihre Verfassungen, und in sechs bis acht Versen ihre Geschichte anschauend darzustellen.[2]

In keeping with his view that Homer's *Iliad* can serve as a model for the poet and the historian alike, Schiller presents the historical particulars of the story of Wallenstein in such a way that they shed light on the general history of mankind.

If one compares Schiller's *Geschichte des dreißigjährigen Krieges* with, for instance, Ranke's *Geschichte Wallensteins* or Mann's *Wallenstein: Sein Leben erzählt*, one will see a difference not so much in facts as in presentation. Whereas Ranke reports facts in clipped words that leave no room for fancy, Mann allows for fancy, only to be reduced to facts, as in, "Wir jedoch dienen der Wissenschaft, nicht der Poeterei. Darum ist hier der Ort, die Geschichte von Wallensteins Ruhestand ein wenig aufs Faktische zurückzuführen."[3] As Hellmut Diwald, in his introduction to Ranke's *Geschichte Wallensteins*, remarks, "Wenn Schiller als Wallensteins Homer bezeichnet wurde, so dürfte Ranke als des Friedländers Thukydides gelten."[4] This judgment covers more ground than intended. Schiller's presentation of the rise and fall of Wallenstein, even in his *Geschichte des dreißigjährigen Krieges*, seems to involve a conscious assimilation of Homer. The historical figures and events of the Thirty Years' War, with Wallenstein and the Emperor on one side, and Gustavus Adolphus on the other, seem to fit the poetic panorama of Homer's *Iliad*, where the natural enmity between Achilles, the hero, and Agamemnon, the ruler, almost outweighs the national enmity against Hector, who is at once both hero and ruler.

The distinction of Wallenstein in the service of the Emperor, followed by his dismissal from power, which offends his boundless pride, recalls the role of Achilles under the leadership of Agamemnon, and Achilles's angry withdrawal from battle, following their fateful clash in the assembly.[5] Wallenstein's reception of the Emperor's two envoys who inform him of his dismissal makes one think of Achilles's welcome to Agamemnon's two heralds who request that he surrender Briseis.[6] Wallenstein's retirement to private life and the ostentatious arrogance of his solitude parallel Achilles's staying away from assembly and battle and the stubborn indulgence of his proud heart.[7] Gustavus Adolphus's presentation of his daughter to the Swedish parliament and his solemn departure from the land of his fathers echo Hector's goodbye to wife and child on the wall of Troy.[8] Wallenstein's vindictive joy over Gustavus Adolphus's advances in Germany reads like Achilles's glorying in Hector's breakthrough to the Greek ships.[9] Wallenstein's brooding over his revenge against the Emperor and the Emperor's attempt to regain his services, working through a delegation of friends, recall Achilles's wrath against Agamemnon and Agamemnon's offer of gifts and honors through the embassy of Odysseus, Phoinix, and Ajax.[10]

Schiller's account of the battle of Lützen suggests, in addition to the parallel between Gustavus Adolphus and Hector, a parallel between Gustavus Adolphus and Patroclos. Both Patroclos, in his assault on Troy, and Gustavus Adolphus, in the battle of Lützen, advance too far and are killed by several blows, the main one in the back. Both their dead bodies are fought over furiously till sunset and nightfall. Suspicion of a plot against Gustavus Adolphus by the Duke of Lauenburg, who follows him like an evil demon, makes one think of the hidden force of Apollo, who strikes Patroclos from behind.[11] With a shift of sides, but still in the same context, Pappenheim, saving the battle for the Emperor, is called "der Telamonier des Heeres."[12] Before the walls of Troy, it is Ajax, the son of Telamon, who rescues the body of Patroclos. The end of the battle of Lützen, with its triple attack at sunset and its final rage in fog and night,[13] echoes the end of Patroclos and his defeat by Apollo veiled in dark night. The description of the sorrow felt at the death of Gustavus Adolphus reminds one of the grief, both in Troy and in Achilles's tent, at the meeting between Achilles and Priam.[14]

Besides the allusions to characters and events in Homer's *Iliad*, Schiller's *Geschichte des dreißigjährigen Krieges* refers to comparable causes and circumstances. The abduction of Helen is as controversial a cause for the Trojan War as the "abduction" of Protestantism from Catholicism for the Thirty Years' War,[15] and the calm of winds that delays Agamemnon's Trojan expedition is as ominous a circumstance as the gale of winds that delays Gustavus Adolphus's German expedition.[16]

Schiller's interest in the richness of the historical episodes, for which he finds no better model than the *Iliad*, leads to what Diwald calls Schiller's "Verlebendigung der äußerlichen Geschichtsfakta." Though admiring the "Glanz der Worte" in Schiller's *Geschichte des dreißigjährigen Krieges*, Diwald nevertheless states: "Nein, Schiller war nicht nur deshalb ein großer Historiker, weil er ein großer Dichter war. Die Leuchtkraft des Berichts hat ihm durchaus nicht die Korrektheit des Faktischen ersetzt."[17] Schiller himself, considering history merely a "warehouse" for his imagination, grants his being "but a bad source for a future historian." Yet his claim to a poetic truth at the cost of historical truth in the narrow sense of the word implies the claim to a "first philosophical truth."[18]

Commenting on Schiller as historian, Wilhelm von Humboldt attempts to explain how history can be invested with poetic truth:

Wer, wie Schiller, durch seine innerste Natur aufgefordert war,
die Beherrschung und freiwillige Übereinstimmung des Sinnen-
stoffes durch und mit der Idee aufzusuchen, konnte nicht da zu-
rücktreten, wo sich gerade die reichste Mannigfaltigkeit eines ungeheuren Gebietes eröffnet; wessen beständiges Geschäft es war,
dichtend, den von der Phantasie gebildeten Stoff in eine, Notwendigkeit atmende Form zu gießen, der mußte begierig sein zu versuchen, welche Form, da das Darstellbare es doch nur durch ir-
gend eine Form ist, ein durch die Wirklichkeit gegebener Stoff
erlaubt und verlangt. Das Talent des Geschichtsschreibers ist dem
poetischen und philosophischen nahe verwandt, und bei dem,
welcher keinen Funken dieser beiden in sich trüge, möchte es sehr
bedenklich um den Beruf zum Historiker aussehen. Dies gilt aber
nicht bloß von der Geschichtsschreibung, sondern auch von der
Geschichtsforschung. Schiller pflegte zu behaupten, daß der Ge-
schichtsschreiber, wenn er alles Faktische durch genaues und
gründliches Studium der Quellen in sich aufgenommen habe, nun
dennoch den so gesammelten Stoff erst wieder aus sich heraus
zur Geschichte konstruieren müsse, und hatte darin gewiß vollkommen recht, obgleich allerdings dieser Ausspruch auch gewaltig mißverstanden werden könnte. Eine Tatsache läßt sich ebenso-
wenig zu einer Geschichte, wie die Gesichtszüge eines Menschen
zu einem Bildnis bloß abschreiben. Wie in dem organischen Bau
und dem Seelenausdruck der Gestalt, gibt es in dem Zusammen-
hange selbst einer einfachen Begebenheit eine lebendige Einheit,
und nur von diesem Mittelpunkt aus läßt sie sich auffassen und
darstellen. Auch tritt, man möge es wollen oder nicht, unvermeid-
lich zwischen die Ereignisse und die Darstellung die Auffassung
des Geschichtsschreibers, und der wahre Zusammenhang der Begebenheit wird am sichersten von demjenigen erkannt werden,
der seinen Blick an philosophischer und poetischer Notwendigkeit
geübt hat. Denn auch hier steht die Wirklichkeit mit dem Geist in
geheimnisvollem Bunde.[19]

Seen in the light of this highly revealing analysis, the reminiscences
of Homer's *Iliad* in Schiller's *Geschichte des dreißigjährigen Krieges* seem
to have something to do with a "mysterious bond" between "reality"
and "mind." That he was used to "living in Homer"[20] and valued the
Iliad as a model for the poet and historian alike lends a new key to
the startling *palinode* with which Schiller concludes his account of
Wallenstein's life:

So endigte Wallenstein, in einem Alter von fünfzig Jahren, sein tatenreiches und außerordentliches Leben; durch Ehrgeiz empor-gehoben, durch Ehrsucht gestürzt, bei allen seinen Mängeln noch groß und bewundernswert, unübertrefflich, wenn er Maß gehalten hätte. Die Tugenden des *Herrschers* und *Helden*, Klugheit, Gerechtigkeit, Festigkeit und Mut, ragen in seinem Charakter kolossalisch hervor; aber ihm fehlten die sanftern Tugenden des *Menschen*, die den Helden zieren, und dem Herrscher Liebe erwerben.[21]

Reinterpreting Homer's "Atreus' Sohn, der Herrscher des Volks, und der edle Achilleus,"[22] Schiller endows his Wallenstein with naturally opposed but artistically complementary characteristics. True to his historical sources, yet enriching them with symbolic significance,[23] he presents the heightened complexity of human nature in the course of history as a response to the myth where extreme natures, in archetypal form, contend with one another. Seen from this point of view, the epilogue of the historian leads directly to the prologue of the poet which, through the power of art, promises to bring the character of Wallenstein "auch menschlich" closer to our eyes and our heart.[24]

For his planned epic poem about Frederick II, Schiller considers "a deep study of our time" and "an equally deep study of Homer" the best preparation. Willing to invent a machinery suited for such a task, he states: "Diese Maschinerie aber, die bei einem so modernen Stoffe in einem so *prosaischen* Zeitalter die größte Schwierigkeit zu haben scheint, kann das Interesse in einem hohen Grade erhöhen, wenn sie eben diesem modernen Geiste angepaßt wird."[25] What Schiller means by "machinery" may become clearer if we consider his change of plans. Not afraid of the difficulty arising from the "apparent incompatibility of the epic tone with a contemporary subject matter,"[26] Schiller nevertheless finds Frederick II not inspiring enough to warrant the "gigantic task of idealization." As he muses about the machinery of idealization that would make a historical character suitable for poetry, Schiller decides:

Von den Requisiten, die den epischen Dichter machen, glaube ich alle, eine einzige ausgenommen, zu besitzen: Darstellung, Schwung, Fülle, philosophischen Geist und Anordnung. Nur die Kenntnisse fehlen mir, die ein homerisierender Dichter notwendig brauchte, ein lebendiges Ganze seiner Zeit zu umfassen und dar-zustellen, der allgemeine, über alles sich verbreitende Blick des

Beobachters. Der epische Dichter reicht mit der Welt, die er in sich hat, nicht aus, er muß in keinem gemeinen Grad mit der Welt außer ihm bekannt und bewandert sein. Dies ist, was mir fehlt, aber auch alles, wie ich glaube. Freilich würde ein mehr entlegenes Zeitalter mir diesen Mangel bedecken helfen, aber auch das Interesse des gewählten Stoffes notwendig schwächen.[27]

In his search for a more remote historical subject matter, Schiller views Gustavus Adolphus as the figure in whom "poetic interest" would combine with "national and political interest" and, at the same time, shed light on the history of mankind, the "most noble theme for the epic poet, if it ever could be a theme for a poet."

Finally though, immersed in his *Geschichte des dreißigjährigen Krieges*, Schiller shifts from Gustavus Adolphus, as the hero of an epic, to Wallenstein, as the hero of a dramatic poem:

Ich bin jetzt voll Ungeduld, etwas Poetisches vor die Hand zu nehmen; besonders juckt mir die Feder nach dem *Wallenstein*. Eigentlich ist es doch nur die Kunst selbst, wo ich meine Kräfte fühle, in der Theorie muß ich mich immer mit Prinzipien plagen. Da bin ich bloß ein Dilettant. Aber um der Ausübung selbst willen philosophiere ich gern über die Theorie; die Kritik muß mir jetzt selbst den Schaden ersetzen, den sie mir zugefügt hat—und geschadet hat sie mir in der Tat; denn die Kühnheit, die lebendige Glut, die ich hatte, ehe mir noch eine Regel bekannt war, vermisse ich schon seit mehreren Jahren. Ich *sehe* mich jetzt *erschaffen* und *bilden*, ich beobachte das Spiel der Begeisterung, und meine Einbildungskraft beträgt sich mit minder Freiheit, seitdem sie sich nicht mehr ohne Zeugen weiß. Bin ich aber erst so weit, daß mir *Kunstmäßigkeit* zur *Natur* wird, wie einem wohlgesitteten Menschen die Erziehung, so erhält auch die Phantasie ihre vorige Freiheit zurück, und setzt sich keine andere als freiwillige Schranken.[28]

The allusion he makes here to his study of Kant's critical philosophy is, at the same time, a reference to the initial formation of his own aesthetic theories.

What Schiller states about his creative process can be stated about the resulting creations as well. His conviction that not historical existence itself, but the potential made known through that existence constitutes the poetic substance of a historical subject matter[29] leaves room for modern historical characters to incorporate traits from ancient mythical characters that both extend and interpret them. Looking back on the years when Schiller, in a circle of family and friends, would read every evening from Homer or Greek tragedy, Caroline von Wolzogen speculates, "daß dies Leben und Weben in diesen Urgebilden auch ein Wendepunkt für seinen eigenen Geist wurde, ja auf den *Wallenstein* mächtig einwirkte, ist wohl nicht zu verkennen."[30] Schiller himself, highly gratified by his reading of Aristotle's *Poetics* and Aristotle's judgment about poetry being more philosophical than history, confesses: "Mich hat er [Aristotle] mit meinem *Wallenstein* keineswegs unzufriedener gemacht. Ich fühle, daß ich ihm, den unvertilgbaren Unterschied der neuen von der alten Tragödie abgerechnet, in allen wesentlichen Forderungen Genüge geleistet habe, und leisten werde."[31] With its claim that art "defining and binding everything leads all extremes back to nature," Schiller's *Prolog* to *Wallenstein* reformulates the demand of Aristotle's *Poetics* that poetry deal more with the universal than the particular.

Intent on portraying the universal as well as the particular, Schiller, in his *Wallenstein*, echoes Homer's *Iliad* even more than in his *Geschichte des dreißigjährigen Krieges*. There only episodes, in the vividness of their description, carry Homeric overtones. Here however, the theme of War and Peace common to both works not only polarizes characters and events in a comparable way, but also affects fundamental elements of the poetic structure.

In noteworthy contrast to his *Geschichte des dreißigjährigen Krieges*, Schiller's *Wallenstein*, like Homer's *Iliad*, begins in the middle of the war.[32] Focusing on the conflict between conventional authority and natural leadership, Homer presents the clash between Agamemnon and Achilles, Schiller the enmity between the Emperor and Wallenstein.[33] Both Homer's *Iliad* and Schiller's *Wallenstein*, with the Catalogue of Ships and *Wallensteins Lager*, exhibit the army and its various elements in a set picture.[34] Both Homer's *Iliad* and Schiller's *Wallenstein*, in comparable moments of dramatic suspense, show the most tender human relationship, the love between Hector and Andromache, and that between Max and Thekla, exposed to the harsh reality of war.[35] Both Homer and Schiller, with the Shield of Achilles and the chalice of the banquet at Pilsen, use the detailed description of an artifact to highlight the world view implicit in each work.[36] Both poets invoke the theme of fate in anticipation of how the action will unfold: Homer, in the first book of the *Iliad*, tells of Achilles's meeting with Thetis, and of her visit to Zeus on Olympus; Schiller, in the opening scene of *Wallensteins Tod*, presents Wallenstein concentrating on the long expected moment of conjunction between the planets Venus and Jupiter.[37] In striking contrast to his *Geschichte des dreißig-*

jährigen Krieges, Schiller models the friendship between Wallenstein and Max, the only nonhistorical character in the trilogy, on the friendship between Achilles and Patroclos in Homer's *Iliad*.[38]

Schiller's view that *Wallenstein* satisfies the demands of Aristotle's *Poetics*, "except for the indelible difference between ancient and modern tragedy," calls attention to this very reservation. A detailed comparison of Schiller's *Wallenstein* and Homer's *Iliad* as well as Euripides's *Iphigenia in Aulis*—the dramatization of the pregnant moment before the action portrayed in the *Iliad*—will show that the echoes of Greek epic and tragic poetry, like catalysts in the process of establishing an ideal mode of poetic expression, only tend to accentuate the modernity of Schiller's work.

II. *Wallenstein* and *The Iliad*

Schiller's familiarity with the story and the heroes of the Trojan War goes back to his early years in Ludwigsburg. Later, at the military academy of the Duke of Württemberg, Schiller especially distinguishes himself in Greek.[1] Readings of Vergil's *Aeneid* and Homer's *Iliad* find their first resonances in his translation "Der Sturm auf dem Tyrrhener Meer" and in his poem "Hektors Abschied," which, as an integral part of *Die Räuber*, interprets the love between Karl and Amalia.[2]

In almost all of his plays, but to varying degrees, Schiller employs this method of highlighting his own dramatic poetry with allusions to Homer. Daniel, like Eurycleia recognizing Odysseus, knows Karl Moor by the old scar from days gone by.[3] King Philipp's queen, another muse, welcomes Marquis Posa with lines echoing the invocation to the *Odyssey*:

> . . . Sie haben viele Höfe
> Besucht auf Ihren Reisen, Chevalier;
> Und viele Länder, vieler Menschen Sitte
> Gesehn—[4]

With his statement, "Auch Patroklos ist gestorben / Und war mehr als du," Fiesco interprets the murder of Gianettino in the light of Achilles's revenge against Lycaon.[5] The same scene is the model for Johanna's refusal of Montgomery's plea for life.[6] Her sparing Lionel, on the other hand, recalls the encounter in which Diomedes and Glaucos recognize each other as "guest friends."[7] In all these and other examples, the parallels Schiller draws to Homer exhibit the similarity as well as the dissimilarity between the ancient and the modern poetic works. In Werner Keller's formulation (though with reference to the relationship between history and drama): "Um den 'Geist' eines historischen Dramas zu erfassen, bedarf es einer Akribie, die sich frei weiß von Stoffhuberei und Parallelenjagd und nicht die Abhängigkeit, sondern vielmehr die Rezeption des Stoffs in der individuellen Konzeption des Dramas erkennt."[8]

Schiller's early readings of Homer must have relied on August Bürger's incomplete translation of the *Iliad* in iambs. By 1788, when Schiller speaks of "reading almost nothing but Homer,"[9] Johann Heinrich Voß had translated the *Odyssey* in hexameters, Friedrich

Stolberg the *Iliad* more or less in prose. Schiller's letters of the time playfully employ Homeric similes and revel in the spirit of the old epic poems.[10] With poetic statements such as "Lang, eh die Weisen ihren Ausspruch wagen, / Löst eine Ilias des Schicksals Rätselfragen / Der jugendlichen Vorwelt auf,"[11] Schiller openly expresses his admiration for Homer. In a contest with Bürger about the meter best suited for a translation of Vergil's *Aeneid*, Schiller chooses the lighter eight-line stanza over the heavier hexameter.[12] His translation "Die Zerstörung von Troja," completed during the work on his *Geschichte des dreißigjährigen Krieges*, is an exercise in transformation as well as in translation. As such—notwithstanding the differences between myth and history—it is a preparation for *Wallenstein*.

While at work on his aesthetic writings and on the plan for *Wallenstein*, Schiller requests Johann Heinrich Voß's new translation of Homer's *Iliad*. His use of this first complete translation in hexameters, which surpassed all previous ones in accuracy and poetic flow, is confirmed in Friedrich von Hoven's remark: "Von Voß war er ein großer Verehrer. Seine Übersetzung Homers, die damals erschienen war, und die er in meiner Gegenwart erhielt, machte ihm große Freude. Beinahe alle Abende las er daraus vor, und pries wechselsweise das Original und die Übersetzung."[13] Schiller's admiration for Voß and his work suggests that a comparison between Schiller's *Wallenstein* and Homer's *Iliad* should rest on Voß's translation rather than on the original text.

The *Prolog* to Schiller's *Wallenstein*, which stands apart from the dramatic poem, and the opening of Homer's *Iliad*, which is an integral part of the epic poem, paradigmatically illustrate the difference between the two works. Whereas Homer in the first seven lines describes the wrath of Achilles and the fateful clash between Achilles and Agamemnon, Schiller in the *Prolog* discusses the role of art and art's relationship to history and nature. Befitting the ancient epic poem, Homer's description, rich in concrete images, centers on Zeus and the fulfillment of his will; befitting the modern dramatic poem, Schiller's discussion, rich in abstract terms, centers on the phenomenon of the great historical personality.[14]

Schiller's *Prolog* to *Wallenstein*, an introduction to the whole dramatic poem as well as to *Wallensteins Lager*,[15] recognizes both the muse and the poet as responsible for the work of art. In a comparable place, before the Catalogue of Heroes and Ships, Homer lavishly invokes the muse:

Sagt mir jetzt, ihr Musen, olympische Höhen bewohnend,
Göttinnen seid ihr wahrlich und waret bei allem und wißt es,
Unser Wissen ist nichts, wir horchen allein dem Gerüchte:
Welche waren die Fürsten der Danaer und die Gebieter?
Nie vermöcht ich das Volk zu verkündigen oder zu nennen,
Wären mir auch zehn Kehlen zugleich, zehn redende Zungen,
Wär unzerbrechlicher Laut und ein ehernes Herz mir gewähret,
Wenn die olympischen Musen mir nicht, des Aigiserschüttrers
Töchter, die Zahl ansagten, wieviel vor Ilios kamen.

Homer's muse is only asked to *name* the leaders of the Trojan War,
but Schiller's muse, in concert with the poet, is expected to perform
much more:

Ja danket ihrs, daß sie [die Muse] das düstre Bild
Der Wahrheit in das heitre Reich der Kunst
Hinüberspielt, die Täuschung, die sie schafft,
Aufrichtig selbst zerstört und ihren Schein
Der Wahrheit nicht betrüglich unterschiebt,
Ernst ist das Leben, heiter ist die Kunst.[16]

In accord with Schiller's request that the poet distance himself from
reality and call attention to his doing so,[17] the muse—another name
for the poet's imagination—is here expected to present the extremi-
ties of life within the boundaries of nature and thus, by transforming
historical into poetic truth, to represent life in art. Promising to unfold the great subject matter in a series of pictures only, the last part
of the *Prolog* prepares the audience for the encounter with Wallenstein's "shadow image," presented on the "shadow stage of art" vying with the "stage of life."[18]

As a still-life display of the army, which the *Prolog* openly blames
for Wallenstein's crime, *Wallensteins Lager* reads like the modern rep-
lica of a passage in Homer's Catalogue of Heroes and Ships:

Aber er, bei den schnellen gebogenen Schiffen des Meeres,
Ruhete, zürnend im Geist dem Hirten des Volks Agamemnon,
Atreus' Sohn; und die Völker am wogenden Strande des Meeres
Freuten sich, mit Scheiben und Jägerspießen zu schleudern,
Und mit Geschoß. Auch standen an jeglichem Wagen die Rosse
Müßig, den Lotos rupfend und sumpfentsprossenen Eppich;
Aber die Wagen, umhüllt mit Teppichen, standen den Herrschern
In den Zelten: sie selber, den streitbaren Führer vermissend,
Wandelten hier im Lager und dort und mieden das Schlachtfeld.[19]

Even before he wrote his historical account of the Thirty Years' War, Schiller had judged Homer's "characteristic enumeration of the allied Greeks and Trojan confederates" the best model for a representative account of a given historical age.[20] From the peasant's corrupt dealing with the soldiers (sc.1), to the Sergeant's arbitration among soldiers discussing the war (sc.6), to the final display of all the types of soldiers in the camp (sc.11),[21] the series of scenes in *Wallensteins Lager* presents itself not unlike a common, and therefore comical, version of book II of the *Iliad*, which moves from the uproar in the assembly caused by Thersites to the conversation among Odysseus, Agamemnon, and Nestor about the war and, finally, to the Catalogue of Heroes and Ships. Yet where the Catalogue of Ships, preceded by an invocation to the muse, merely lists the leaders of the Trojan War, *Wallensteins Lager* depicts the dissolution of life in the state of war which, as a state of nature in the midst of the state of society, debases all human values. The figure of the Sergeant dominating the stage with his baton appears to be a base version of Agamemnon, with his scepter wrought by Hephaistos, bestowed by Zeus on a succession of mortal kings, and used by Odysseus to beat Thersites.[22] Continuing this train of associations, the Capuchin Friar's violent sermon against Wallenstein echoes Thersites's vile railing against Agamemnon as leader of the Trojan War.[23] Reminiscent of the Homeric Nestor posturing as father of the army, the Sergeant even serves as a mock shadow image of Wallenstein.

The grotesqueness of the chaotic, yet static scenes of *Wallensteins Lager*, accentuated by the Homeric overtones, largely stems from the discrepancy between the play's character-types and its themes. War and peace, freedom and dominion, nature and convention, the universal themes of Schiller's *Wallenstein*, loudly resound throughout the rough-and-tumble exchanges among the soldiers who fancy themselves in the role of deciding the fate of the world. The modern touch of this poetic tour de force, to have commoners discuss matters of such universal consequence, heightens its comic effect. *Wallensteins Lager*, especially with its stylized doggerel verse, seems to be a perfect example of Schiller's notion of comedy: ". . . überall mehr Zufall als Schicksal zu finden, und mehr über Ungereimtheit zu lachen als über Bosheit zu zürnen oder zu weinen."[24]

Portrayed on a common level in *Wallensteins Lager*, the conflict between nature and convention reappears on a higher level in *Die Piccolomini*. The discussion between Max, speaking for the natural leadership of Wallenstein, and Octavio, speaking for the conventional authority of the Emperor, moves Questenberg to exclaim: "O! hören

Sie den Vater—hören Sie / *Ihn*, der ein Held ist und ein Mensch zugleich." This exclamation, with the terms "Held" and "Mensch," seems to refer back to Schiller's final portrait of Wallenstein in his *Geschichte des dreißigjährigen Krieges*: "Die Tugenden des *Herrschers* und *Helden*, Klugheit, Gerechtigkeit, Festigkeit und Mut, ragen in seinem Charakter kolossalisch hervor; aber ihm fehlten die sanftern Tugenden des *Menschen*, die den Helden zieren, und dem Herrscher Liebe erwerben."[25] With the watchwords "Herrscher" und "Held," echoing Homer's "Atreus' Sohn, der Herrscher des Volks und der edle Achilleus," Schiller draws attention to the naturally opposed, but artistically complementary aspects of Wallenstein's character. Questenberg's implicit reference to Wallenstein, in calling Octavio "Held und Mensch zugleich," makes one wonder whether the dramatic poem meant to bring Wallenstein "menschlich" closer to us, with its last line, "Dem *Fürsten* Piccolomini,"[26] does not strike a balance between the heroic suffering of both Wallenstein and Octavio, the one to die as "Mensch," the other to live as "Herrscher." In drawing attention to the positive and negative aspects of mythical simplicity and historical complexity alike, the traces of the archetypal figures of Homer's *Iliad* within Schiller's *Wallenstein* contribute to the "symbolic extension"[27] of the modern dramatic characters.

The reference to Octavio as "Held" and "Mensch" introduces another series of Homeric overtones crucial for the understanding of Wallenstein's political entourage. Octavio's presentation of Buttler and Isolani as "Stärke" and "Schnelligkeit" recalls the Homeric pair of Ajax, son of Telamon, known for his strength, and Ajax, son of Oileus, known for his speed. Questenberg's recognition of Octavio as "Erfahrner Rat" between Buttler and Isolani alludes to the Homeric Odysseus, known for his experience and versatility.[28] Comparable to Odysseus who, in successive games at Patroclos's funeral, only ties Ajax, the son of Telamon, but with the help of Athena defeats Ajax, the son of Oileus, Octavio—in successive scenes of *Wallensteins Tod*—wins an easy game over Isolani, but in the end pays bitterly for his victory over Buttler.[29]

Continuing the parallel with the Achilles line in Homer's *Iliad*, Questenberg's mission from the Emperor to Wallenstein recasts the embassy of Odysseus, Phoinix, and Ajax from Agamemnon to Achilles.[30] Like Odysseus, Octavio supports Questenberg in his diplomatic game of speaking for the conventional authority without openly condemning the rebel power; like Phoinix, Questenberg invokes examples from the past in order to reconcile the offended parties; like Ajax, Buttler appeals to valor and decency in his call for equity on both sides; like Achilles, Wallenstein only vows resignation. That both Agamemnon's embassy and Questenberg's mission fail is crucial, for in each case the failure of diplomacy sparks the beginning of dramatic events which, in the end, turn the tide against the protagonist—in the one instance, Achilles, in the other, Wallenstein.

In a comment on the broad exposition of *Die Piccolomini* (acts I and II), Schiller remarks, "es kommt mir vor, als ob mich ein gewisser epischer Geist angewandelt habe," and concludes: "So habe ich diesen ruhigen Anfang dazu benutzt, die Welt und das Allgemeine, worauf sich die Handlung bezieht, zu meinem eigentlichen Gegenstand zu machen."[31] Whether, in this connection, he did think of Homer's epic poetry Schiller never openly states. As to the epic breadth of *Wallenstein*, and the tendency of his characters to speak a great deal, he later explains:

> Aber das Beispiel der Alten, welche es auch so gehalten haben und in demjenigen was Aristoteles die Gesinnungen und Meinungen nennt, gar nicht wortkarg gewesen sind, scheint auf ein höheres poetisches Gesetz hinzudeuten, welches eben hierin eine Abweichung von der Wirklichkeit fordert. Sobald man sich erinnert, daß alle poetischen Personen symbolische Wesen sind, daß sie, als poetische Gestalten, immer das Allgemeine der Menschheit darzustellen und auszusprechen haben, und sobald man ferner daran denkt, daß der Dichter so wie der Künstler überhaupt auf eine öffentliche und ehrliche Art von der Wirklichkeit sich entfernen und daran erinnern soll, daß ers tut, so ist gegen diesen Gebrauch nichts zu sagen.[32]

Schiller's distancing himself from reality becomes clearest in the figure of Max. Deviating drastically from his *Geschichte des dreißigjährigen Krieges*, Schiller models the friendship between Wallenstein and Max, the only nonhistorical character in the play,[33] on the friendship between Achilles and Patroclos in Homer's *Iliad*. Like Achilles's friend Patroclos, singled out by Homer's personal address, Wallenstein's friend Max holds a special place in Schiller's heart.[34] Like Patroclos, waiting out Achilles's wrath, Max is mentioned early in a foreboding way during Buttler's condemning report about Gallas.[35] Similarly, Max's declaration of his love for Wallenstein occurs between Terzky's entry with bad news, and the reminder to attend the assembly that, in the end, will provide the basis for Wallenstein's treason.[36] But where Patroclos, through book IX of the *Iliad*, appears only as faithful follower and silent companion of Achilles, Max, like

Buttler earlier, defends Wallenstein before Questenberg and Octavio.[37] Max's belief that the one superior by nature should not be subject to the one superior only by convention moves him to openly oppose Wallenstein's resignation from the army. The sense of responsibility expressed in Max's move and his decision to take the initiative where Patroclos only waits for orders accentuate the modern self-consciousness of Schiller's dramatic character.[38]

In accordance with Schiller's practice of blending Homeric roles, Max is primarily modeled on Patroclos, yet in the central act of *Die Piccolomini* and, therefore, of *Wallenstein* as a whole, he reminds one more of Hector.[39] (By contrast, in Schiller's *Geschichte des dreißigjährigen Krieges*, Gustavus Adolphus is primarily modeled on Hector, yet in the account of his death he reminds one more of Patroclos.) On his return from the battlefield, eager to have the women implore Athena with prayers, Hector first meets Hekabe, his mother, then Helen, Paris's lover, and finally, after missing her at home, Andromache, his wife, with their infant son, who are witnessing the battle from the walls of Troy. The placement of Helen, the cause of the war, between Hekabe and Andromache painfully points to the frailty of human relationships, and to the difficulty of separating the private from the public sphere. Like Hector and Andromache, Max and Thekla have to overcome obstacles to find each other. In order to meet with Thekla, Max must agree to the manipulative terms of Countess Terzky. Max's account of his visit to the church and of his being moved by the image of the Virgin Mary recalls Hector's concern about the prayer to Athena. Max's wait for Thekla and his earlier shock at seeing her adorned with jewels repeats Hector's search for Andromache and their child's terror at the sight of Hector's glittering helmet.

Once before, in *Die Räuber*, Schiller incorporated "Hektors Abschied"[40] into the poetic structure of his own work. More subtle now, Schiller's allusion to this favorite Homeric scene of his highlights the "poetically most important" part of *Wallenstein*.[41] As in *Die Räuber*, Schiller's transposition of the Homeric scene contains an intrinsic commentary. Where Homer, in the parting of Hector from wife and child, focuses on the conflict between family and society, Schiller, in the love scenes between Max and Thekla, focuses on the conflict between individuals and society. For Andromache, family life is of the utmost value:

Hektor, siehe, du bist mir Vater jetzt und auch Mutter
Und mein Bruder allein, o du mein blühender Gatte!

Aber erbarme dich nun und bleib allhier auf dem Turme!
Mach nicht zur Waise das Kind und zur Witwe die Gattin!

Thekla, however, refuses to play the role of Wallenstein's daughter as
she begins to recognize her autonomy as an individual:

Ernst liegt das Leben vor der ernsten Seele.
Daß ich mir selbst gehöre, weiß ich nun.
Den festen Willen hab ich kennenlernen,
Den unbezwinglichen, in meiner Brust,
Und an das Höchste kann ich alles setzen.[42]

In a monologue fraught with premonitions of doom Thekla finally
asks:

So ists denn wahr? Wir haben keinen Freund
Und keine treue Seele hier—wir haben
Nichts als uns selbst.

Founded on nothing but their "heart,"[43] another form of Kant's
Moral Law,[44] love creates an island of freedom in the sea of historical
necessity. Full of regret over its loss, Max confesses:

Auf einer Insel in des Äthers Höhn
Hab ich gelebt in diesen letzten Tagen,
Sie hat sich auf die Erd herabgelassen,
Und diese Brücke, die zum alten Leben
Zurück mich bringt, trennt mich von meinem Himmel.

But Thekla, more sober, warns:

Laß nicht zu viel uns an die Menschen glauben,
Wir wollen diesen Terzkys dankbar sein
Für jede Gunst, doch ihnen auch nicht mehr
Vertrauen, als sie würdig sind, und uns
Im übrigen—auf unser Herz verlassen.[45]

While the presence of Helen, luring Paris into adultery, implies the
interference of nature with the life of family and city, the presence of
Countess Terzky, plotting political connections between the houses
of Friedland and Piccolomini, implies the interference of history with
the life of individuals.

   History rather than nature is evoked again in the presentation of
the golden chalice used during the banquet at Pilsen. Like Homer's
Shield of Achilles, described in great detail, Schiller's chalice reflects
the world view implicit in the poetic work.[46] While the scenes on the

shield depict human life within the timeless order of nature and, therefore, are self-explanatory, the scenes on the chalice require an explanation not only for their reference to a specific moment in human history, but also for their allegorical representation of that moment. As artifacts, used for dramatic suspense, both shield and chalice have a deeper significance. The completion of the shield marks Achilles's return to his political community, while the presentation of the chalice signals Wallenstein's turning away from his.

Together with a report on sketching out a detailed scenario for *Wallenstein*, and thinking about his own task in connection with Greek tragedy, Schiller relates to Goethe how much his recent reading of Sophocles's *Philoctetes* impressed him with its exhausting the "particular case" for the expression of the "eternal ground of human nature."[47] In accordance with Schiller's problematic ideal of a union between ancient and modern poetry, the conversation between Odysseus and Neoptolemos at the beginning of Sophocles's *Philoctetes* provides a mythical horizon for the painful scenes between Octavio and Max at the end of *Die Piccolomini*.[48] Octavio's plan to wrest the army from Wallenstein, and Odysseus's plan to capture the bow of Philoctetes are equally loathsome to Max and Neoptolemos. Max's vision of Wallenstein as the only one able to bring peace to Europe reflects the mythical figure of Philoctetes, whose bow will be instrumental in ending the Trojan War.[49]

The parallels linking Octavio and Max in Schiller's *Wallenstein* with Odysseus and Neoptolemos in Sophocles's *Philoctetes* are the more interesting as they raise the question of the mutual compatibility of epic and dramatic elements in Schiller's dramatic poem. The series of events involving Max more or less parallels the plot of Sophocles's *Philoctetes*.[50] Interwoven with other events, however, and portraying characters more complex than their ancient counterparts, this series leads through a maze of poetic implications. While Neoptolemos, by nature, is Achilles's son, Max, by choice, wants to become Wallenstein's son (Wallenstein in the place of the Homeric Achilles).[51] While Odysseus, with conventional authority, bids Neoptolemos to capture the bow of Philoctetes, Octavio, with natural as well as conventional authority, begs Max to follow him in his effort to wrest the army from Wallenstein (Wallenstein in the place of the Sophoclean Philoctetes). While Neoptolemos, before the intervention of the deus ex machina, resolves the conflict in agreement with his nature, Max, in his death reminiscent of Wallenstein's dream before the battle at Lützen,[52] follows both his nature and his choice. True to the conventional authority, he follows his nature. True to the idea of friendship, a middle ground between a natural and a conventional bond, he follows his choice. Conscious of the enormity of the conflict in question, Max describes the impending fall of Wallenstein with a Homeric simile:

> Denn dieser Königliche, wenn er fällt,
> Wird eine Welt im Sturze mit sich reißen,
> Und wie ein Schiff, das mitten auf dem Weltmeer
> In Brand gerät mit einem Mal, und berstend
> Auffliegt, und alle Mannschaft, die es trug,
> Ausschüttet plötzlich zwischen Meer und Himmel,
> Wird er uns alle, die wir an sein Glück
> Befestigt sind, in seinen Fall hinabziehn.[53]

Max's resolve to fulfill duty and friendship alike blends the roles of both Neoptolemos in Sophocles's *Philoctetes* and Patroclos in Homer's *Iliad*. But whereas Neoptolemos is governed by Odysseus and Patroclos by Achilles, Max, responding only to his inner sense of right and wrong, contradicts Wallenstein as well as Octavio and thus is caught in a conflict that no deus ex machina, but only death, can solve.[54] The fact that it is Max's tragic despair which, in the context of Greek epic overtones, evokes Greek tragedy may illustrate Schiller's judgment about Greek epic poetry as unable to sustain the emotional depth of the modern poetic character.

The development of Schiller's *Wallenstein* from the *Prolog* to *Die Piccolomini* parallels the development of Homer's *Iliad* from book I to book IX. Reaching into books II, VI, and XVIII, this sequence of events sketches a parallel to the Homeric Achilles line. In accordance with Schiller's view of the last play as the true tragedy of his dramatic poem,[55] a second and much fuller parallel begins with *Wallensteins Tod*.

The opening of *Wallensteins Tod*, Wallenstein's observation of the heavenly conjunction between the planets Venus and Jupiter, corresponds to the second half of book I of the *Iliad*, in which Achilles calls upon Thetis, and Thetis meets with Zeus on Olympus.[56] The change of perspective from the trust in divine powers, moved by will and fate, to the reliance on heavenly bodies, moving in accordance with universal laws, does not affect the precariousness of either position.[57] Counting too much on a support that distinguishes them from other men, both Wallenstein and Achilles misjudge the world. But whereas Achilles's religious attitude leaves room for alternative explanations, Wallenstein's scientific stance, comprehending everything in terms of cosmic laws, makes him much more vulnerable. Wallenstein's reaction to the capture of Sesina with his repeated "es ist ein böser Zufall"[58] points to the insufficiency of a position that tries to explain human as well as natural events in terms of necessity.

The dominant theme of Wallenstein's great monologue, his reflection on freedom and necessity in human nature, corresponds to Achilles's song about the glorious deeds of men:

> Als sie die Zelt' und Schiffe der Myrmidonen erreichten,
> Fanden sie ihn, erfreuend sein Herz mit der klingenden Leier,
> Schön und künstlich gewölbt, woran ein silberner Steg war,
> Die aus der Beut' er gewählt, da Eetions Stadt er vertilget;
> Hiermit erfreut' er sein Herz und sang Siegstaten der Männer.
> Gegen ihn saß Patroklos allein und harrete schweigend
> Dort auf Aiakos' Enkel, bis seinen Gesang er vollendet.

While Achilles, in the company of Patroclos, presents a living example of tradition, his restful repose expressing the harmony of his song, Wallenstein, in a monologue on the dubious bond between freedom and necessity, questions the phenomenon of tradition, his restless stopping and starting expressing the disharmony of his reflective state of mind.[59]

Just as the embassy of Odysseus, Phoinix, and Ajax, in their attempts to convince Achilles, spells out the implications of Achilles's song, so the conversations with Wrangel, with Illo and Terzky, and finally with the Countess, explicate the sections on freedom, on necessity, and on tradition that constitute Wallenstein's monologue.[60] But where the progression from the slippery tongue of Odysseus to the stout heart of Ajax bodes well for the chances of Achilles, the progression from the stout heart of Wrangel to the slippery tongue of the Countess bodes ill for the chances of Wallenstein ever to return to his political community. Comparable to the embassy of Odysseus, Phoinix, and Ajax, which prepares Achilles for his encounter with Patroclos, the exchanges with Wrangel, with Illo and Terzky, and with the Countess prepare Wallenstein for his confrontation with Max.[61] Max's failure to gain admittance before Wallenstein's traitorous decision has been reached weighs as heavily as the delay in Patroclos's return to Achilles because of Eurypylos.[62]

Max's confrontation with Wallenstein, like Patroclos's encounter with Achilles, comes too late to avoid tragedy. Similar in setting and dramatic flow,[63] the two scenes paradigmatically show the difference between Schiller and Homer. Judged to be mere followers of Wallenstein and Achilles respectively, both Max and Patroclos dare to affront their friends with bitter criticism. However, Max envisions a betrayal of ideals:

> Nein, du wirst *so* nicht endigen. Das würde
> Verrufen bei den Menschen jede große
> Natur und jedes mächtige Vermögen,
> Recht geben würd es dem gemeinen Wahn,
> Der nicht an Edles in der Freiheit glaubt,
> Und nur der Ohnmacht sich vertrauen mag.

By contrast, Patroclos simply exclaims:

> Nie doch fülle der Zorn die Seele mir, welchen du hegest,
> Unglücksheld! Wie soll ein Spät'rer sich an dir freuen,
> Wenn du nicht die Argeier vom schmählichen Jammer errettest?[64]

Deeply offended by the conventional authorities, neither Wallenstein nor Achilles is willing to give in. But whereas Wallenstein rejects Max's offer to intercede for him at the Court, Achilles agrees to have Patroclos fight in his stead.[65] Accordingly, while Achilles's prayer to Zeus for the glory and the safe return of Patroclos is partially granted, Wallenstein's trust in Octavio, confirmed by a sign of fate from the World Spirit during the night before the battle at Lützen, is answered by Octavio's assertion, "Denn meines Kalkuls halt ich mich gewiß," and Octavio's own view of the incident at Lützen as merely an insignificant event.[66]

Welcoming the necessity for action after Octavio's betrayal, Wallenstein, in armor, reflects on his inner power:

> Den Schmuck der Zweige habt ihr abgehauen,
> Da steh ich, ein entlaubter Stamm! Doch innen
> Im Marke lebt die schaffende Gewalt,
> Die sprossend eine Welt aus sich geboren.[67]

In a variant text of act II, scene 4, of *Die Piccolomini*, Max speaks of Wallenstein's bounteous powers:

> Ja, unversiegt ist seiner Großmut Quelle,
> Und mir besonders war er gütig stets
> Und herrlich wie ein Gott und unerschöpflich wie
> Das reiche Jahr, die nimmer alternde Sonne.
> Gleich einem guten Acker gibt er nie
> Zurück, wie man ihm gab, es sprosset gleich
> Aus jedem Kern ein königlicher Baum,
> Von jeder Aussaat wallet, körnerschwer,
> Dem Überraschten eine goldne Ernte.[68]

In another variant, the one of act II, scene 7, of *Die Piccolomini*, Buttler warns against a change in command:

Versuchs die Jugend mit der neuen Sonne!
Ists in dem Spätjahr unsers Lebens Zeit,
Neu auszusäen, neu Verdienst zu pflanzen?
Der dürre Stamm treibt keine Sprossen mehr.
Von jenem Vorrat müssen wir jetzt zehren,
Den wir im warmen Sommer unsrer Kraft
Bei dem gerechten Fürsten aufgeschüttet.
Verloren ist uns das vergangne Leben,
Beherrscht uns der nicht mehr, der uns erprobet,
Der Buch gehalten über unser Tun,
Und in sich trägt lebendig, was wir gelten.[69]

Wallenstein's metaphor of the tree trunk, the branches and foliage of which were cut off, recalls Achilles's vow made upon a scepter used in the assembly:

Wahrlich bei diesem Zepter, das niemals Blätter und Zweige
Wieder zeugt, nachdem es den Stamm im Gebirge verlassen;
Nie mehr sproßt es empor, denn ringsum schälte das Erz ihm
Laub und Rinde hinweg, und edele Söhne Achaias
Tragen es jetzt in der Hand, die Richtenden, welchen Kronion
Seine Gesetze vertraut: dies sei dir die hohe Beteurung!
Wahrlich, vermißt wird Achilleus hinfort von den Söhnen Achaias
Allzumal; dann suchst du umsonst, wie sehr du dich härmest,
Rettung, wenn sie in Scharen, vom männermordenden Hektor
Niedergestürzt, hinsterben; und tief in der Seele zernagt dich
Zürnender Gram, daß den besten der Danaer nicht du geehret!
Also sprach der Peleid', und warf auf die Erde das Zepter,
Rings mit goldenen Buckeln geschmückt; dann setzt er sich
    nieder.[70]

This scepter, cut off from its natural source and studded with golden nails, had become a symbol of just power, combining nature and convention as human society combines the good of the individual with the good of the community. Throwing the scepter to the earth where it can neither regain its natural nor retain its conventional power symbolizes that Achilles is neither a part of nor apart from society. Wallenstein, on the other hand, comparing himself to the tree trunk, relies on an inner power to sprout again and create new life. The ground in which Wallenstein, like the tree trunk, is rooted seems to be man's freedom over and against natural necessity.[71] The acknowledgment of natural necessity, together with the claim to freedom—in Schiller's understanding, the Kantian distinction between heteronomy and autonomy—seems to be expressed in another set of passages relating to the night before the battle at Lützen. Speaking to Questenberg, Octavio reports:

> Es war der Morgen vor der Lützner Schlacht—
> Mich trieb ein böser Traum, ihn [Wallenstein] aufzusuchen,
> Ein ander Pferd zur Schlacht ihm anzubieten.
> Fern von den Zelten, unter einem Baum
> Fand ich ihn eingeschlafen.[72]

Speaking to Illo and Terzky, Wallenstein recalls:

> Es gibt im Menschenleben Augenblicke,
> Wo er dem Weltgeist näher ist, als sonst,
> Und eine Frage frei hat an das Schicksal.
> Solch ein Moment wars, als ich in der Nacht,
> Die vor der Lützner Aktion vorher ging,
> Gedankenvoll an einen Baum gelehnt,
> Hinaussah in die Ebene.[73]

Whereas Octavio, convinced of the necessity of man's earthbound actions, speaks of Wallenstein as under a tree (in a level position), Wallenstein, convinced of man's heavenbound reflections, speaks of himself as leaning against a tree (in an upright position). Such a reference to a tree, in Schiller's mind very likely a reference to the tree of the knowledge of good and evil,[74] does not occur in Wallenstein's remembrance of Octavio waking him on the morning of the battle. It does, however, occur in Wallenstein's concluding statement:

> Des Menschen Taten und Gedanken, wißt!
> Sind nicht wie Meeres blind bewegte Wellen.
> Die innre Welt, sein Mikrokosmus, ist
> Der tiefe Schacht, aus dem sie ewig quellen.
> Sie sind notwendig, wie des Baumes Frucht,
> Sie kann der Zufall gaukelnd nicht verwandeln.
> Hab ich des Menschen Kern erst untersucht,
> So weiß ich auch sein Wollen und sein Handeln.[75]

Wallenstein's insistence on freedom, against the background of necessity, in his assertion, "Es ist der Geist, der sich den Körper baut, / Und Friedland wird sein Lager um sich füllen," is refuted immediately by the scene with the Cuirassiers. Achilles's success in arming the Myrmidons to be sent out with Patroclos provides the background for Wallenstein's failure to persuade Max's troops[76] and throws an ominous shadow over Wallenstein's readiness for action. Wallenstein's mistaking one of the soldiers for his older brother credited with having brought a captured Swedish colonel to the camp at Nuremberg, together with the information about his younger brother's service in the Emperor's army,[77] might reflect the fateful polarity of Octavio and Max around Wallenstein himself.

Echoes of the encounter between Patroclos and Achilles, which signals the beginning of Achilles's return to his place in the community, make the parting of Max from Wallenstein and Thekla even more heart-rending.[78] Max's fourfold "ich kann nicht," pitted against a threefold "ich muß," recalls his first reaction to Octavio's report on Wallenstein's treason.[79] Desperate about Wallenstein's lack of humanity, Max exclaims:

> Gleichgültig
> Trittst du das Glück der Deinen in den Staub,
> Der Gott, dem *du* dienst, ist kein Gott der Gnade.
> Wie das gemütlos blinde Element,
> Das furchtbare, mit dem kein Bund zu schließen,
> Folgst du des Herzens wildem Trieb allein.

Equally bitter, Patroclos reproaches Achilles:

> Grausamer! Nicht dein Vater war, ach, der reisige Peleus,
> Noch auch Thetis die Mutter; dich schuf die finstere Meerflut,
> Dich hochstarrende Felsen: denn starr ist dein Herz und
>   gefühllos![80]

But whereas Patroclos pleads for the community, Max, in an illusionary attempt to find a refuge for their hearts, speaks only of Thekla and himself: "Doch wie gerieten *wir*, die nichts verschuldet, / In diesen Kreis des Unglücks und Verbrechens?"[81] Both Max's and Patroclos's similes for their friend's lack of humanity remain within the limits of our world. Wallenstein, on the other hand, comparing himself to a heavenly body, breaks out of those limits:

> Und wenn der Stern, auf dem du lebst und wohnst,
> Aus seinem Gleise tritt, sich brennend wirft
> Auf eine nächste Welt und sie entzündet,
> Du kannst nicht wählen, ob du folgen willst,
> Fort reißt er dich in seines Schwunges Kraft,
> Samt seinem Ring und allen seinen Monden.

As if signing the portrait of Wallenstein with his own initials, Schiller uses the same set of metaphors as in his *Geschichte des dreißigjährigen Krieges*: "Durch keine Beleidigung gereizt, hätte er folgsam seine Bahn um die Majestät des Thrones beschrieben, zufrieden mit dem

Ruhme, der glänzendste seiner Trabanten zu sein; erst nachdem man ihn gewaltsam aus seinem Kreise stieß, verwirrte er das System, dem er angehörte, und stürzte sich zermalmend auf seine Sonne."[82] In striking contrast, Max's initial image of Wallenstein is of a firm pillar of strength:

> Wohl dem Ganzen, findet
> Sich einmal einer, der ein Mittelpunkt
> Für viele tausend wird, ein Halt;—sich hinstellt
> Wie eine feste Säul, an die man sich
> Mit Lust mag schließen und mit Zuversicht.

However, anticipating Max's later disillusionment, the Duchess, with horror, recalls how Wallenstein lost his bearings:

> Denn gleich wie an ein feurig Rad gefesselt,
> Das rastlos eilend, ewig, heftig, treibt,
> Bracht ich ein angstvoll Leben mit ihm zu,
> Und stets an eines Abgrunds jähem Rande
> Sturzdrohend, schwindelnd riß er mich dahin.[83]

Just as Patroclos's encounter with Achilles recasts the embassy of Odysseus, Phoinix, and Ajax in more urgent language, meant to touch and challenge Achilles's heart, so Max's parting from Wallenstein reaps its bitter fruits from their earlier conversation which, in turn, illustrated Wallenstein's first monologue.[84] Both Wallenstein and Phoinix remind their young friends of the fatherly role they have played in the past. In the case of Phoinix, the remembrance is calmly expressed:

> Dich auch macht ich zum Manne, du göttergleicher Achilleus,
> Liebend mit herzlicher Treu; auch wolltest du nimmer mit andern
> Weder zum Gastmahl gehn, noch daheim in den Wohnungen
>   essen,
> Eh ich selber dich nahm, auf meine Knie dich setzend,
> Und die zerschnittene Speise dir reicht und den Becher dir
>   vorhielt.
> Oftmals hast du das Kleid mir vorn am Busen befeuchtet,
> Wein aus dem Munde verschüttend in unbehilflicher Kindheit.
> Also hab ich so manches durchstrebt und so manches erduldet
> Deinethalb; ich bedachte, wie eigene Kinder die Götter
> Mir versagt, und wählte, du göttergleicher Achilleus,
> Dich zum Sohn, daß du einst vor traurigem Schicksal mich
>   schirmtest.

There then follows a respectful admonition:

> Zähme dein großes Herz, o Achilleus! Nicht ja geziemt dir
> Unerbarmender Sinn; oft wenden sich selber die Götter,
> Die doch weit erhabner an Herrlichkeit, Ehr und Gewalt sind.[85]

However, Wallenstein pleads, "Max, bleibe bei mir.—Geh nicht von
mir, Max!"—and insists on his love with the protestation:

> . . . dich hab ich *geliebt*,
> Mein Herz, mich selber hab ich dir gegeben.
> Sie alle waren Fremdlinge, *du* warst
> Das Kind des Hauses—Max! du kannst mich nicht verlassen!
> Es kann nicht sein, ich mags und wills nicht glauben,
> Daß mich der Max verlassen kann.

Those statements of Wallenstein, which frame the account of his fatherly, and even motherly, services end by his setting himself up as
absolute authority:

> Auf *mich* bist du gepflanzt, ich bin dein Kaiser,
> Mir angehören, mir gehorchen, *das*
> Ist deine Ehre, dein Naturgesetz.[86]

Wallenstein's words suggesting a fight between himself and Max—
"Willst du den Gang mit mir versuchen?"—recall Achilles's wish that
he and Patroclos storm the ramparts of Troy:

> Wenn doch, o Vater Zeus und Pallas Athen' und Apollon,
> Auch kein einziger Troer sich rettete, aller, die da sind,
> Auch der Danaer keiner, und wir nur entflöhn der Vertilgung,
> Daß wir allein abrissen die heiligen Zinnen von Troja![87]

But whereas Achilles speaks of himself and Patroclos fighting side by
side, Wallenstein speaks of himself and Max fighting on opposite
sides. Max's refusal to fight against Wallenstein is,[88] nevertheless, a
preparation for his fighting in Wallenstein's stead. Just as Achilles, in
his fight against Hector, seems to be fighting against himself because
Hector is wearing the armor Achilles had given Patroclos to wear in
his stead, so Wallenstein, in Max's fight against the Swedes, seems to
partake of an action he should have, but did not take up.[89] Reminiscent of Achilles, standing in front of the wall, his head in a blaze of
light, shouting to dispel the Trojans from Patroclos's dead body, Wallenstein decides to show himself before his rebellious troops:

> Hinweg! Zu lange schon hab ich gezaudert.
> Das konnten sie sich freventlich erkühnen,

Weil sie mein Angesicht nicht sahn—sie sollen
Mein Antlitz sehen, meine Stimme hören—
Sind es nicht *meine* Truppen? Bin ich nicht
Ihr Feldherr und gefürchteter Gebieter?
Laß sehn, ob sie das Antlitz nicht mehr kennen,
Das ihre Sonne war in dunkler Schlacht.
Es braucht der Waffen nicht.[90]

Yet where Athena's help and Achilles's violent sorrow make up for his lack of armor, Wallenstein, in armor, but a traitor, and merely human, fails utterly.

Interspersed between Max's attempt to leave and his final words— "Wer mit mir geht, der sei bereit zu sterben!"—echoes of events after Patroclos's death anticipate Max's own death. Likewise, reports of his death, interspersed between Buttler's and Gordon's conversations, anticipate the death of Wallenstein.[91] Bearing out Wallenstein's dream before the battle at Lützen, Max, another Patroclos dying his friend's death, succumbs in the fight against the Swedes.[92] Terzky's report about Max's death, "Nach Sonnenuntergang hab's angefangen . . . ," resounds in Buttler's comment, "Der Sonne Licht ist unter," which anticipates the death of Wallenstein. Both remarks echo Homer's "Aber sobald die Sonne zum Stierabspannen sich neigte."[93] Buttler's "Schad ists doch um den heldenmütgen Jüngling, / Dem Herzog selbst gings nah, man sah es wohl," and Illo's "Auch jetzo noch, ich schwörs bei meiner Seele, / Säh er uns alle lieber zehnmal tot, / Könnt er den Freund damit ins Leben rufen" once more recall Achilles's wish for the death not only of the Trojans, but of the Greeks as well, so that he and Patroclos could storm the ramparts of Troy.[94]

Against the background of Patroclos's humiliation by Apollo, Max's death shines forth with human dignity. Patroclos, warned by the god not to try to capture Troy, has his helmet struck off his head and his armor dashed to the ground:

Aber Patroklos stürzte mit feindlicher Wut in die Troer.
Dreimal stürzt' er hinein, dem stürmenden Ares vergleichbar,
Schreiend mit grausem Getön, dreimal neun Männer erschlug er.
Als er das vierte Mal drauf anstürmete, stark wie ein Dämon,
Jetzt war dir, Patroklos, genaht das Ende des Lebens.
Denn dir begegnete Phoibos im Ungestüme der Feldschlacht
Fürchterlich. Doch nicht merkt er den Wandelnden durch das
    Getümmel,
Weil in finstere Nacht der begegnende Gott sich gehüllet.

Hinten stand und schlug er den Rücken ihm zwischen den
  Schultern,
Mit gebreiteter Hand; da schwindelten jenem die Augen.
Auch ihm hinweg vom Haupte den Helm schlug Phoibos Apollon;
Dieser rollte dahin und erklang von den Hufen der Rosse
Hell, der gekegelte Helm, und besudelt war ihm der Haarbusch
Ganz in Blut und Staube.[95]

Max, on the other hand, recognized by his helmet, is asked by the
Rhinegrave to yield in honorable battle, as Thekla learns from the
Swedish captain:

Doch unbesonnen hatte sie [die Pappenheimer] der Mut
Vorausgeführt den andern, weit dahinten
War noch das Fußvolk, nur die Pappenheimer waren
Dem kühnen Führer kühn gefolgt—
Von vorn und von den Flanken faßten wir
Sie jetzo mit der ganzen Reiterei,
Und drängten sie zurück zum Graben, wo
Das Fußvolk, schnell geordnet, einen Rechen
Von Piken ihnen starr entgegenstreckte.
Nicht vorwärts konnten sie, auch nicht zurück,
Gekeilt in drangvoll fürchterliche Enge.
Da rief der Rheingraf ihrem Führer zu,
In guter Schlacht sich ehrlich zu ergeben,
Doch Oberst Piccolomini—ihn machte
Der Helmbusch kenntlich und das lange Haar,
Vom raschen Ritte wars ihm losgegangen—
Zum Graben winkt er, sprengt, der erste, selbst
Sein edles Roß darüber weg, ihm stürzt
Das Regiment nach—doch—schon wars geschehn!
Sein Pferd, von einer Partisan durchstoßen, bäumt
Sich wütend, schleudert weit den Reiter ab,
Und hoch weg über ihn geht die Gewalt
Der Rosse, keinem Zügel mehr gehorchend.[96]

Whereas Patroclos's death is marked by the cruelty of an immortal
god and his funeral by the ruthlessness of a godlike mortal, sacrific-
ing "auch zwölf tapfere Söhne der edelmütigen Troer," Max's funeral, as well as his death, carries the mark of humanity:

Heut früh bestatteten wir ihn. Ihn trugen
Zwölf Jünglinge der edelsten Geschlechter,
Das ganze Heer begleitete die Bahre.

Ein Lorbeer schmückte seinen Sarg, drauf legte
Der Rheingraf selbst den eignen Siegerdegen.
Auch Tränen fehlten seinem Schicksal nicht,
Denn viele sind bei uns, die seine Großmut
Und seiner Sitten Freundlichkeit erfahren,
Und alle rührte sein Geschick. Gern hätte
Der Rheingraf ihn gerettet, doch er selbst
Vereitelt' es, man sagt, er wollte sterben.[97]

In her sorrow over Patroclos's death, Briseis laments:

> . . . du versprachst mir, des göttergleichen
> Achilleus
> Jugendlich Weib zu werden, der einst in Schiffen gen Phthia
> Heim mich brächt und fei'rte den Myrmidonen das Brautmahl.
> Ach, du starbst, und ohn End bewein ich dich, freundlicher
> Jüngling.[98]

Terrified even at the thought of Hector's death, Andromache swoons at the sight of his being dragged on the battlefield behind Achilles's chariot:

> Sprachs und hinweg aus der Kammer enteilte sie, gleich der
> Mänade,
> Wild ihr pochte das Herz; und es folgten ihr dienende Weiber.
> Aber nachdem sie den Turm und die Schar der Männer erreichet,
> Stand sie und blickt' auf der Mauer umher und schauete jenen
> Hingeschleift vor Ilios' Stadt; und die hurtigen Rosse
> Schleiften ihn sorglos hin zu den räumigen Schiffen Achaias.
> Schnell umhüllt' ihr die Augen ein mitternächtliches Dunkel,
> Und sie entsank rückwärts und lag entatmet in Ohnmacht.[99]

Blending the roles of Briseis and of Andromache, Thekla anticipates Max's death:

> Sie scheint
> Unglück geahnt zu haben. Das Gerücht
> Von einer Schlacht erschreckte sie, worin
> Der kaiserliche Oberst sei gefallen.
> Ich sah es gleich. Sie flog dem schwedischen
> Kurier entgegen und entriß ihm schnell
> Durch Fragen das unglückliche Geheimnis.
> Zu spät vermißten wir sie, eilten nach,
> Ohnmächtig lag sie schon in seinen Armen.[100]

Recovered from her swoon, she insists on hearing the report about the fateful battle. But while Briseis is joined by others, and Andromache, surrounded by the women of Troy, mourns the loss of her fulfillment in Hector's love, Thekla, in a monologue, mourns what she possessed only as a promise never to be fulfilled. In her echoing both Briseis and Andromache, Thekla gives voice to a sorrow that in its humanity goes beyond the narrow limits of national enmity.

In its impersonal formulation, Thekla's "Das ist das Los des Schönen auf der Erde!"[101] reminds one of Schiller's "Nänie," which culminates in the poet's lament over the death of Achilles:

> Nicht errettet den göttlichen Held die unsterbliche Mutter,
> Wann er, am skäischen Tor fallend, sein Schicksal erfüllt.
> Aber sie steigt aus dem Meer mit allen Töchtern des Nereus,
> Und die Klage hebt an um den verherrlichten Sohn.
> Siehe! Da weinen die Götter, es weinen die Göttinnen alle,
> Daß das Schöne vergeht, daß das Vollkommene stirbt.
> Auch ein Klaglied zu sein im Mund der Geliebten, ist herrlich,
> Denn das Gemeine geht klanglos zum Orkus hinab.[102]

In the *Iliad*, however, it is the death of Patroclos that brings Achilles's mother and all the daughters of Nereus from the depths of the sea to lament with her son:

> Hört mich all', ihr Schwestern, unsterbliche Töchter des Nereus,
> Daß ihr vernehmt den Jammer, wie viel mir die Seele belastet!
> Weh mir armen, o mir unglücklichen Heldenmutter,
> Die ich den Sohn mir gebar, so edelen Sinns und so tapfer,
> Hoch vor Helden geschmückt! Er schwang sich empor wie ein
>   Sprößling;
> Und ich erzog ihn mit Fleiß, wie die Pflanz' im fruchtbaren Acker;
> Drauf in geschnäbelten Schiffen gen Ilios sandt ich daher ihn,
> Troias Volk zu bekämpfen; doch nie empfang ich ihn wieder,
> Wann er zur Heimat kehrt in Peleus' ragende Wohnung!
> Aber solang er mir lebt und das Licht der Sonne noch schauet,
> Duldet er Qual, und nichts vermag ich ihm nahend zu helfen![103]

The connection between the death of Achilles and the death of Patroclos in Schiller's transfiguration of the Homeric text interprets the connection between the death of Wallenstein and the death of Max in Thekla's "Nänie" for "the Beautiful on earth." Thekla's "Sein Geist ists, der mich ruft" reminds one of Patroclos's coming to Achilles in his dream to ask him for burial. This reminder, together with

Thekla's "Lassen Sie mich jetzt bald schlafen gehen . . . ich brauche Ruh," foreshadows not only Thekla's, but also Wallenstein's death, anticipated in his last words, "Ich denke einen langen Schlaf zu tun," and thus unites Max and Thekla in more than one way.[104]

Echoing Homer's description, "Ihn nun fand er vorn an des Meers hochhauptigen Schiffen, / Dem nachsinnend im Geist, was schon zur Vollendung genahet," Schiller's stage direction, "Wallenstein sitzt in tiefen Gedanken, starr vor sich hinsehend, den Kopf in die Hand gesenkt," prepares for Wallenstein's reaction to Max's death. Against the background of Achilles's violent lament over Patroclos's death, Wallenstein's sorrow appears, at first, almost distracted. In Homer's words:

> . . . und jenen umhüllte der Schwermut finstere Wolke.
> Siehe, mit beiden Händen des schwärzlichen Staubes ergreifend,
> Überstreut' er sein Haupt und entstellte sein liebliches Antlitz;
> Auch das ambrosische Kleid umhaftete dunkele Asche.
> Aber er selber, groß, weithingestreckt, in dem Staube
> Lag, und entstellete raufend mit eigenen Händen das Haupthaar.
> Mägde zugleich, die Achilleus erbeutete und Patroklos,
> Laut mit bekümmerter Seel aufschrien sie; all' aus der Türe
> Liefen sie her um Achilleus, den feurigen, und mit den Händen
> Schlugen sich alle die Brust, und jeglicher wankten die Knie.
> Drüben Antilochos auch wehklagte, Tränen vergießend,
> Haltend Achilleus' Händ', als beklemmt sein mutiges Herz rang:
> Daß er nicht die Kehle sich selbst mit dem Eisen durchschnitte.
> Fürchterlich weint' er empor.[105]

Schiller, on the other hand, has Wallenstein rise, remark, "es ist schon finstre Nacht," and step up to the window:

> Am Himmel ist geschäftige Bewegung,
> Des Turmes Fahne jagt der Wind, schnell geht
> Der Wolken Zug, die Mondessichel wankt,
> Und durch die Nacht zuckt ungewisse Helle.
> —Kein Sternbild ist zu sehn! Der matte Schein dort,
> Der einzelne, ist aus der Kassiopeia,
> Und dahin steht der Jupiter—Doch jetzt
> Deckt ihn die Schwärze des Gewitterhimmels![106]

That statement ends in the stage direction "er versinkt in Tiefsinn und sieht starr hinaus."

Whereas Thetis and all the Nereids (their musical names suspending the mortal anguish for more than ten lines) indulge Achilles's grief, the Countess tries to dispel Wallenstein's melancholy mood. Godlike in his bearing, Achilles stands in front of the wall, his head in a blaze of light:

> Aber Achilles erhob sich, der göttliche. Selber Athene
> Hängt um die mächtigen Schultern die quastumbordete Aigis,
> Auch sein Haupt mit Gewölk umkränzte die heilige Göttin,
> Goldenem, und ihm entstrahlt' ein ringsumleuchtendes Feuer.

But Wallenstein has to be reminded of his power: "O bleibe stark! Erhalte du uns aufrecht, / Denn du bist unser Licht und unsre Sonne."[107] Even Achilles, however, has to be stirred from his grief by Thetis, who points out:

> Liebes Kind, was weinst du, und was betrübt dir die Seele?
> Sprich, verhehle mir nichts! Dir ward doch alles vollendet
> Jenes von Zeus, wie vordem mit erhobenen Händen du flehtest,
> Daß, um die Steuer zusammengedrängt, die Männer Achaias,
> Schmachtend nach deiner Hilfe, unwürdige Taten erlitten!

In a similar vein, the Countess remarks, "Auch dich, mein Bruder, find ich nicht wie sonst. / Nach einem Sieg erwartet ich dich heitrer," and counsels, "Freu dich des Siegs, vergiß was er dir kostet. / Nicht heute erst ward dir der Freund geraubt, / Als er sich von dir schied, da starb er dir."[108] As a testimony to Max's plea,

> Wirf ihn heraus, den schwarzen Fleck, den Feind.
> Ein böser Traum bloß ist es dann gewesen,
> Der jede sichre Tugend warnt,

Wallenstein confirms,

> . . . sein Leben .
> Liegt faltenlos und leuchtend ausgebreitet,
> Kein dunkler Flecken blieb darin zurück,
> Und unglückbringend pocht ihm keine Stunde.[109]

An expression of feeling lost between the world of his heart and the world of his duty, Max's "mir machte sie [die kriegerische Bühne] mein wirklich Glück zum Traum" is answered in Wallenstein's sad, but fond remembrance, "er [Max] machte mir das Wirkliche zum Traum."[110] Even though Wallenstein's subdued melancholy is worlds apart from Achilles's wild laments, Wallenstein speaks with the same deep feeling:

> . . . mir fiel
> Der liebste Freund, und fiel durch meine Schuld.
> So kann mich keines Glückes Gunst mehr freuen,
> Als dieser Schlag mich hat geschmerzt.

Those words echo Achilles's cry:

> Aber was frommt mir solches, nachdem mein teurer Patroklos
> Mir hinsank, den ich wert vor allen Freunden geachtet,
> Wert wie mein eigenes Haupt![111]

Like the death of Patroclos for Achilles, the death of Max brings Wallenstein closer to realizing the tragic connection between freedom and necessity, borne out in the problematic relationship of nature and convention. Wallenstein, conscious of the responsibility of choice, concedes he might have acted otherwise:

> Hätt ich vorher gewußt, was nun geschehn,
> Daß es den liebsten Freund mir würde kosten,
> Und hätte mir das Herz wie jetzt gesprochen—
> Kann sein, ich hätte mich bedacht—kann sein
> Auch nicht—

However, Achilles only curses his anger and shares the responsibility with Patroclos, with Agamemnon and, finally, with the gods:

> Vater Zeus, fürwahr! Verblendung gibst du den Männern!
> Nimmermehr wohl hätte den Mut in der Tiefe des Herzens
> Atreus' Sohn mir empört so fürchterlich, oder das Mägdlein
> Weg mir geführt mit Gewalt, der Unbiegsame; sondern fürwahr,
>   Zeus
> Wollte nur vielen den Tod in Argos' Volke bereiten![112]

Instead of blaming the gods, or even the stars, Wallenstein rephrases the Countess's statement:

> Denn Recht hat jeder eigene Charakter,
> Der übereinstimmt mit sich selbst, es gibt
> Kein andres Unrecht, als den Widerspruch.

Thus he says in the first act of *Wallensteins Tod*:

> Geschehe denn, was muß.
> Recht stets behält das Schicksal, denn das Herz
> In uns ist sein gebietrischer Vollzieher.

This in turn reformulates the Countess's remark to Thekla, "Dein Herz, mein liebes Kind, und nicht das Schicksal," and Thekla's answer, "Der Zug des Herzens ist des Schicksals Stimme."[113]

The polarity between Buttler and Max,[114] representing the two sides of Wallenstein's character, is carried on, after Max's death, in the polarity between Buttler and Gordon. Gordon's statement, "ich aber war der ältre," recalls Menoitios's advice to Patroclos:

Lieber Sohn, an Geburt ist zwar erhabner Achilleus,
Älter dafür bist du; doch ihm ward größere Stärke;
Aber du hilf ihm treulich mit Rat und kluger Erinnrung
Und sei Lenker dem Freund; er folgt dir gerne zum Guten.[115]

In turn, that statement continues the parallel between Wallenstein and Achilles in their relationship to Max and Patroclos. In the light of an earlier analogy drawn between Buttler and Ajax, on the one hand, and Octavio and Odysseus, on the other, the last two scenes of Schiller's *Wallenstein* echo the outcome of the contest between Ajax and Odysseus over the weapons of Achilles.[116] Alluding to the questionable character of that outcome, the last words of the trilogy, "Dem *Fürsten* Piccolomini," together with the stage direction, "Octavio erschrickt und blickt schmerzvoll zum Himmel," acknowledge the bitterness of a victory that, in a deeper sense, is a defeat.

III. "No *Iliad* Possible Any More after *The Iliad*"

Schiller's *Geschichte des dreißigjährigen Krieges*, in the development of its central books, recalls the plot of Homer's *Iliad*. Schiller's *Wallenstein*, recalling not only the plot but also the characters of the *Iliad*, surrounds the historical field of action with a mythical horizon of Homeric overtones. Recasting the themes of the ancient epic in the form of a modern dramatic poem, Schiller calls attention to both their similarity and dissimilarity.

The dominant theme of Homer's *Iliad*, presented in the archetypal figures of Achilles and Agamemnon, is the conflict between nature and convention. Looming large over Schiller's *Wallenstein*, the same conflict shapes the dramatic constellations of the trilogy. With reference to his own historical moment Schiller, in the *Prolog*, speaks of "Herrschaft" and "Freiheit" as "der Menschheit große Gegenstände." With reference to past as well as present history, the *Prolog* points to the permanency of the conflict between nature and convention.[1] Yet the order of the terms "Herrschaft" and "Freiheit" holds out the hope for a recovery of man's natural legacy from the bondage of conventional authority.

Present on all levels of the trilogy, the conflict between nature and convention appears in many forms. The quarrel between the peasant father and son in *Wallensteins Lager* prefigures the disagreement between Octavio and Max in *Die Piccolomini* and prepares for the opposition between the Emperor and Wallenstein in *Wallensteins Tod*. At the same time it introduces the rift between civilians and soldiers in their judgment about war and peace as advocated by the Emperor and Wallenstein. Compounding the differences between fathers and sons as well as civilians and soldiers, the opposition between the Emperor and Wallenstein consists in the conflict between conventional authority and natural leadership.

The dominant theme of Schiller's *Wallenstein* and Homer's *Iliad* alike, the conflict between nature and convention is transfigured in the idea of friendship which, as a freely chosen relationship of naturally kindred souls, can be seen as a middle ground between a natural and a conventional bond. Failing to resolve the conflict, friendship becomes the turning point for tragedy in both works.

46

The similarity of themes between Schiller's *Wallenstein* and Homer's *Iliad* allows at the same time for a striking dissimilarity of expression. Again and again Schiller conveys in abstract language what Homer presents in concrete images. Insisting on a special affinity to the Greeks, Schiller nevertheless concedes:

> Das mag sein, daß meine *Sprache* immer künstlicher organisiert sein wird, als sich mit einer homerischen Dichtung verträgt, aber den Anteil der Sprache an den Gedanken unterscheidet ein kritisches Auge leicht, und es wäre der Mühe und Aufopferung nicht wert, eine so mühsam gebildete Organisation, die auch nicht an Tugenden leer ist, auf gut Glück wieder zu zerstören.[2]

In its artful organization, however, Schiller's abstract language lends itself to portraying characters who are torn between action and reflection and thus expresses the differentiation of human nature in the course of history.

Compared with the characters in Homer's *Iliad*, the characters in Schiller's *Wallenstein* reflect more than they act, reflect in monologues[3] more than in dialogues, and reflect on a world where history, man's expression of self-consciousness, claims autonomy from the restrictive rule of nature. As examples of the fragmentation of human nature, some of Schiller's characters parallel more than one Homeric character: Max, both Patroclos and Hector; Thekla, both Briseis and Andromache. This double role of the modern characters is the more significant as it obliterates the enmity between Greeks and Trojans and thus points to an individuality that transcends the political nature of man.

Complementary to the parallels of characters, parallels of plots create a maze of poetic affinities between Schiller's *Wallenstein* and Homer's *Iliad*. Used for internal cross-references, the parallels of plots increase in complexity towards the end of the trilogy. Discontinuous and staggered, they seem to point not only to the fragmentation of human nature in modern times, but also to a new totality made possible through history.

The complexity of plots and characters increases in the most political part of Schiller's *Wallenstein* to include not only parallels with Homer's *Iliad*, but also with Sophocles's *Philoctetes*. Wallenstein, the tragic hero, reflects both Achilles and Philoctetes; Max, Wallenstein's idealistic self, both Patroclos and Neoptolemos; Octavio, Wallenstein's realistic self, both Homer's and Sophocles's Odysseus. By reflecting characters and plots from both Greek epic and dramatic poetry, Schiller's modern historical drama raises the question of the mutual compatibility of epic and dramatic as well as ancient and modern poetry.

This question, brought to the fore with Goethe's *Hermann und Dorothea*, becomes a burning issue for both Schiller and Goethe:

> Das epische Gedicht von Goethen, das ich habe entstehen sehen, und welches, in unsren Gesprächen, alle Ideen über epische und dramatische Kunst in Bewegung brachte, hat, verbunden mit der Lektüre des Shakespeare und Sophokles, die mich seit mehrern Wochen beschäftigt, auch für meinen *Wallenstein* große Folgen, und da ich bei dieser Gelegenheit tiefere Blicke in die Kunst getan, so muß ich manches in meiner ersten Ansicht des Stücks reformieren. Diese große Krise hat indes den eigentlichen Grund meines Stücks nicht erschüttert, ich muß also glauben, daß dieser echt und solid ist: aber freilich bleibt mir das Schwerste noch immer übrig, nämlich die poetische Ausführung eines so schweren Plans, wie der meinige es in der Tat ist.[4]

Eager to hear the voice of a Homeric rhapsode in this "new politically rhetorical world,"[5] Schiller welcomes the completion of Goethe's *Hermann und Dorothea*.

Under the names of the nine muses, starting with Calliope, the muse of epic poetry, and ending with Urania, the muse of philosophical poetry, the nine cantos of *Hermann und Dorothea* present the whole realm of poetic expression. A unity of material and form, the story of individual lives against the background of history embedded in the world of nature, together with the different modes of poetry evolving from each other, Goethe's *Hermann und Dorothea* seems to be a modern version of Homer's Shield of Achilles.[6] The muse of epic poetry, however, not only governs the first canto, but her spirit pervades the poem as a whole: Homeric meter, Homeric diction, Homeric epithets and episodes, though softened from heroic to idyllic tone, echo the *Iliad* as well as the *Odyssey* throughout Goethe's poem.

Though delighted with Goethe's *Hermann und Dorothea*, and even envious of the later *Achilleis*,[7] Schiller voices his doubts about merely imitating Homer:

> Da es wohl seine Richtigkeit hat, daß keine Ilias nach der Ilias mehr möglich ist, auch wenn es wieder einen Homer und wieder ein Griechenland gäbe, so glaube ich Ihnen nichts Besseres wünschen zu können, als daß Sie Ihre Achilleis, so wie sie jetzt in Ihrer Imagination existiert, bloß mit sich selbst vergleichen, und beim Homer bloß Stimmung suchen, ohne Ihr Geschäft mit seinem eigentlich zu vergleichen.[8]

This statement, made during Schiller's work on *Wallensteins Tod*, ends with a reminder about the modern poet's advantage over his ancient counterpart: "Ihr schöner Beruf ist, ein Zeitgenosse und Bürger beider Dichterwelten zu sein, und gerade um dieses höhern Vorzugs willen werden Sie keiner ausschließend angehören." Despite his appreciation of Homer,[9] Schiller cannot help but observe:

Homers Werke haben zwar einen hohen *subjectiven* Gehalt (sie geben dem Geist eine reiche Beschäftigung), aber keinen so hohen *objectiven* (sie *erweitern* den Geist ganz und gar nicht, sondern bewegen nur die Kräfte, wie sie wirklich sind). Seine Dichtungen haben eine unendliche Fläche, aber keine solche Tiefe. Was sie an Tiefe haben, das ist ein Effekt des Ganzen, nicht des einzelnen; die Natur im Ganzen ist immer unendlich und grundlos.[10]

Commenting on the unsatisfactory attempt to approach the Greek spirit, even in the case of Goethe, Schiller claims a certain "reality" as the advantage of the modern poet:

Ich habe zugleich bemerkt, daß diese *Annäherung* an den griechischen Geist, die doch nie *Erreichung* wird, immer etwas von jener "modernen Realität" nimmt, gerade herausgesagt, daß ein Produkt immer ärmer an *Geist* ist, je mehr es *Natur* ist. Und nun fragt sich, sollte der moderne Dichter nicht Recht haben, auf seinem ihm ausschließend eigenen Gebiet sich einheimisch und vollkommen zu machen, als in einem fremden, wo ihm die Welt, seine Sprache und seine Cultur selbst ewig widersteht, sich von dem Griechen übertreffen lassen? Sollten, mit Einem Wort, neuere Dichter nicht besser tun, das *Ideal* als die *Wirklichkeit* zu bearbeiten?[11]

In an exchange about Schiller's poetic talent, Körner reflects on the requirements for harmony within a work of art. Considering the harmony between "infinite unity" and "infinite freedom" characteristic of "the spirit of antiquity," he remarks:

Was ich an Dir vorzüglich schätze, ist, daß Du Dich immer mehr diesem Ziele näherst, ohne den *Reichtum* des *Einzelnen* aufzuopfern. Ich begreife die Schwierigkeit dieses Unternehmens, und merke wohl, daß Goethe auf einem bequemeren Wege die Forderungen des Geschmacks zu befriedigen sucht. Aber wenn es möglich ist, die Alten zu übertreffen, so ist es auf dem Wege, den Du einschlägst.[12]

With reference to his *Ästhetische Versuche über Goethes "Hermann und Dorothea,"* a detailed discussion of Goethe's work in its relation to

Homer, Humboldt proposes, "das vollkommene Gegenstück zu dieser Arbeit würde eine ähnliche über Ihren Wallenstein sein."[13]
Though Humboldt does not make explicit in what sense he uses the
term "Gegenstück," the difference between Goethe and Schiller in
their relation to Homer certainly would have entered the discussion.
Dependent on Homer in every aspect of form, Goethe's *Hermann und
Dorothea* is an example of new wine in old bottles; independent of
Homer in this respect, Schiller's *Wallenstein* is an example of new
wine in new bottles.[14] Yet, in keeping with the last verse of the par-
able, "No man also having drunk old wine straightway desireth new:
for he saith, The old is better." Schiller adds some old wine to the
new.[15] Like catalysts in the process of establishing an ideal mode of
poetic expression, allusions to Homeric characters and plots enrich
the modern ingredients of Schiller's historical drama and thus contribute to the transformation of historical into poetic truth.

Even though Humboldt never wrote a review of Schiller's *Wallenstein* comparable to his work on Goethe's *Hermann und Dorothea*, letters between Humboldt and Schiller and Humboldt's "Über Schiller
und den Gang seiner Geistesentwicklung" amply discuss Schiller's
relation to the Greeks. In answer to Schiller's notion of "Geist" as
the modern poet's prerogative and "Natur" as the Greek poet's,
Humboldt claims to be able to justify "the seemingly paradoxical
statement,"

> daß auf der einen Seite Sie, da Ihre Produkte gerade das Gepräge
> der Selbsttätigkeit an sich tragen, das gerade Gegenteil der Grie-
> chen, und ihnen doch unter allen Modernen wiederum am näch-
> sten sind, da aus Ihren Produkten, nächst den griechischen, am
> meisten die Notwendigkeit der Form spricht, nur daß Sie dieselbe
> aus sich selbst schöpfen, indem die Griechen sie aus dem An-
> blick der gleichfalls in ihrer Form notwendigen äußern Natur
> nahmen.[16]

Subtly expressed in the second to the last line (italicized here) of his
elegy "Der Spaziergang,"

> Unter demselben Blau, über dem nämlichen Grün[17]
> *Wandeln die nahen und wandeln vereint die fernen Geschlechter,*
> Und die Sonne Homers, siehe! sie lächelt auch uns,

Schiller's relationship to the Greeks never loses its problematic character. Delayed till the end of the line, the subject ("Geschlechter")
carries two, but the same, predicates ("wandeln"). Meaningless in
itself, "die nahen" has to wait past "die fernen" in order to reach

"Geschlechter." The critical position of "vereint," after the second predicate, but before the common subject, seems to express the problematic character of the modern dependence on and independence from the Ancients. The line, as a whole, seems to be a miniature statement of Schiller's aesthetic theories where the relative perfection of the Moderns is understood to complement that of the Ancients.[18] Schiller's impression that his conversations with Goethe about epic and dramatic poetry and his reading of Shakespeare and Sophocles "greatly influenced" his *Wallenstein*, but in the end did not "shake its foundations," is true for his reading of Homer as well.[19] As Humboldt formulates it:

> Es lag in Schillers Eigentümlichkeit, von einem großen Geiste neben sich nie in dessen Kreis herübergezogen, dagegen in dem eignen, selbstgeschaffenen durch einen solchen Einfluß auf das mächtigste angeregt zu werden; und man kann wohl zweifelhaft bleiben, ob man dies in ihm mehr als Größe des Geistes, oder als tiefe Schönheit des Charakters bewundern soll. Sich fremder Individualität nicht unterzuordnen, ist Eigenschaft jeder größeren Geisteskraft, jedes stärkeren Gemüts, aber die fremde Individualität ganz, als verschieden, zu durchschauen, vollkommen zu würdigen, und aus dieser bewundernden Anschauung die Kraft zu schöpfen, die eigne nur noch entschiedner und richtiger ihrem Ziele zuzuwenden, gehört Wenigen an, und war in Schiller hervorstechender Charakterzug.[20]

Part II. Euripides

Aber eben so, wie der bildende Künstler die faltige Fülle der
Gewänder um seine Figuren breitet, um die Räume seines Bildes
reich und anmutig auszufüllen, um die getrennten Partien desselben
in ruhigen Massen stetig zu verbinden, um der Farbe, die das Auge
reizt und erquickt, einen Spielraum zu geben, um die menschlichen
Formen zugleich geistreich zu verhüllen und sichtbar zu machen,
eben so durchflicht und umgibt der tragische Dichter seine streng
abgemessene Handlung und die festen Umrisse seiner handelnden
Figuren mit einem lyrischen Prachtgewebe, in welchem sich, als wie
in einem weit gefalteten Purpurgewand, die handelnden Personen
frei und edel mit einer gehaltenen Würde und hoher Ruhe bewegen.

(Schiller, Preface to *Die Braut von Messina*)

IV. Dramatic versus Epic Poetry

A historical drama of epic dimensions, Schiller's *Wallenstein* reflects the different stages of Schiller's infatuation with the story of the historical Wallenstein. Even years after sketching out the dramatic structure of *Wallenstein*, Schiller wrestles with the problem of its poetic execution. Convinced more than ever of an ideal correspondence between poetic material and poetic form, he searches for the form most suited to express the poetic potential of the Wallenstein story.[1] Schiller's choice of a dramatic rather than an epic poem, but a dramatic poem of epic dimensions, therefore, has as much to do with his poetic conception of the character of Wallenstein as with his understanding of the differences between epic and dramatic poetry.

Classifying dramatic or, for that matter, tragic poetry under the category of causality, and epic poetry under the category of substantiality, Schiller points both to their difference and to the complementary nature of their differentiating characteristics. Struck by their difference, he defines tragedy as concerned only with "singular extraordinary moments of mankind," but epic poetry with "the permanent, ongoing whole thereof."[2] In answer to Goethe's summary of their ideas on epic and dramatic poetry, however, Schiller concludes:

> Die Tragödie in ihrem höchsten Begriffe wird also immer zu dem epischen Charakter *hinauf* streben und wird nur dadurch zur Dichtung. Das epische Gedicht wird eben so zu dem Drama *herunter* streben und wird nur dadurch den poetischen Gattungsbegriff ganz erfüllen; just das, was beide zu poetischen Werken macht, bringt beide einander nahe.[3]

A presentation of "singular extraordinary moments of mankind" and, as such, a testimony to man's "causality," tragedy focuses on places in human history defining the space of human nature. A presentation of "the permanent, ongoing whole thereof" and, as such, a testimony to man's "substantiality," epic poetry focuses on the space of human nature defining places in human history.[4] Despite his appreciation of the complementary nature of the two poetic species, Schiller insists, "daß dieses wechselseitige Hinstreben zu einander nicht in eine Vermischung und Grenzverwirrung ausarte, das ist eben die eigentliche Aufgabe der Kunst."[5] Inspired by their exchange of ideas about epic and dramatic poetry, Schiller tells Goethe in July

1797 of his intention to use it "immediately" and "productively" in his "*Wallenstein* and in any other future work of significance."[6]

Interrupted by long years of historical and philosophical studies, Schiller's dramatic work, in a sense, takes up from where it left off. His translation of Euripides's *Iphigenia in Aulis*, the last dramatic work before those studies, is reflected in his *Wallenstein*, the first dramatic work thereafter.

Schiller's immersion in Homer and his pursuit of a classical simplicity of style through the temporary avoidance of modern authors culminates in his translation of Euripides's *Iphigenia in Aulis* and his plan for a future translation of Aeschylus's *Agamemnon*.[7] His pleasure in Euripides's portrayal of human nature does not, however, sweep away his reservation: "Setze noch hinzu, daß ich mir, bei mehrerer Bekanntschaft mit griechischen Stücken, endlich das Wahre, Schöne und Wirkende daraus abstrahiere und mir mit Weglassung des Mangelhaften ein gewisses Ideal daraus bilde, wodurch mein jetziges corrigiert und vollends geründet wird."[8] This liberty of using the Ancients for the fuller pursuit of his own modern goals seems to be a lasting trait in Schiller's attitude. Remembering the years when Schiller, in the evenings, would read from Homer or Greek tragedy, Caroline von Wolzogen speculates about their influence on him and his work, particularly on his *Wallenstein*.[9] Anticipating a lively exchange of ideas about the most important matters in poetry, Schiller himself suggests utilizing Goethe's next visit in May 1798 for reading Homer, and later the Greek tragedians, together.[10] Focusing on Greek epic poetry, the first part of this study traced the presence of Homeric archetypes in Schiller's *Wallenstein*. Schiller's conception of *Wallenstein* as a dramatic rather than an epic poem seems to imply the final consummation of a long-standing vow: "Ehe ich der griechischen Tragödie durchaus mächtig bin und meine dunklen Ahnungen von Regel und Kunst in klare Begriffe verwandelt habe, lasse ich mich auf keine dramatische Ausarbeitung ein."[11] His elaborate ideas on the complementary nature of epic and dramatic poetry suggest that archetypes from Greek tragic as well as epic poetry might be present in Schiller's *Wallenstein*.

At work on sketching out a detailed plan for *Wallenstein*, Schiller criticizes the modern concern for historical rather than poetic truth:

> Ich finde, je mehr ich über mein eigenes Geschäft und über die Behandlungsart der Tragödie bei den Griechen nachdenke, daß der ganze Cardo rei in der Kunst liegt, eine poetische Fabel zu erfinden. Der Neuere schlägt sich mühselig und ängstlich mit Zufälligkeiten und Nebendingen herum, und über dem Bestreben, der

Wirklichkeit recht nahe zu kommen, beladet er sich mit dem Leeren und Unbedeutenden, und darüber läuft er Gefahr, die tiefliegende Wahrheit zu verlieren, worin eigentlich alles Poetische liegt. Er möchte gern einen wirklichen Fall vollkommen nachahmen und bedenkt nicht, daß eine poetische Darstellung mit der Wirklichkeit eben darum, weil sie absolut wahr ist, niemals koinzidieren kann.[12]

Respecting the historical reality of the Thirty Years' War, Schiller presents *Wallenstein* as a modern historical drama. Yet as he extends the historical horizon into mythical spheres by including archetypes from Greek tragedy he makes historical truth the bearer of poetic or natural truth. Schiller's consideration of his own task and of the mode of tragedy among the Greeks leads him to emphasize the art of inventing a poetic plot. In the process of sketching out his detailed plan for *Wallenstein*, he seems to rethink the poetic plot of Euripides's *Iphigenia in Aulis*, the translation of which had been his last dramatic work before *Wallenstein*. The poetic plot in both dramas proceeds from a skeleton of dramatic action. Crucial for the complications in both, the leader of the army orders members of his family to join him at his camp. In both, the political reasons for this move are disguised as personal reasons. In both, the heroic action of a youth close to the leader interferes with the leader's plan and finally causes tragedy and death.[13]

There probably is more than one reason for Schiller's choice of a Euripidean play as his source for archetypal patterns from Greek tragedy. As Wilhelm von Humboldt reports: "Ich liebte sonst den Euripides gar nicht und stritt oft mit Schiller darüber, dem er vorzugsweise gefiel. Es kam wirklich daher, daß er in der Tat moderner ist und daß Schiller doch nicht sehr antik gestimmt war."[14] Complementary to his view of Homer as the naive poet par excellence, Schiller considers Euripides as a poet on the way from naive to sentimental poetry.[15] The presence of both Homeric and Euripidean archetypes in Schiller's *Wallenstein* provides a continuity of poetic truth which, at the same time, adheres to and transcends history and thus coincides with the truth of nature.

In the light of Schiller's understanding of tragedy as concerned only with "singular extraordinary moments of mankind," and of epic poetry as concerned with "the permanent, ongoing whole thereof," Euripides's *Iphigenia in Aulis* can be seen as the presentation of the moment before the Trojan War, and Homer's *Iliad* as the presentation of the whole thereof.

In the first part of this study, a comparison between Schiller's *Wal-*

lenstein and Homer's *Iliad*, the main parallels were drawn between the Emperor and Agamemnon, Wallenstein and Achilles, and Max and Patroclos. In this second part, a comparison between Schiller's *Wallenstein* and Euripides's *Iphigenia in Aulis*,[16] the main parallels will be drawn between Wallenstein and Agamemnon, Max and Achilles, and Thekla and Iphigenia. Seen from this angle, the fundamental theme of Schiller's trilogy, the necessary connection between nature and convention, emerges in the "living shape"[17] of Wallenstein who, in one modern historical figure, presents Achilles, the archetype of the natural hero, and Agamemnon, the archetype of the conven tional ruler. The fact that the poetic figure of Wallenstein reflects archetypes from Homer and Euripides in a cross between naturally opposed, but artistically complementary characters demonstrates both the fragmentation and the striving for a new totality of human nature in the course of history. By reflecting the *Iliad* as well as the pregnant moment before the action portrayed in the *Iliad*, Schiller's *Wallenstein* presents a living example of the complementary unity of substantiality[18] and causality or, in less technical terms, of timeless-ness and time. With his integration of Greek "imitation of nature" into his own "presentation of the ideal," Schiller seems to assert the importance of history for the progress of art towards a fuller repre-sentation of nature.

V. *Wallenstein* and *Iphigenia in Aulis*

Compared to Euripides's *Iphigenia in Aulis*, Schiller's *Wallenstein* appears to be infinitely more complex. A comparison between the two is of interest insofar as it sheds light on the function of comparable elements within fundamentally different contexts. Appended remarks of Schiller's to his translation of Euripides's *Iphigenia in Aulis* are rather critical:

> Diese Tragödie ist vielleicht nicht die tadelfreieste des Euripides, weder im ganzen, noch in ihren Teilen. Agamemnons Charakter ist nicht fest gezeichnet und durch ein zweideutiges Schwanken zwischen Unmensch und Mensch, Ehrenmann und Betrüger nicht wohl fähig, unser Mitleiden zu erregen. Auch bei dem Charakter des Achilles bleibt man zweifelhaft, ob man ihn tadeln oder bewundern soll.[1]

Strange as it may seem, these judgments of character apply to Wallenstein and Max as much as to Agamemnon and Achilles. Another remark concerns the poet's liberty of inserting his own sentiments into the poetic fabric of his work:

> Ist es dem Dichter erlaubt, seine eigenen Gesinnungen in Begebenheiten einzuflechten, die ihnen so ungleichartig sind, und handelt er nicht gegen sich selbst, wenn er den Verstand seiner Zuschauer in eben dem Augenblicke aufklärt oder stutzen macht, wo er ihren Augen einen höhern Grad von Glauben zumutet? Sollte er nicht vielmehr die so leicht zu zerstörende Illusion durch die genaueste Übereinstimmung von Gesinnungen und Begebenheiten zusammenzuhalten und dem Zuschauer den Glauben, der ihm fehlt, durch die handelnden Personen unvermerkt mitzuteilen beflissen sein?[2]

What seems objectionable in Euripides, whether in itself or only in Euripides's mode, Schiller himself certainly practices in *Wallenstein*. The question of the immanence of the poet's reflections in his work becomes an all-pervasive theme for the sentimental poet, much more so than for the poet on the way from naive to sentimental poetry.

Held, as it were, within the concentric circles of the outer and the inner parts of its first and last lines, the *Prolog* to *Wallenstein* explores the relationship between art and life.[3] According to this display of form and content, the *Prolog*'s first and last sections, concerned with art and its relationship to nature, contain its middle section, concerned with life and its relationship to history.[4] Within this overall framework of the *Prolog*, each section follows a linear progression, the first and last ones, in the spirit of nature, from "place" through "time" to "art," the middle one, in the spirit of history, from "time" through "place" to "art."[5] Emphasizing the power of art to transcend the narrow limits of place and time, the tripartite division of each section is reflected further in the first part of the *Prolog*'s first section. The description of the theater, in its new splendor, giving rise to expectations of artistic excellence, culminates in a discussion of the art of the mime who, as human being, exists in place and time but, as artist, transcends the given boundaries of the here and now.[6] The architecture of the *Prolog*, with art as the final perspective from all vantage points, is mirrored in the order of the three plays to come: *Wallensteins Lager*—a definition of place, *Die Piccolomini*—a definition of time, *Wallensteins Tod*—a definition of art. That art, in this case, means the tragic transfiguration of human life might be exemplary for all great art.

The prologue to Euripides's *Iphigenia in Aulis* consists of three parts, Agamemnon's opening dialogue, his monologue, and his closing dialogue with Clytemnestra's slave.[7] Though similar in form, the openings to Schiller's *Wallenstein* and Euripides's *Iphigenia in Aulis* differ greatly in content. Set apart from the trilogy, Schiller's *Prolog* frames the historical subject matter of the plays between the poet's discussions about art and its relationship to history and nature. As a part of the drama, Euripides's prologue frames Agamemnon's recollection of the fateful past between dialogues about his choice for or against the sacrifice of Iphigenia. With man, the natural being moved by choice, put in stark contrast to the regular cyclical motion of the natural world, the paling stars giving way to the rising sun symbolize the inescapability of Agamemnon's lot. While the natural situation at Aulis forces Agamemnon to reflect on the permanently tragic condition of man, the historical moment at the close of the century moves the poet to envision the possibility of a fulfillment of human nature through art.

In both Schiller's *Wallenstein* and Euripides's *Iphigenia in Aulis* the prologue is followed by the impressive sight of an army waiting for action.[8] In trying to justify the mass of the army represented on stage through the various types of foreign mercenaries, Schiller recalls the opening of Shakespeare's *Julius Caesar*: "Hier, bei der Darstellung des Volkscharakters, zwang ihn schon der Stoff, mehr ein poetisches Abstraktum als Individuen im Auge zu haben, und darum finde ich ihn hier den Griechen äußerst nah." Admiring Schiller's ingenuity in using *Wallensteins Lager* for the exposition of his drama, Goethe likens the mass of the army to the chorus of the Ancients.[9]

Crucial for the human significance of the exposition, the first scene of *Wallensteins Lager* focuses not on soldiers, but on peasants, on a son and a father about to play at dice with the soldiers.[10] This allusion to peace, to family life and being rooted in the land, together with the illusion of manipulating chance symbolizing the hazards of war, sets the stage for the conflict between soldiers, representing the state of nature, and civilians, representing the state of society, a conflict which is explored in every scene of *Wallensteins Lager*. Like concentric circles, the eleven scenes of this first play of *Wallenstein* spread around scene six, the central statement about war creating the conditions for freedom. Scene five, the Sutlerwoman's story about her own life, ties in with scene seven, the induction of the young boy into the army, both scenes setting the soldiers' life against and above the life of family and society. Scene four, the reference to Regensburg recalling Wallenstein's earlier dismissal from power correlates with scene eight, the appearance of the Capuchin friar who heaps blame and insult on the life of the army and its controversial leader. In contrast to scenes five and seven, scenes four and eight show the life encouraged under Wallenstein as a corruption of human existence. Scene three, the bargaining between the Croat and the Sharpshooter, is reflected in scene nine, the discussion of rumors about Wallenstein's alliance with the devil, where the Sergeant's "denn *er* denkt gar zu tiefe Sachen" carries over into the soldiers' "greift *ihn*, den Schelm!"[11]—meaning the peasant caught at foul play. Scene two, the Sergeant's suspicions about the assembly at Pilsen,[12] rather ironically fits with scene ten where the peasant, first condemned to hang, is let go because the war situation explains his desperation.

In the form of thesis and antithesis leading to synthesis, scene one, the view of necessity, and scene six, the view of freedom, lead to scene eleven, the view of freedom and necessity joined in the idea of discipline imposed on oneself. This proud view of life, expressed in the chorus's final words, "Und setzet ihr nicht das Leben ein, / Nie wird euch das Leben gewonnen sein," appears to be an answer to the *Prolog*'s challenge to present the great objectives of mankind on the shadow stage of art vying with the stage of life. In Gerhard Kaiser's formulation: "Die für Schillers Klassik charakteristische Verklärung der Existenz . . . ereignet sich für die *Wallenstein*-Trilogie im

Chorlied des Lagers, das im Sinne der griechischen Tragödie Kommentar und Deutung, zugleich aber auch Bestandteil des Vorganges ist."[13] Aware of the contrast between the solemn tone of the *Prolog* and the doggerel verse of *Wallensteins Lager*, we are supposed to thank the muse for playing the sinister truth of history over into the serene realm of art. The *Prolog's* closing line, "Ernst ist das Leben, heiter ist die Kunst," seems to be more than fulfilled in the final chorus of *Wallensteins Lager* where the curtain falls over the soldiers' claim about staking one's life in order to win it. The fact, however, that the curtain falls before the end of the chorus suggests that the soldiers' vision of life pretending to the serenity of art is,[14] at best, insufficient.

Following the prologue of Euripides's *Iphigenia in Aulis*, the first choral interlude describes the overwhelming spectacle of the Greek army encamped at Aulis. With the chorus divided evenly, the first half is devoted to the sight of the heroes, the second half to that of their ships.[15] Admiring the heroes at various sports, the chorus of foreign women begins with the Aiaces playing at dice, and ends with Achilles racing in full armor to overtake a chariot. With the effect of perfect symmetry for the whole, the second half of the chorus begins with the ships of Achilles, and ends with those of Ajax, the son of Telamon. Befitting the foreign women's ignorance of the true causes for the army's stay at Aulis, the figure of Agamemnon is missing from their account; only his ships are mentioned in the center between those of Achilles and Ajax.

Strikingly similar, the first play of Schiller's *Wallenstein* and the first choral interlude of Euripides's *Iphigenia in Aulis* present an army at leisure, open the view on a game of dice, and focus their attention, in the center of a highly symmetrical sequence of scenes or strophes, on the figure of a leader. Despite all these traits in common, the dissimilarity of the two beginnings is even more striking. Set between spatial or natural limits, between Chalkis, the home of the foreign women, and Troy, the destination of the army, the splendor of the Greek heroes, with Achilles in the center, is seen in harmonious beauty, almost like an idyllic landscape. Set between temporal or historical limits, between the peasant (the lowest type in society) and the Cuirassier (the highest type in the camp), the mass of Wallenstein's army, with the Sergeant and other soldiers in the center, is heard in unruly contentiousness that reveals the corruption of its life as a perversion of heroism. Where the classical play presents outstanding individuals and groups of friends diverting themselves with games of leisure, the modern play confronts us with common men, part of a mass, one cheating at dice and almost losing his life over it.[16] In contrast to the display of grace and beauty against the background of the story of Helen, the scenes around the Sutler-woman's tent against the background of her wretched story convey the impression of humanity both lost and gained. The loss of beauty and apparent[17] unity with nature is balanced by the gain of self-consciousness expressed in opinions by everyone about everything, be it within their range of understanding or not. The gamut of opinions about human nature, and the goals of life, reaches a climax in the various judgments about Wallenstein: "Doch in den kühnen Scharen, / Die sein Befehl gewaltig lenkt, sein Geist / Beseelt, wird euch sein Schattenbild begegnen."[18] While Achilles, truly a half-god, stands out in the center of Euripides's first choral interlude, Wallenstein, though only as shadow image, is present twice: once as half-god, in the opinion of his soldiers, once in the figure of the Sergeant conversing with them. Even in Euripides, the central presence of Achilles is challenged by the central position of Agamemnon's ships outnumbering all others. But whereas Agamemnon and Achilles complement each other as leaders, the commonness of the Sergeant compromises Wallenstein's leadership and makes it suitable for comedy rather than tragedy.

Corresponding to the middle section of Schiller's *Prolog* to *Wallenstein*, the middle play focuses on the historical situation of the Thirty Years' War. On a higher level than *Wallensteins Lager*, *Die Piccolomini* presents the political atmosphere among Wallenstein's generals and, for a few scenes, even Wallenstein himself. In pursuance of the parallel in "poetic plot" between Schiller's *Wallenstein* and Euripides's *Iphigenia in Aulis*, acts I, II, and III of *Die Piccolomini* correlate with acts II, III, and IV of *Iphigenia in Aulis*. The parallel, interrupted during acts IV and V of *Die Piccolomini*, is completed in *Wallensteins Tod*.

Gallas's attempt to detain Buttler, later the one to mastermind Wallenstein's murder, takes on a foreboding sense in the light of the capture by Menelaus of Clytemnestra's slave, later the one to betray Agamemnon to Clytemnestra and Achilles.[19] The heated argument about Wallenstein's usurpation of power that arises between Octavio and Questenberg on the one side, and Wallenstein's generals on the other side, reminds one of the argument between Menelaus and Agamemnon about Agamemnon's claim to leadership and his justification for trying to prevent the sacrifice of Iphigenia.[20]

Reminiscent of the messenger's announcement of the arrival of Clytemnestra, Iphigenia, and Orestes at Aulis, welcoming music indicates the arrival of Wallenstein's wife and daughter escorted by

Max. The added presence of Orestes and Max is the more significant if one considers their future roles: Orestes to avenge the murder of Agamemnon, Max to expiate the murder of Wallenstein by dying a death in the image of Wallenstein's dream before the battle at Lützen.[21] Max's defense of Wallenstein against Questenberg's accusations recalls Agamemnon's defense of himself against Menelaus's complaints. In the end, Questenberg is as moved by Max's plea for the idea of peace in Europe as Menelaus is by Agamemnon's plea for the life of Iphigenia.[22]

Octavio's curse upon Max's trip as Thekla's escort, and the chorus's curse upon Paris's abduction of Helen touch on similar points. While Paris and Helen, following Aphrodite, offend against society, Max and Thekla, following only their hearts, seem to offend against history. In a world marked by the fragmentation of human nature, where the completion of the individual is supposed to depend on the progress of mankind through history,[23] Max and Thekla's reliance on the natural force of the heart seems to be almost as grave an offense as Paris and Helen's reliance on the supernatural force of Aphrodite clashing with the laws of society.

Comparable to the chorus's fearful hope that no evil omen overshadow the arrival of Iphigenia and Clytemnestra, the astrologer's insistence on twelve rather than eleven chairs for the assembly of the generals throws a fateful light on Wallenstein's first appearance.[24] Seni's explanation that eleven transgresses the ten commandments, but that twelve encompasses both the planets (seven) and the human soul (five), the latter mixing good and evil as five mixes even and odd, provides a clue for the use of numbers in Schiller's *Wallenstein*: Only *Wallensteins Lager*, admittedly the basis for Wallenstein's crime,[25] has eleven scenes. The five acts of *Die Piccolomini*, with a significant imbalance between two scenes more in act III (the act dominated by love) and two scenes less in act V (the act dominated by hate), imply a balance of five scenes and seven scenes.[26] The five acts of *Wallensteins Tod*, the actual tragedy of the *Wallenstein* trilogy, balance out in units and compounds of seven scenes and twelve scenes.[27] The center of *Wallensteins Tod* (III, 12), surrounded on each side by eleven scenes, is the first and last open acknowledgment of Wallenstein's failure. Together with their corporal who voices the regiment's request for the truth about Wallenstein's treason from the general's own mouth, the contingent of ten Cuirassiers numbers eleven.[28] After forsaking her mother (IV, 11) in order to be united with Max at his grave (IV, 10), Thekla in her *Nänie* for him (IV, 12) not only mourns her beloved, borne to his rest by twelve noble youths, but also, in the spirit of Schiller's aesthetic reflections, the fate of "the Beautiful on earth." Wallenstein's murderers are supposed to gather "wenns elf geschlagen," but the murder will take place shortly after midnight.[29] The eleventh scene of act V in *Wallensteins Tod* does not present the murder itself, but rather the argument between Buttler and Octavio over the responsibility for the murder. Despite this damning fact, the fifth act of *Wallensteins Tod* is the only act of eleven in the trilogy to have twelve scenes, completing the dramatic poem and fulfilling, as it were, the *Prolog*'s closing line "Ernst ist das Leben, heiter ist die Kunst."[30] The *Prolog*, as opening statement to the whole of Schiller's *Wallenstein*, rounds out the number of acts to twelve.

Though inconspicuous in its effect on the theater audience, this number symbolism in Schiller's *Wallenstein* is the more striking as it is revealed directly before Wallenstein's first appearance. With the astrologer's explanation about the numbers eleven and twelve still in the air, Wallenstein's first appearance stands under the motto:

> Fünf ist
> Des Menschen Seele. Wie der Mensch aus Gutem
> Und Bösem ist gemischt, so ist die Fünfe
> Die erste Zahl aus Grad und Ungerade.[31]

Like the first scene of *Wallensteins Lager*, with its conversation between peasants rather than soldiers, Wallenstein's first appearance occurs in conversation with his family rather than his generals. Yet this allusion to the interdependence between the natural preconditions of political life (family) and political life itself (society) works both ways. Reminiscent of Agamemnon's manipulations at Aulis, Wallenstein uses a family affair, the anticipation of his daughter's wedding, as pretext for his political schemes.[32] After Iphigenia's arrival the messenger reports on the speculations about a royal wedding with the intention, "der Göttin von Aulis die Verlobte vorzustellen." While Agamemnon's wife is unaware of the pretext, Wallenstein's wife knowingly states:

> Ich tat nach Ihrer Vorschrift, führte an,
> Sie hätten über unser Kind bestimmt,
> Und möchten gern dem künftigen Gemahl
> Noch vor dem Feldzug die Verlobte zeigen.[33]

Like an echo of Clytemnestra's response to the chorus,

Ein glücklich Zeichen, schöne Hoffnungen
Und eines frohen Hymens Unterpfand,
Dem ich die Tochter bringe, nehm ich mir
Aus eurem Gruß und freundlichen Empfange,

Wallenstein welcomes Thekla with, "Ja! Schön ist mir die Hoffnung aufgegangen. / Ich nehme sie zum Pfande größern Glücks." The same words, in connection with his veneration for the name of Friedland, express Max's hope for becoming, through Thekla, Wallenstein's son, ". . . darin blühen soll / Mir jedes Glück und jede schöne Hoffnung."[34] Yet the stage direction about Wallenstein holding Thekla in his arms as Max enters[35] seems to imply that this hope for the personal happiness of the lovers is no more than an illusion.

The parallel between the first few scenes of act II of *Die Piccolomini* and of act III of *Iphigenia in Aulis* points to a crucial difference between the plays. In *Iphigenia in Aulis*, the third scene of act III, the central meeting between Agamemnon and Iphigenia, is at the same time the center of the whole play. In *Die Piccolomini*, the third scene of act II, the meeting between Wallenstein and Thekla, is not even the central scene of that act, let alone of the whole trilogy. While the conflict between father and king in Agamemnon determines the play as a whole, the conflict between father (scene 3) or friend (scene 4) and commanding general in Wallenstein expresses only one part of his complex character.

Act III of *Iphigenia in Aulis* pivots around scene three, correlating Clytemnestra's hope for the happiness of Iphigenia (scene 2) with Agamemnon's information about Achilles (scene 4), and the chorus's desire to avert any unhappy omen (scene 1) with the third choral interlude about the grief of the Trojan women. Likewise, act II of *Die Piccolomini* pivots around scene four, correlating Wallenstein's hopes for a royal crown on Thekla's head (scene 3) with his political dealings all over Europe (scene 5), Wallenstein's reaction to the news from the court (scene 2) with his insistence on the army's unconditional commitment to himself (scene 6), and the astrologer's reflections on the numbers eleven and twelve (scene 1) with the meeting of Wallenstein and Questenberg in the presence of Wallenstein's generals (scene 7). The correlation of the beginning and the end of act II of *Die Piccolomini* (scenes 1 and 7) with the beginning and the end of act III of *Iphigenia in Aulis* (scene 1 and the third choral interlude) points to the apparent futility of human deliberations in a world governed by the complexity of circumstances. The chorus's final doubts about the existence of the gods in act III of *Iphigenia in Aulis* and the servants' doubtful remarks about astrology in act II of *Die Piccolomini* suggest that Wallenstein's answer to Questenberg reflects the mixture of good and evil in the human soul as much as the grief of the Trojan women overshadows the deceptive happiness of Clytemnestra.

One of the dominant themes of both Schiller's *Wallenstein* and Euripides's *Iphigenia in Aulis* is the conflict between the private and the public realms. But whereas the central meeting between Agamemnon and Iphigenia presents it as a conflict between family and society, the central meeting between Max and Thekla presents it as a conflict between individuals and society.[36] Against the background of the banquet given for Wallenstein's generals, Max and Thekla meet in a world of their own, created by their love and sustained only by their hearts. Reminiscent of Achilles's impatience with Agamemnon, "anstatt noch länger ein Spiel zu sein der zögernden Atriden," the annoyance of Illo and Terzky with Wallenstein's indecision—elaborating on Terzky's "so hast du stets dein Spiel mit uns getrieben!"—sets the stage for the political background of the lovers' meeting.[37] Reminiscent of the compromising encounter of Clytemnestra and Achilles, the Terzkys' speculations about Wallenstein's intentions for Max throw a dubious light over the anticipated meeting. Thus the Countess says:

> Errat ich etwa nicht,
> Warum die Tochter hergefordert worden,
> Warum just *er* gewählt, sie abzuholen?
> Denn dieses vorgespiegelte Verlöbnis
> Mit einem Bräutigam, den niemand kennt,
> Mag andre blenden![38]

The sequence of scenes between Countess Terzky, Max, and Thekla parallels the long scene between Clytemnestra, the slave, and Achilles, revealing in each case the background for the situation. But where the slave reports on Agamemnon's pretext of marriage for the fateful sacrifice to Diana, Max tells of his love that made him seek refuge from the camp in a church with an image of the Virgin Mary.[39] When Clytemnestra laments,

> Doch hab ich sie
> Als deine Braut hieher geführt, *dir* hab ich
> Mit Blumen sie geschmücket—Ach! ein Opfer
> Hab ich geschmückt, ein Opfer hergeführt!

Achilles is moved to condemn Agamemnon not only for the sacrifice of Iphigenia, but also for the abuse of his name. Max, on the other hand, confesses:

> O! diesen Morgen, als ich Sie im Kreise
> Der Ihrigen, in Vaters Armen fand,
> Mich einen Fremdling sah in diesem Kreise!
> Wie drängte michs in diesem Augenblick,
> Ihm um den Hals zu fallen, *Vater* ihn
> Zu nennen! Doch sein strenges Auge hieß
> Die heftig wallende Empfindung schweigen,
> Und jene Diamanten schreckten mich,
> Die wie ein Kranz von Sternen Sie umgaben.
> Warum auch mußt er beim Empfange gleich
> Den Bann um Sie verbreiten, gleich zum Opfer
> Den Engel schmücken, auf das heitre Herz
> Die traurge Bürde seines Standes werfen!
> Wohl darf die Liebe werben um die Liebe,
> Doch solchem Glanz darf nur ein König nahn.[40]

Whereas Achilles, out of respect for custom, prevents Clytemnestra from having Iphigenia embrace his knees in supplication, Max and Thekla, left alone, hold each other, against all custom, in an embrace dictated only by their hearts.[41] Yet the complicated cross-relationships between Illo, the Terzkys, and Max, on the one hand, and the slave and Achilles, on the other hand,[42] point to the impossibility of Max and Thekla's extricating themselves from the political world to escape to "an island in ethereal heights."[43] Set against the background of the festive banquet given in honor of Wallenstein's generals, Thekla's premonitions in the last few scenes of act III of *Die Piccolomini* sound like an accompaniment to the fourth choral interlude of *Iphigenia in Aulis*, which contrasts the festive wedding of Peleus and Thetis with the bitter sacrifice of Iphigenia. As if transposing the description of that sacrifice,

> Dir flechten einen Kranz von Blüten
> Die Griechen in das schöngelockte Haar.
> Gleich einem Rinde, das der wilde Berg gebar,
> Das, unberührt vom Joch, aus Felsenhöhlen,
> Unfern dem Meer, gestiegen war,
> Wird dich der Opferstahl entseelen,[44]

onto a figurative level, the Countess warns Thekla:

Blick um dich her. Besinn dich, wo du bist—
Nicht in ein Freudenhaus bist du getreten,
Zu keiner Hochzeit findest du die Wände
Geschmückt, der Gäste Haupt bekränzt. Hier ist
Kein Glanz, als der von Waffen. Oder denkst du,
Man führte diese Tausende zusammen,
Beim Brautfest dir den Reihen aufzuführen?
Du siehst des Vaters Stirn gedankenvoll,
Der Mutter Aug in Tränen, auf der Waage liegt
Das große Schicksal unsers Hauses![45]

Even stronger than the choral interlude's conclusion,

Die Tugend ist aus dieser Welt geflohn,
Und dem Geschlecht der Menschen drohn
Nicht ferne mehr die göttlichen Gerichte,

Thekla's final monologue anticipates doom and destruction:

O! wenn ein Haus im Feuer soll vergehn,
Dann treibt der Himmel sein Gewölk zusammen,
Es schießt der Blitz herab aus heitern Höhn,
Aus unterirdschen Schlünden fahren Flammen,
Blindwütend schleudert selbst der Gott der Freude
Den Pechkranz in das brennende Gebäude![46]

Act IV of *Iphigenia in Aulis* pivots around scene three (the revelation of Agamemnon's deceit), correlating scene two (the meeting of Clytemnestra and Achilles) with strophe and antistrophe (his parents' wedding), and scene one (Achilles's eagerness for Troy) with the epode of the fourth choral interlude (Iphigenia's impending sacrifice). Likewise, act III of *Die Piccolomini* pivots around scene five (the embrace of the lovers), correlating scene four (their meeting) with scene six (their separation), scene three (Max's hope) with scene seven (Thekla's despair), scene two (the Terzkys' intrigue) with scene eight (its discussion), and scene one (the political speculations of Wallenstein's henchmen) with scene nine (Thekla's forebodings of doom and destruction). The symmetry expressed in these concentric circles of scenes around the intimate meeting of the lovers adds significance to that meeting as the center both of *Die Piccolomini* and of *Wallenstein* as a whole. Schiller's understanding of these scenes as the "poetically most important part"[47] of *Wallenstein* brings out the difference between Schiller's modern historical drama and Euripides's classical tragedy. Evolving the same poetic plot in a comparable sequence of symmetrically ordered scenes and acts, *Wallenstein*, with its focus on the conflict between individuals and society, stresses the freedom of self-consciousness, while *Iphigenia in Aulis*, with its focus on the conflict between the family and society, stresses the political nature of man.

In the comparison between Schiller's *Wallenstein* and Homer's *Iliad*, a complication of parallels was shown, in the last act of *Die Piccolomini*, by the addition of a parallel to Sophocles's *Philoctetes*. This additional parallel, by focusing on a pregnant moment after the action portrayed in the *Iliad*, raised the question of the mutual compatibility of epic and tragic poetry. In the comparison between Schiller's *Wallenstein* and Euripides's *Iphigenia in Aulis*, which focuses on a pregnant moment before the action portrayed in the *Iliad*, another complication of parallels can be shown, in the second to the last act of *Die Piccolomini*, by the addition of a parallel to Judas's betrayal of Jesus. This additional parallel, by focusing on the messianic character of Wallenstein as tragic hero, raises the question of the mutual compatibility of Greek tragedy with the spirit of Christianity. In either case the complication of parallels could point to the increasing insufficiency of Greek epic and tragic archetypes to sustain the symbolic extension of the modern poetic characters. At the end of his preface to *Die Braut von Messina*, Schiller remarks:

> Eine andere Freiheit, die ich mir erlaubt, möchte schwerer zu rechtfertigen sein. Ich habe die christliche Religion und die griechische Götterlehre vermischt angewendet . . . Und dann halte ich es für ein Recht der Poesie, die verschiedenen Religionen als ein kollektives Ganze für die Einbildungskraft zu behandeln, in welchem alles, was einen eignen Charakter trägt, eine eigne Empfindungsweise ausdrückt, seine Stelle findet. Unter der Hülle aller Religionen liegt die Religion selbst, die Idee eines Göttlichen, und es muß dem Dichter erlaubt sein, dieses auszusprechen, in welcher Form er jedesmal am bequemsten und am treffendsten findet.[48]

Why this part of *Wallenstein* should be the one to warrant Christian overtones is not immediately clear. It might be that the extraordinary historical moment demands a sanction accredited neither by nature nor by convention but by a power that appeals to the human heart without being humanly accountable.

"Anstatt eines körperlichen Eides," and within the limits of the oath to the Emperor, the pledge of allegiance to Wallenstein alludes to the New Law, written in the spirit rather than in the flesh and claiming to fulfill rather than to destroy the Old Law. The subsequent removal of the clause concerning the oath to the Emperor and the various generals' awareness of it point to the questionable character of that claim.[49] The chalice requested for the banquet at Pilsen, decorated with the symbols of religious freedom and the historical events leading to the Thirty Years' War, recalls the chalice used at the Last Supper and symbolizing the spirit of the New Testament.[50] Buttler's reminder that thirty signatures are required alludes to the thirty pieces of silver promised Judas for his betrayal of Jesus.[51] Buttler's later taunting one of the murderers with "Erschreckts dich, feige Memme? Wie? Du hast / Schon deine dreißig Seelen auf dir liegen—"[52] indicates that the killing of Wallenstein surpasses even the killing of Jesus. Terzky's statement, "ein Kreuz steht hier," Tiefenbach's "das Kreuz bin ich," and Isolani's "er kann nicht schreiben, doch sein Kreuz ist gut, und wird ihm honoriert von Jud und Christ" signify the three crosses on Golgotha, the middle one, between the two murderers, to bear Jesus of Nazareth, the king of the Jews.[53] Illo, in his drunkenness kissing Octavio, telling Max, "wer nicht ist *mit* mir, der ist wider mich," and confronting him, at sword's point, with "schreib—Judas!" reminds one of Judas's kissing Jesus, Jesus' rebuke of the Pharisees' accusation that he cast out Satan by the power of Satan, and Peter's striking one of Jesus' assailants at Gethsemane.[54] The confusion between Illo and Max as Judas, and Octavio and Wallenstein as Jesus, prefigures the fusion of traitor and hero in both Max and Octavio, the one to die, the other to live, for an ideal unable to sustain either of them.

Just as the parallel between Wallenstein and the Homeric Achilles leads over into the parallel between Wallenstein and the Sophoclean Philoctetes, so the parallel between Wallenstein and the Euripidean Agamemnon leads over into the parallel between Wallenstein and Jesus. In both cases, a hero of great suffering takes on the task of obtaining peace where the conventional powers have failed. Wallenstein's vision of peace for Europe, disregarding the differences of religion and territorial interests between the powers at war, recalls Jesus' attempt to unite mankind under the precepts of love rather than law.[55] Buttler's comment in act V of *Wallensteins Tod*, "Sie sehn im Herzog einen Friedensfürsten / Und einen Stifter neuer goldner Zeit,"[56] a variation on Luther's "Friedefürst," echoes Isaiah 9:6, the most outspoken prophecy on the coming of the Messiah. The messianic references to Wallenstein in *Wallensteins Lager*, called into question by Octavio's expectations for the Emperor's own son,[57] point back to the conflict between Jesus' disciples and the Pharisees over his claim to be the son of God.[58] Continuing the parallel between Schiller's *Wallenstein* and the story of the sacrifice of Iphigenia, the story of the sacrifice of Jesus seems to underline the problematic relationship between politics and religion, and the failure of each one without the other.[59]

As in the comparison with Homer's *Iliad*, the comparison with Euripides's *Iphigenia in Aulis* reveals a new parallel at the beginning of *Wallensteins Tod*. Against the background of Agamemnon's restless star watch, Wallenstein's observation of the conjunction between the planets Venus and Jupiter takes on a rather dubious meaning. At the brink of the Trojan War brought on by the favor of Venus to Paris, Agamemnon has to make a choice about his sacrifice of Iphigenia. Waiting for the favorable influence of Venus and Jupiter on the sinister power of Mars,[60] Wallenstein has to make a choice about his sacrifice of the idea of freedom. Like the sunrise over Aulis, Terzky's knocks at the door symbolize time's indifference to the human situation, and bear out Illo's earlier warning:

> O! du wirst auf die Sternenstunde warten,
> Bis dir die irdische entflieht! Glaub mir,
> In deiner Brust sind deines Schicksals Sterne.
> Vertrauen zu dir selbst, Entschlossenheit
> Ist deine Venus! Der Maleficus,
> Der einzge, der dir schadet, ist der *Zweifel*.[61]

The capture of Wallenstein's and Agamemnon's couriers, and the interception of their letters suggest that both leaders tend to be one step behind the events.[62] But where Menelaus blames Agamemnon for changing his decision about the sacrifice of Iphigenia, Illo and Terzky blame Wallenstein for his lack of decision.[63] Agamemnon's "Unglücklichster, was nun?" and his despair over the arrival of Iphigenia are echoed in Wallenstein's "Wärs möglich? Könnt ich nicht mehr, wie ich wollte?" and in his reflections on freedom and necessity in human nature.[64] Haunted by his decision about the sacrifice of a life, Agamemnon cries out, "In welche Schlingen hat das Schicksal mich / Verstrickt—ein Dämon, listiger als ich, / Vernichtet alle meine Künste," and laments, "Götter, wozu bringt ihr mich in diesem fürchterlichen Drange!"[65] Taunted by his decision about the sacrifice of an idea, the idea of the freedom to act or not to act, Wallenstein exclaims,

> Wie? Sollt ichs nun im Ernst erfüllen müssen,
> Weil ich zu frei gescherzt mit dem Gedanken?
> Verflucht, wer mit dem Teufel spielt!—

and observes, "Ich bin es nicht gewohnt, daß mich der Zufall / Blind waltend, finster herrschend mit sich führe."[66]

The three parts of II, 4 of *Iphigenia in Aulis* spell out the consequences of Iphigenia's arrival, announced to Agamemnon in the central scene of that act.[67] Likewise, the last three scenes of act I of *Wallensteins Tod* not only balance the first three scenes of it, but also elaborate on the three parts of Wallenstein's central monologue that discuss the connection between freedom and necessity in human nature manifested in the age-old authority of custom.[68]

While custom is a dominant theme in Agamemnon and Clytemnestra's exchange about the wedding of Iphigenia and Achilles, it plays only a negative role in the conversation between Wallenstein and Countess Terzky. Unlike Clytemnestra, who wants to hear about not only the parentage (nature) but also the education (custom) of Achilles, the Countess, in a rational argument for self-preservation, appeals only to nature.[69] Reminiscent of the serpent in the Garden of Eden, the Countess, instrumental in all the crucial moments of Wallenstein's fall, finally does effect a decision. Once aware of his fall, and of the evil to follow upon it, Wallenstein, like Agamemnon, defers to necessity. However, Agamemnon is overwhelmed by necessity,

> Doch ach! Dies wendet die entsetzliche
> Notwendigkeit nicht ab. Ich muß, ich muß
> Die Hände tauchen in ihr Blut,

and he cannot do anything but bewail his utter helplessness, "Daß ichs könnte! Ach! / Ich kann es nicht—ich kann nicht, wie ich wünsche— / Das ist es eben, was mir Kummer macht." By contrast, in reformulating Countess Terzky's statement,

> Denn recht hat jeder eigene Charakter,
> Der übereinstimmt mit sich selbst, es gibt
> Kein andres Unrecht, als den Widerspruch,

Wallenstein asserts, "Geschehe denn, was muß. / Recht stets behält das Schicksal, denn das Herz / In uns ist sein gebietrischer Vollzieher."[70]

Suspecting only personal motives, Countess Terzky makes light of Max's urgent request for an audience with Wallenstein. In a similar way, Clytemnestra's joyous anticipation of their future bond startles Achilles in his endeavor to question Agamemnon about the delay of the Trojan expedition. Shock and embarrassment turn to anger and grief upon the slave's information that the wedding of Iphigenia is only a pretext for her sacrifice.[71] Following the same pattern, Max's

"Mein General!" meets with Wallenstein's rejoinder, "Der bin ich nicht mehr, wenn du des Kaisers Offizier dich nennst,"[72] which buries Max's wish for personal happiness in his grief over Wallenstein's traitorous decision. Whereas Achilles, mostly for his own honor, agrees to defend the life of Iphigenia, Max tries to defend the idea of noble freedom.[73] Reminiscent of Agamemnon's anguished decision, "Entsetzlich ist mirs, solches zu beschließen, / Entsetzlich, mich ihm zu entziehn—sein muß es," Wallenstein reformulates his answer to the Countess, "Geschehe denn, was muß. / Recht stets behält das Schicksal, denn das Herz / In uns ist sein gebietrischer Vollzieher," in his more noble reply to Max, "Wir handeln, wie wir müssen. / So laß uns das Notwendige mit Würde, / Mit festem Schritte tun—."[74]

Just as the nobility in his conversation with Max gives meaning to Wallenstein's recollection of the night before the battle at Lützen, so the subtlety in Countess Terzky's persuasion of Wallenstein is matched by Octavio's assuredness, "Denn meines Kalkuls halt ich mich gewiß."[75] This statement of Octavio's in the central scene of act II of *Wallensteins Tod* serves as a counterpart not only to Wallenstein's usurpation of fate masked as acceptance of necessity, but also to his reflections on freedom and necessity in human nature expressed in the central monologue of act I of *Wallensteins Tod*.[76] Correlated with the seven scenes of act I of *Wallensteins Tod*, the seven scenes of the second act reveal a direct cause-and-effect relationship: Wallenstein's realization of the pregnant moment for action (I, 1) leads to his directives for Octavio, (II, 1); the report of Sesina's capture (I, 2) moves Max to confront Wallenstein (II, 2); Wallenstein's interpretation of Sesina's capture as accident (I, 3) makes mockery of his view that fate, not accident, brought Octavio to rouse him from his dream before the battle at Lützen (II, 3); Wallenstein's reflections on freedom and necessity in human nature (I, 4) are carried out in Octavio's "Kalkul" for action (II, 4); Wrangel's doubts about the army's willingness to defect (I, 5) are dubiously confirmed in Octavio's clever game with Isolani (II, 5); Wallenstein's belated respect for trust (I, 6) reaps its fruits in Octavio's winning back Buttler (II, 6); and finally, Wallenstein's fall to the guile of the Countess (I, 7) is caught in Max's refusal to play along with Octavio's "Kalkul" (II, 7). The same superposition of centers and correlating scenes could be done not only between different acts of one play but also between corresponding acts of different plays of *Wallenstein*, bearing out Schiller's claim that a work of art is "a living work where everything hangs together with everything and where nothing can be moved without dislocating everything."[77]

Compared with the first parallel between Schiller's *Wallenstein* and Euripides's *Iphigenia in Aulis*—which stretches from the *Prolog* (cf. *IA*, I) through *Wallensteins Lager* (cf. *IA*, first choral interlude) to acts I–III of *Die Piccolomini* (cf. *IA*, II–IV)—the second parallel starting over with *Wallensteins Tod* (*WT*, I–II; cf. *IA*, I–IV) is much less continuous. By act III of *Wallensteins Tod*, the interrupted first parallel is resumed and, together with the second, continues into act IV of *Wallensteins Tod*, but fades out before the last act of the *Wallenstein* trilogy begins.

Clytemnestra's reckoning with Agamemnon in her account of their marriage provides a background for the Duchess's reminiscence about her anguished life with Wallenstein.[78] Thekla's trembling denial of Wallenstein's request that she give proof of her enchanting voice[79] sounds like an echo of Iphigenia's tearful words to her father:

Mein Vater, hätt ich Orpheus' Mund, könnt ich
Durch meiner Stimme Zauber Felsen mir
Zu folgen zwingen, und durch meine Rede
Der Menschen Herzen, wie ich wollte, schmelzen,
Jetzt würd ich diese Kunst zu Hülfe rufen.
Doch meine ganze Redekunst sind Tränen.

That denial of Thekla's prompts the Countess to tell Wallenstein of the love between Max and Thekla.[80] His reaction, much more so than Agamemnon's agony about the fate of Iphigenia, deserves Clytemnestra's response, "Er hat sein Kind dem Orkus hingegeben."[81]

In their bitter union through death, Max and Thekla follow the fate of Iphigenia, who is finally willing to be sacrificed for the freedom of Greece. But whereas Achilles, surrounded by his men, pledges to counter the army's violent demand for the sacrifice of Iphigenia, Max, preceded by his Cuirassiers, stands torn between his love and his loyalty. Shortly before the end of Euripides's play, Iphigenia exclaims to her father:

Was geht mich Paris' Hochzeit an? Kam er
Nach Griechenland, mich Arme zu erwürgen?
O gönne mir dein Auge! Gönne mir
Nur einen Kuss, wenn auch nicht mehr Erhörung,
Daß ich *ein* Denkmal deiner Liebe doch
Mit zu den Toten nehme!

In the same spirit, Max asks:

Doch wie gerieten *wir*, die nichts verschuldet,
In diesen Kreis des Unglücks und Verbrechens?
Wem brachen *wir* die Treue? Warum muß

Der Väter Doppelschuld und Freveltat
Uns gräßlich wie ein Schlangenpaar umwinden?
Warum der Väter unversöhnter Haß
Auch uns, die Liebenden, zerreißend scheiden?

A while later, Max begs of Wallenstein:

—O wende deine Augen
Nicht von mir weg! Noch einmal zeige mir
Dein ewig teures und verehrtes Antlitz.
Verstoß mich nicht—[82]

Blending the roles of Iphigenia and Achilles, the tragedy of Max and
Thekla begins with the Countess's command, "Trennt euch!" and
reaches a climax with Wallenstein's command, "Scheidet!" Iphigenia's farewell, "Ein schöner Stern ging den Achivern auf / In deinem
Schoß—Doch nein. Ich will ja freudig sterben," ties together Wallenstein's greeting,

Sei mir willkommen, Max. Stets warst du mir
Der Bringer irgendeiner schönen Freude,
Und, wie das glückliche Gestirn des Morgens,
Führst du die Lebenssonne mir herauf,

and the Swedish captain's comment about Max's death: "man sagt, er
wollte sterben."[83] It also shines through Thekla's remembrance of her
love, which at the same time is a lament over the fate of "the Beautiful on earth."[84]

Even though Euripides's *Iphigenia in Aulis* ends either with a messenger's speech about the sacrifice of Iphigenia or the intervention of
a deus ex machina,[85] Schiller, emphasizing the human heroism, ends
his translation with Iphigenia's farewell. His plan for a future translation of Aeschylus's *Agamemnon*[86] seems to provide the missing section of the parallel between the last act of *Wallenstein* and Euripides's
Iphigenia in Aulis. As in the comparison with Homer's *Iliad*, Schiller's
modern dramatic poem, in the end, outstrips its ancient counterpart.

There is almost no limit to the complexity of Schiller's *Wallenstein*
as compared with Euripides's *Iphigenia in Aulis*.[87] Correlating with
the three parts of the *Prolog*, the three plays of *Wallenstein* correspond
to each other in centers and surrounding acts, balancing out in centers and surrounding scenes. Reminiscent of the relationship between the physical, the aesthetic, and the moral states, discussed in
Über die aesthetische Erziehung des Menschen, *freedom*, in the center of
Wallensteins Lager, and *necessity*, in the center of *Wallensteins Tod*,
pivot around *love*, in the center of *Die Piccolomini*, and therefore in

the center of *Wallenstein* as a whole.[88] The fact that *freedom*, in *Wallensteins Lager*, is proclaimed in the central scene of eleven scenes, and that *necessity*, in *Wallensteins Tod*, is affirmed in the twelfth scene of the third act, surrounded on either side by eleven scenes, points to the ambivalence of these aspects of human life. The fact that *love*, in *Die Piccolomini*, is celebrated in the fifth scene of the central act, but against the backdrop of the banquet which prepares the ground for Wallenstein's treason, reminds one of Seni's statement about the number five:

> Fünf ist
> Des Menschen Seele. Wie der Mensch aus Gutem
> Und Bösem ist gemischt, so ist die Fünfe
> Die erste Zahl aus Grad und Ungerade.[89]

It also points to the precariousness of the aesthetic state, possible in the realm of art, but an illusion in the realm of life. In regard to Wallenstein himself, the central claim of the *Prolog* reads:

> Von der Parteien Gunst und Haß verwirrt
> Schwankt sein Charakterbild in der Geschichte,
> Doch euren Augen soll ihn jetzt die Kunst,
> Auch eurem Herzen, menschlich näher bringen.
> Denn jedes Äußerste führte *sie*, die alles
> Begrenzt und bindet, zur Natur zurück,
> Sie sieht den Menschen in des Lebens Drang
> Und wälzt die größre Hälfte seiner Schuld
> Den unglückseligen Gestirnen zu.[90]

That claim seems to be fulfilled in the presentation of Wallenstein as a modern historical figure—a figure who reflects at the same time, however, the archetypes of Greek epic and tragic poetry. Such reflection of Greek art, a poetic device in the process of "individualizing the ideal" and "idealizing the individual," becomes an integral part in Schiller's presentation of the tragic hero as a paradigm of the "idea of mankind."[91]

VI. *Wallenstein*—"Not a Greek Tragedy"

Looking forward to a visit of Goethe's and a reading of the finished parts of *Wallenstein* in Goethe's presence, Schiller writes

> Aber freilich ist es keine griechische Tragödie und kann keine sein; wie überhaupt das Zeitalter, wenn ich auch eine daraus hätte machen können, es mir nicht gedankt hätte. Es ist ein zu reicher Gegenstand geworden, ein kleines Universum. . . .[1]

Shortly after the completion of *Wallenstein*, Johann Wilhelm Süvern published a book bearing the title *Über Schillers "Wallenstein" in Hinsicht auf griechische Tragödie*. Measuring *Wallenstein* against Sophoclean tragedy, Süvern takes issue mainly with Schiller's notion of fate. In his reply to Süvern, Schiller confesses his "unqualified veneration" for Sophocles, but rejects the imposition of a past product of art as "standard and model" for an "altogether heterogeneous time":

> Unsere Tragödie wenn wir eine solche hätten, hat mit der Ohnmacht, der Schlaffheit, der Charakterlosigkeit des Zeitgeistes und mit einer gemeinen Denkart zu ringen, sie muß also Kraft und Charakter zeigen, sie muß das Gemüt zu erschüttern, zu erheben, aber nicht aufzulösen suchen.[2]

As if in answer to this statement of Schiller's, Hegel voices his critique of the ending of *Wallenstein*: "Dies ist nicht tragisch, sondern entsetzlich! Dies zerreißt das Gemüt, daraus kann man nicht mit erleichterter Brust springen."[3] That statement seems to defy the mockery in Schiller's *Xenion* "Entgegengesetzte Wirkung":

> Wir Modernen, wir gehn erschüttert, gerührt aus dem Schauspiel,
> Mit erleichterter Brust hüpfte der Grieche heraus.

Less openly mocking is Schiller's *Xenion* "Griechische und moderne Tragödie":

> Unsre Tragödie spricht zum Verstand, drum zerreißt sie
> das Herz so,
> Jene setzt in Affekt, darum beruhigt sie so![4]

The comparison nevertheless seems to capitalize on the sting of contradiction offending our sensibilities. The logical force of "drum" and "dárum," the one contracted and without a stress, the other full and with a more than usual stress because of its position in the pentameter, is called into question by the opposition between "Verstand" and "Herz" as well as "Affekt" and "beruhigt." Yet the fact that both "drum" and "dárum" occur after caesuras, but "drum" after the fourth stress, and therefore off balance, and "dárum" after the third stress, and therefore in balance, emphasizes the difference between the two forms of tragedy. Considered in the light of Aristotle's definition of tragedy, according to which the arousal of pity and fear is supposed to achieve a purgation and a purification of such affects,[5] the pentameter of Schiller's *Xenion* loses its explicit contradiction. As a sign of Greek tragedy's achievement "das Gemüt . . . aufzulösen," no separate powers of the soul intrude on the pentameter.

After reading Aristotle's *Poetics*, Schiller reports: "Mich hat er mit meinem Wallenstein keineswegs unzufriedener gemacht. Ich fühle, daß ich ihm, den unvertilgbaren Unterschied der neuen von der alten Tragödie abgerechnet, in allen wesentlichen Forderungen Genüge geleistet habe, und leisten werde." Judging from the second *Xenion* quoted above, the ineradicable difference between ancient and modern tragedy may have something to do with the possibility or impossibility of a catharsis resulting from the arousal of pity and fear.[6]

The calming effect from the catharsis of Greek tragedy depends on the restoration of a balance between the extremes portrayed in the work of art towards an understanding of human nature within the framework of nature as a whole. Nature, in this view, provides standards not only for what we would call the natural world, but also for man who as a natural being endowed with reason is part of an ordered universe. According to a Kantian view of human nature, however, the standards for the understanding derive from the world of nature governed by necessity, but the standards for the heart from the world of morality governed by freedom.[7] Speaking to the understanding, modern tragedy tries to analyze this contradiction that causes man to remain forever an alien in the world. Rent by the failure of the understanding to justify man's suffering as part of a higher world order, the heart, thrown back upon itself, is left to a despair that Hegel refuses even to call tragic.

Attesting to both Schiller's modernity and kinship with the Greeks, Wilhelm von Humboldt comments on his first reading of *Wallenstein*:

Solche Massen hat noch niemand in Bewegung gesetzt; einen so viel umfassenden Stoff noch niemand gewählt; eine Handlung, deren Triebfedern und Folgen, gleich den Wurzeln und Zweigen eines ungeheuren Stamms, so weit verbreitet und so vielfach gestaltet zerstreut liegen, niemand in einer Tragödie dargestellt. Sie haben Wallensteins Familie zu einem Haus der Atriden gemacht, wo das Schicksal haust, wo die Bewohner vertrieben sind, aber wo der Betrachter gern und lang an der verödeten Stätte verweilt.[8]

On the basis of the preceding chapter, this statement of Humboldt's sounds less "metaphorisch über das Stück hinaus gesprochen"[9] than it might otherwise seem. Far from attempting[10] a "nachdichtende Wiederbelebung der antiken Tragödie," Schiller both did and did not seize on "einem mythischen und bereits von antiken Tragikern behandelten Stoff."[11] True to the supremacy of modernity in Schiller's *Wallenstein*, Humboldt's remarks about Wallenstein's family as a house of Atreus comment on the modern complexity of the work. Despite the similarity in poetic plot between Schiller's *Wallenstein* and Euripides's *Iphigenia in Aulis*, Humboldt's comments call more attention to the dissimilarity between modern and Greek tragedy. Impressed with Schiller's view of *Wallenstein* as the "touchstone" for his "poetic capacity," Humboldt marvels at the tragic grandeur resulting from the complexity of Schiller's characters and plots.

In comparison with Homer's *Iliad* and Euripides's *Iphigenia in Aulis* as representative works of Greek epic and tragic poetry, Schiller's *Wallenstein* is no doubt closer to the latter. It, nevertheless, "ist keine griechische Tragödie und kann keine sein." Shifting the implication of "kann" from an inconceivability for the poetic work to be otherwise than it is to the poet's being determined by the circumstances of his time, Florian Prader asserts, "die Modernität des eigenen Dichtertums, die Humboldt ihm zuspricht, kann er nicht verleugnen."[12] That this is not a question of poetic capacity but of poetic will seems to me indisputable.

Compared with the characters in Euripides's *Iphigenia in Aulis*, the characters in Schiller's *Wallenstein* reflect more than they act. Caught up in reflections, they express themselves in rather abstract language.[13] In the expression of their modern self-consciousness, they seem to be a living example of the progress of mankind in the course of history. As a sign of this progress, staggered parallels between the plots of Schiller's *Wallenstein* and Euripides's *Iphigenia in Aulis* indicate a greater differentiation of human nature in the species at the cost of a fragmentation of it in the individuals. Highlighting both the gain and the loss of mankind in its historical development, the central scene of Schiller's *Wallenstein* (III, 5 of *Die Piccolomini*) focuses on the conflict between individuals and society, whereas the central scene of Euripides's *Iphigenia in Aulis* (III, 3) focuses on the conflict between the family and society. In support of this emphasis on individual rather than political morality, a parallel to Judas's betrayal of Jesus raises the question of the mutual compatibility between the classical and the Christian spirit within the context of the modern historical drama.

Commenting on Schiller's genius in blending diverse traditions, Hugo von Hofmannsthal speaks of him as:

> Der große Schüler des Rousseau und des Euripides, nicht geringer als einer von ihnen. Ein Geist, der in großer Weise sich Resultate aneignete. Der die Sittlichkeit Kants, die Hingerissenheit und Fülle des Katholizismus, die Gebundenheit der Antike in sein Bauwerk hineinnahm, wie die normännischen Seekönige ihre Burgen aus antikem und sarazenischem Getrümmer aufrichteten. Der mit seinem Adlerblick nirgends Schranken sah, nicht der Zeiten, nicht der Länder.[14]

Verifying this intuition of Hofmannsthal's, scholars have taken note of Schiller's incorporating foreign elements into his own dramatic work. In the context of a small survey of such passages, Emil Staiger claims:

> Die Trimeter und die ungereimten Strophen der Chöre, auch die häufigen Stichomythien, erinnern uns an die attische Tragödie und sollen uns offenbar auch an sie erinnern. Der Anklang wird noch verstärkt durch eine Menge von Versen, die jeder, der Aischylos, Sophokles und Euripides kennt, schon oft gelesen zu haben glaubt.[15]

Much more radically, but only with respect to Schiller's *Die Braut von Messina*, Wolfgang Schadewaldt interprets the wealth of "intentionally and consciously wrought" quotes from Sophocles's *Oedipus* and "the same sequence of scenes, situations, images" from Schiller's own translation of Euripides's *Phoenician Women* as "regulative forces" within Schiller's "free shaping of modern materials." Trying to assess the function of such foreign elements in the one work of Schiller's that comes closest to Greek tragedy, Schadewaldt concludes:

> Was sein jahrelanges Lernen an den Griechen ihm eingebracht hat, ist ein vielseitiges, vielschichtiges Ganzes. Im Stofflichen: Ar-

chetypen und Motive, die er neu faßte, im Dramaturgischen: eine
Fülle von Handlungsformen, die er überbot, indem er sie neu ab-
wandelte, kombinierte, vervielfältigte.[16]

With only a general acknowledgment of the influence of Greek
tragedy on Schiller's *Wallenstein*, Schadewaldt likens the alternating
of the subsequent plays between a "stricter" and a "looser" form of
tragedy to the natural rhythm of systolic and diastolic movement.[17]
Using "stricter" and "looser" as respective synonyms for "Greek"
and "modern," Schadewaldt seems to claim an organic give and take
between those elements in Schiller's dramatic work.

With a similar approach, Harold Jantz considers Schiller's incorporating a scene from Aeschylus's *Persians* into *Wilhelm Tell* as "one of
the symbolic extensions of the drama."[18] In a more general context,
Jantz explores the artistic phenomenon of the intentional transposition of seemingly foreign material into a poet's own work. The effec-
tiveness of this artistic phenomenon to be found in the poetry of all
ages depends not only on the subtlety of its writers, but also on the
keenness of its readers:

> In einem zeitgenössischen Werk wird der gut informierte Leser
> den "Fremdkörper" oft leicht erkennen, auch wenn er sorgfältig
> verhüllt und eingeblendet ist. Bei älteren Werken darf das funda-
> mentale und notwendige Wissen und Verständnis des modernen
> Lesers nicht vorausgesetzt werden. Wenn ein Forscher nun die
> übersehenen Züge aufweist und erklärt, dann bewirkt das allzu-
> leicht die falsche Beschuldigung der Quellenjagd und dadurch
> wird die richtige Erkenntnis der symbolischen Bedeutung der
> eingefügten Artefakten erschwert.[19]

Whether and to what extent Schiller's plays include echoes from
Greek tragedy or Homer, from Shakespeare or the Bible, or even
from a more or less variegated mixture of these, depends on their
theme as well as on their time in the poet's life. The Bible seems to
predominate in the earlier, Greek tragedy in the later plays. Though
more all-pervasive, Homer seems to predominate in the plays beginning with *Wallenstein*, and Shakespeare in those ending with *Wallenstein*. Besides this difference in predominant voices, some of Schiller's plays are more, some less open about these symbolic extensions. While *Die Räuber*, in so many words, interprets the love
between Karl and Amalia through their song about Hector's parting
from Andromache,[20] and the despair of old Moor through the reading about Jacob's grief over the loss of Joseph,[21] *Wallenstein* never so

much as hints at either Homer's *Iliad* or Euripides's *Iphigenia in Aulis*, which this study identifies as the principal symbolic extensions of the trilogy.[22] A statement of Schiller's from the early months of his work on *Wallenstein* might apply here too:

> Vordem legte ich das ganze Gewicht in die Mehrheit des Einzelnen; jetzt wird alles auf die Totalität berechnet, und ich werde mich bemühen, denselben Reichtum im einzelnen mit eben sovielem Aufwand von Kunst zu verstecken, als ich sonst angewandt ihn zu zeigen, und das Einzelne recht vordringen zu lassen.[23]

Schiller's letters are full of remarks about his literary studies and their influence on his own dramatic work. Yet these remarks rarely go beyond general comments such as intending to use a Euripidean method for *Maria Stuart* or hoping to write *Wilhelm Tell* in the spirit of antiquity newly quickened in him by his reading of Aeschylus.[24] There are, however, a few comments on the poetic integration of foreign material into his own dramatic work. One is about the character of Karl Moor in *Die Räuber*:

> Räuber Moor ist nicht Dieb, aber Mörder. Nicht Schurke, aber Ungeheuer. Wofern ich mich nicht irre, dankt dieser seltene Mensch seine Grundzüge dem Plutarch und Cervantes, die durch den eigenen Geist des Dichters nach Shakespearischer Manier in einem neuen, wahren und harmonischen Charakter unter sich amalgamiert sind.[25]

Another such comment is about the Montgomery scene in *Die Jungfrau von Orléans*: "Wer seinen Homer kennt, der weiß wohl, was mir dabei vorschwebt."[26] A third concerns his recent reading of Shakespeare and Sophocles and its consequences for his *Wallenstein*. Not one of these comments is explicit enough to clarify why Schiller, even in his most modern of historical dramas, would resort to symbolic extensions into the mythical worlds of Greek poetry.

Rounding out his remark about *Wallenstein* not being a Greek tragedy nor being able to be one, Schiller claims, "Es ist ein zu reicher Gegenstand geworden, ein kleines Universum."[27] Abstracting now from the intrinsic complexity of *Wallenstein* and focusing only on Schiller's integration of Greek epic and tragic poetry into his own modern historical drama, one cannot help but consider those foreign elements in connection with *Wallenstein* as a "small universe." A comment in one of Schiller's early letters seems to point the way to a fuller understanding:

> Mein Euripides gibt mir noch viel Vergnügen, und ein großer Teil davon kommt auch auf sein Altertum. Den Menschen sich so ewig selbstgleich zu finden, dieselben Leidenschaften, dieselbe Collisionen der Leidenschaften, dieselbe Sprache der Leidenschaften. Bei dieser unendlichen Mannichfaltigkeit immer doch diese Ähnlichkeit, diese Einheit derselben Menschenform.[28]

Schiller's appreciation of his text's antiquity is the more remarkable in that he is speaking of one of Euripides's last plays, which, at the same time, is one of the last plays to be considered a Greek tragedy. Be that as it may, Euripides's portrayal of human nature brings Schiller face to face with archetypal figures whose humanity rings true despite the passing of the ages. His reading of Homer, during the same period of his life, stirs in him an even stronger conviction that the passing of the ages cannot obliterate the truth of nature contained in the *Iliad*.

Surrounding the modern historical world of the Thirty Years' War with a mythical horizon of overtones from Homer and Greek tragedy, Schiller transcends the narrow limits of historical truth. Encompassing historical with poetic truth, he points to the truth of nature and thus substantiates the significance of time as well as of timelessness.[29]

In the language of Schiller's preface to *Die Braut von Messina*, the archetypal forms of Greek epic and tragic poetry allow the modern poet "both to unveil and veil the human forms" of his own picture:

> Wie der bildende Künstler die faltige Fülle der Gewänder um seine Figuren breitet, um die Räume seines Bildes reich und anmutig auszufüllen, um die getrennten Partien desselben in ruhigen Massen stetig zu verbinden, um der Farbe, die das Auge reizt und erquickt, einen Spielraum zu geben, um die menschlichen Formen zugleich geistreich zu verhüllen und sichtbar zu machen, eben so durchflicht und umgibt der tragische Dichter seine streng abgemessene Handlung und die festen Umrisse seiner handelnden Figuren mit einem lyrischen Prachtgewebe, in welchem sich, als wie in einem weit gefalteten Purpurgewand, die handelnden Personen frei und edel mit einer gehaltenen Würde und hoher Ruhe bewegen.[30]

Transposing Schiller's "lyrical" to "mythical," we gain a perspective on the field of Homeric and Euripidean overtones above and beyond the modern historical world of *Wallenstein*. In the light of Homer's *Iliad*, the quarrel between Wallenstein and the Emperor and the friendship between Wallenstein and Max restate the quarrel between Achilles and Agamemnon and the friendship between Achilles and Patroclos. In the light of Euripides's *Iphigenia in Aulis*, Wallenstein's conflict over the sacrifice of his freedom and Max's attempt to save Wallenstein's nobility restate Agamemnon's conflict over the sacrifice of Iphigenia and Achilles's attempt to save her life. Like the death of Patroclos for Achilles and the sacrifice of Iphigenia for Agamemnon, the death of Max brings Wallenstein closer to realizing the tragic connection between freedom and necessity borne out in the problematic relationship of nature and convention.

Encompassing the roles of the Homeric Achilles and the Euripidean Agamemnon, the poetic figure of Wallenstein merges the archetypes of the natural hero and the conventional ruler. The fact that Schiller takes the figures of Achilles and Agamemnon not only from Homer, but from Homer *and* Euripides, the first and the last in the tradition of classical Greek poets, heightens the complexity of his poetic enterprise. Reflecting the difference between the worlds of epic and tragic poetry, their presence in *Wallenstein* is felt differently.[31] Aimed more at the development of characters than of plot, the restatement of epic poetry directly preserves Homer's themes. Aimed more at the development of plot than of characters, the restatement of tragic poetry indirectly preserves Euripides's themes, but substitutes ideas for the life of a human being.[32]

Given Schiller's notion of Homer as the naive poet par excellence and of Euripides as a poet on the way from naive to sentimental poetry, the contrast between *Wallenstein* and the *Iliad* is much stronger than the one between *Wallenstein* and *Iphigenia in Aulis*. By opening a perspective on the archetypal figures of Achilles and Agamemnon, once in the light of the *Iliad*, once in the light of the pregnant moment before the action portrayed in the *Iliad*, Schiller creates a mythical horizon which, at the same time, allows us to see the fragmentation of modern man and his striving for a new totality made possible through history. Schiller's preservation of themes from Homer and Euripides, together with his substitution of ideas for the life of a human being, implies his assumption of the constancy of human nature borne out in its historical development.

This acknowledgment of a mythical horizon that extends the definitive historical time into an atmosphere of poetic timelessness goes far beyond the claim of Helmut Koopmann's "Schillers *Wallenstein*: Antiker Mythos und moderne Geschichte." Koopmann's formulation, "Das antike Erbe ist gerade in der Behandlung Wallensteins als eines Mythos in *Wallensteins Lager* unverkennbar," acknowledges the legacy of antiquity only in a very specific sense:

> Was wie eine antike Tragödie mit einem Mythos beginnt, endet als
> moderne historische Tragödie mit der Entthronung dieses Mythos:
> der über alle Zeit und alles zeitliche Geschehen erhabene Wallen-
> stein des *Lagers* wird in die zerstörerische, den Mythos destruie-
> rende Gewalt der Zeit einbezogen, ihr unterworfen und von ihr
> überwältigt.

Though Koopmann's conclusion is correct in its general outline, "In
diesem eigentlichen Sinne steht die von Schiller modern gesehene
Macht der Geschichte, die Shakespearesche Welt, gegen die zeitlos
antikische Welt des Sophokles,"[33] it does not sufficiently take into
account that Schiller, in his assimilation of Greek tragedy, favors Euripides much more than Sophocles. Euripides's denunciation of *ta
pragmata* as finally responsible for the tragic condition of man is not
too far from Schiller's accusation of circumstances as active powers
within human history.[34]

The complex mythical horizon around Schiller's *Wallenstein*, the
more complex as it intertwines Homeric and Euripidean overtones,
seems to express more than one poetic purpose. Seeing the characters and plots of Schiller's modern historical drama against the background of Greek mythical archetypes, one becomes aware of their
similarity as much as of their dissimilarity. Not necessarily set up as
models, the archetypal figures act as catalysts in our understanding
of Schiller's dramatic conception.[35] Achieving a reciprocal interpretation between modern and Greek poetry, Schiller seems to point to
the relative perfection and imperfection of both.[36]

A look at Schiller's philosophical writings will help us to understand the theoretical foundations of this poetic vision.

Part III. Philosophical Writings

Aber dies Dichtergenie war auf das engste an das Denken in allen seinen Tiefen und Höhen geknüpft, es tritt ganz eigentlich auf dem Grunde einer Intellektualität hervor, die Alles, ergründend, spalten, und Alles, verknüpfend, zu einem Ganzen vereinen möchte. Darin liegt Schillers besondere Eigentümlichkeit. Er forderte von der Dichtung einen tieferen Anteil des Gedankens, und unterwarf sie strenger einer geistigen Einheit, letzteres auf zweifache Weise, indem er sie an eine festere Kunstform band, und indem er jede Dichtung so behandelte, daß ihr Stoff unwillkürlich und von selbst seine Individualität zum Ganzen einer Idee erweiterte.

(W. v. Humboldt, *Über Schiller*)

VII. Philosophical Poems and Aesthetic Writings

In the spirit of his poem "Die Künstler," which traces the role of art from the beginnings of human history to Schiller's own historical moment, Schiller, at the outset of his letters *Über die aesthetische Erziehung des Menschen*, confesses that he would not like to live in and have worked for a different century.[1] Convinced of the responsibility of artists for the humanity of mankind during their time, Schiller challenges them:

> Der Menschheit Würde ist in eure Hand gegeben,
> Bewahret sie!
> Sie sinkt mit euch! Mit euch wird sie sich heben![2]

This sense of urgency about guarding the dignity of mankind stems from Schiller's notion of a necessary historical development of man from a state of nature to a state of civilization where the progress of the species towards a fulfillment of human nature depends on the fragmentation of it in the individuals. As manifestations of these two states of mankind, Schiller contrasts the Greeks and the Moderns.[3] As in "Die Sänger der Vorwelt," where the happiness of a life in harmony with men and gods fills the lines with longing and regret, Schiller, in "Der Genius," laments:

> Aber die glückliche Zeit ist dahin! Vermessene Willkür
> Hat der getreuen Natur göttlichen Frieden gestört.
> Das entweihte Gefühl ist nicht mehr Stimme der Götter,
> Und das Orakel verstummt in der entadelten Brust.
> Nur in dem stilleren Selbst vernimmt es der horchende Geist
>   noch,
> Und den heiligen Sinn hütet das mystische Wort.[4]

Shaped by "all-uniting nature," the Greeks, in Schiller's eyes, exhibit a totality of nature, both in the individuals and in the species; shaped by "all-dividing reason," the Moderns exhibit a fragmentation of nature in the individuals for the sake of a more differentiated totality of it in the species.[5]

Notwithstanding his conviction that the species could have progressed in no other way, Schiller rebels against this sacrifice of the individuals in the cause of humanity:

> Kann aber wohl der Mensch dazu bestimmt sein, über irgendeinem Zwecke sich selbst zu versäumen? Sollte uns die Natur durch ihre Zwecke eine Vollkommenheit rauben können, welche uns die Vernunft durch die ihrigen vorschreibt? Es muß also falsch sein, daß die Ausbildung der einzelnen Kräfte das Opfer ihrer Totalität notwendig macht; oder wenn auch das Gesetz der Natur noch so sehr dahin strebte, so muß es bei uns stehen, diese Totalität in unsrer Natur, welche die Kunst zerstört hat, durch eine höhere Kunst wieder herzustellen.[6]

This credo, which reformulates Schiller's challenge to the artists to preserve the dignity of mankind, assumes that a special kinship between genius and nature exempts them from the curse of the historical development. Mourning a world deprived of gods, and therefore no longer a reflection of man either, "Die Götter Griechenlands" finds the trace of nature's lost beauty only in the land of poetry:

> Ja, sie kehrten heim, und alles Schöne,
> Alles Hohe nahmen sie mit fort,
> Alle Farben, alle Lebenstöne,
> Und uns blieb nur das entseelte Wort.
> Aus der Zeitflut weggerissen, schweben
> Sie gerettet auf des Pindus Höhn,
> Was unsterblich im Gesang soll leben,
> Muß im Leben untergehn.[7]

Relying on the one hand on the heart of the poet to echo the divine voice of nature,[8] Schiller on the other hand refers to reason as the source of a culture which will lead us back to nature: "Leben gab ihr die Fabel, die Schule hat sie entseelet, / Schaffendes Leben aufs neu gibt die Vernunft ihr zurück."[9] Measured against the end of "Die Götter Griechenlands," these two lines of "Die drei Alter der Natur" seem to distill from the life lost with the Greeks a higher form of life possible for the Moderns. Schiller's claim that "nature, even now, is the only flame to nourish the poetic spirit" has to be understood in a dialectical way:

> Aber wenn du über das verlorene *Glück* der Natur getröstet bist, so laß ihre *Vollkommenheit* deinem Herzen zum Muster dienen. Trittst du heraus zu ihr aus deinem künstlichen Kreis, steht sie vor dir in ihrer großen Ruhe, in ihrer naiven Schönheit, in ihrer

kindlichen Unschuld und Einfalt; dann verweile bei diesem Bilde, pflege dieses Gefühl, es ist deiner herrlichsten Menschheit würdig. Laß dir nicht mehr einfallen, mit ihr *tauschen* zu wollen, aber nimm sie in dich auf und strebe, ihren unendlichen Vorzug mit deinem eigenen unendlichen Prärogativ zu vermählen, und aus beidem das Göttliche zu erzeugen. Sie umgebe dich wie eine liebliche *Idylle*, in der du dich selbst immer wiederfindest aus den Verirrungen der Kunst, bei der du Mut und neues Vertrauen sammelst zum Laufe und die Flamme des *Ideals*, die in den Stürmen des Lebens so leicht erlischt, in deinem Herzen von neuem entzündest.[10]

Considering poets as preservers of nature, Schiller distinguishes between two types, the naive poet as "being nature," the sentimental poet as "seeking nature."[11] Striving to give mankind "its fullest expression possible," the naive poet fulfills the task by "imitating nature," the sentimental poet by "presenting the ideal":

Dem naiven Dichter hat die Natur die Gunst erzeigt, immer als eine ungeteilte Einheit zu wirken, in jedem Moment ein selbständiges und vollendetes Ganze zu sein und die Menschheit, ihrem vollen Gehalt nach, in der Wirklichkeit darzustellen. Dem sentimentalischen hat sie die Macht verliehen oder vielmehr einen lebendigen Trieb eingeprägt, jene Einheit, die durch Abstraktion in ihm aufgehoben worden, aus sich selbst wieder herzustellen, die Menschheit in sich vollständig zu machen, und aus einem beschränkten Zustand zu einem unendlichen überzugehen.[12]

This difference expressive of two states of mankind, the one of a union, the other of a separation between man and nature, is viewed by Schiller as the difference between two forms of perfection. By imitating nature (a form of "absolute presentation"), naive poetry is understood to fulfill a finite goal; by presenting the ideal (a form of "presentation of an absolute"), sentimental poetry is understood to strive for an infinite goal.[13]

Granting Wilhelm von Humboldt's doubts about the sharp distinction between naive and sentimental poetry, Schiller agrees that in order to understand the relationship of the different species to the genus he might have overstated their specific differences. Distinguishing between "individualization" and "idealization" as the specific differences between the Greeks and the Moderns,[14] Schiller seems to overstate his thesis in both directions. From the point of view that a strict historicism can never do justice to the complexity of human nature in all ages as well as to the poetry attempting to capture it, Schiller's philosophy of history and the poetic typology built on it appear to be generally misconceived. Their particular application to the Greeks[15] as children of the history of mankind whose original unity with nature, reflected in Greek works of art, is supposed to provide a model for our striving to restore that unity on a higher level equally underestimates and overestimates them.[16] Schiller's image of the Greeks not only as examples of a lost age of natural beauty and nobility, but also as models for an age where beauty and nobility are to be restored through the powers of reason, has been called "Griechenromantik."[17] With his explanation that the poet's lament never concerns a real, but always an ideal loss—"Der elegische Dichter sucht die Natur, aber als eine Idee und in einer Vollkommenheit, in der sie nie existiert hat, wenn er sie gleich als etwas Dagewesenes und nun Verlorenes beweint"—Schiller shifts one's attention from the historical accuracy to the poetic fruitfulness of what one might call his "Griechenerlebnis."[18] Whether this shift tacitly invalidates Schiller's philosophy of history or only suspends the question of its status with respect to his understanding of human nature, remains, I think, a problem.

Like most of the poems written during his work on *Über die aesthetische Erziehung des Menschen* and *Über naive und sentimentalische Dichtung*, Schiller's "Der Spaziergang" reflects his thoughts about the historical development of man. At first conceived under the title "Elegie," it shares the characteristics of that genre: "Setzt der Dichter die Natur der Kunst und das Ideal der Wirklichkeit so entgegen, daß die Darstellung des ersten überwiegt, und das Wohlgefallen an demselben herrschende Empfindung wird, so nenne ich ihn *elegisch*."[19] Yet the further specification that "nature," presented as "lost," and "the ideal," presented as "unattained," become an object of "mourning" appears to be met differently than in Schiller's other elegies. Whereas "Die Götter Griechenlands" and "Die Sänger der Vorwelt" mourn a lost beauty of nature that, only an echo in the recesses of the human heart, might come to life again in poetry, "Der Spaziergang" overlays nature and history in such a way that the live experience of nature, in the description of the poet's walk through a changing natural landscape, transmits a panorama of historical perspectives.[20] Written in the present tense, except for the reminiscence about Greek life and art and the final realization about the intrusion of the historical perspectives on the natural world, the poem begins and ends with nature.[21] The use of the past tense for both the oasis of Greek life and art, in the history of mankind, and the historical self-consciousness of the modern poet may be related to the change of titles from "Elegie" to "Der Spaziergang." By the end of the poem, the "sun" that originally shone upon the mountain top shines upon us as "Homer's sun." In Gerhard Kaiser's formulation: "Es ist, an sich selbst, die gleiche Sonne, die Homer geleuchtet hat, in der Tat. Aber erst der Moderne kann dieses Gleichbleibende erfassen. Die Sonne Homers, als solche erkannt, ist neue Sonne aus imaginativer Reflexion, Symbol neuer Natur aus dem Geist."[22]

Years before, stirred by the beauty of a sunset, Schiller had marveled about the power of the human soul to endow the natural world with life and meaning. Yet speaking of nature as eternally the same and of the human spirit as eternally different, he had also expressed his gratitude for nature's ability to preserve the changing images of the human self.[23] Passing from the creation of nature in human experience to the representation of it in human art, Schiller, clearly distancing himself from the art of the Greeks as he saw it, speaks of art not only as enriching nature,[24] but even as constituting it:

> Die Natur selbst ist nur eine Idee des Geistes, die nie in die Sinne fällt. Unter der Decke der Erscheinungen liegt sie, aber sie selbst kommt niemals zur Erscheinung. Bloß der Kunst des Ideals ist es verliehen, oder vielmehr es ist ihr aufgegeben, diesen Geist des Alls zu ergreifen, und in einer körperlichen Form zu binden. Auch sie selbst kann ihn zwar nie vor die Sinne, aber doch durch ihre schaffende Gewalt vor die Einbildungskraft bringen, und dadurch wahrer sein als alle Wirklichkeit und realer als alle Erfahrung. Es ergibt sich daraus von selbst, daß der Künstler kein einziges Element aus der Wirklichkeit brauchen kann, wie er es findet, daß sein Werk in *allen* seinen Teilen ideell sein muß, wenn es als ein Ganzes Realität haben und mit der Natur übereinstimmen soll.[25]

To see the sun as the sun of Homer, therefore, means not only to see it as endowed with the experience of life in an individual sense, but with the experience of life preserved in the archetypal forms of poetry attesting to the life of mankind as a whole. With the same theoretical understanding of the relationship between man and nature, Schiller's drama, presenting historical characters surrounded by a mythical horizon of archetypal figures from Greek epic and tragic poetry, encompasses the whole of nature.

In recapitulating the results of this study, the next chapter will offer an assessment of the function of Schiller's aesthetic theories in his poetic practice.

VIII. Theory in Practice: Art and Nature in Schiller's Presentation of the Ideal

Schiller's notion of art as building its "ideal edifice" on the "firm and deep foundation of nature," together with his notion of nature as "only an idea of the mind inaccessible to the senses," explains his credo that "the artist cannot use a single element from reality, as he finds it, that his work has to be ideal in *all* its parts, if it is to have reality as a whole and agree with nature."[1] Convinced of the symbolic nature of poetic figures and their implicit universality confirmed by the example of the Ancients, Schiller urges a reform of the drama where the introduction of symbolic devices would displace the common imitation of nature and thus "provide air and light for art."[2] What he means by symbolic devices might become clear from Schiller's portrait of the artist:

> Der Künstler ist zwar der Sohn seiner Zeit, aber schlimm für ihn, wenn er zugleich ihr Zögling oder gar noch ihr Günstling ist. Eine wohltätige Gottheit reiße den Säugling beizeiten von seiner Mutter Brust, nähre ihn mit der Milch eines bessern Alters und lasse ihn unter fernem griechischen Himmel zur Mündigkeit reifen. Wenn er dann Mann geworden ist, so kehre er, eine fremde Gestalt, in sein Jahrhundert zurück; aber nicht, um es mit seiner Erscheinung zu erfreuen, sondern furchtbar wie Agamemnons Sohn, um es zu reinigen.[3]

Clear about not wanting to live in and have worked for a different century, Schiller emphasizes the importance of compensating for the prosaic character of his own time with the poetic spirit of the age of the Greeks. Counseling the poetic genius of his time to remain, through the Greek myths, the relative of a "far off, foreign and ideal age,"[4] he uses the myth of Orestes to intimate the difficulty of such a task. Comparable to Orestes who, under the orders of Apollo, has to kill his mother in order to avenge his father, the modern poet, as if under orders from the god of poetry, has to overcome his time in order to avenge nature.[5]

Even though Schiller judges the antagonism between material and presentation to be part of the poetic interest of a work, he heavily downplays the content for the sake of the form. Expecting a truly beautiful work of art to consummate its form by consuming the material[6] and thus, in the spirit of the Orestes myth to "kill" the mother in order to "avenge" the father, Schiller bids the modern poet to take the material for his work from the present, but the form from a nobler time. As if in answer to his challenge to the artists:

Der Menschheit Würde ist in eure Hand gegeben,
Bewahret sie!
Sie sinkt mit euch! Mit euch wird sie sich heben!

Schiller's notion of the lost dignity of mankind having been preserved in Greek works of art suggests an instrument to be used in the restoration of that dignity on a higher level.[7] Speaking of Greek art, on the basis of its "imitation of nature," as an example of "individuality," and of modern art, on the basis of its "presentation of the ideal," as an example of "ideality," Schiller considers their union in one and the same work of art the "highest peak of all art." Under the regulative assumption of the presentability of the ideal, the aesthetic value of Greek works of art for the modern poet lies in their "imitation of nature," which, in Schiller's eyes, is essentially different from what he calls the "common imitation of nature." Using the "imitation of nature" preserved in Greek works of art as "symbolic devices" in his striving "to give mankind its fullest expression possible," the modern poet displaces the "common imitation of nature" and therefore provides "air and light for art." Pointing beyond all time, the past as well as the present, Schiller refers the artist to the "absolute unchangeable unity of his being" as the ultimate source of his work of art. Asked to strive for the procreation of the ideal out of the union of the "possible" with the "necessary," the modern artist is expected to do justice to time as well as to timelessness.[8]

Capturing time and timelessness in the interrelation between history and nature, Schiller's drama is a foremost example of his own taking up the challenge to the modern artist. The following pages will apply the findings of this chapter to the relationship between Schiller's *Wallenstein* and both Homer's *Iliad* and Euripides's *Iphigenia in Aulis* as examples of Greek art. Schiller's sentiment concerning his aesthetic writings during the planning stage of *Wallenstein* as "so to speak a bridge to poetic production" more than justifies this approach.[9]

Judging the greatness of the historical Wallenstein based on the brutality of his character to be incompatible with the greatness of a tragic hero, Schiller tries to compensate for the "missing (namely sentimental) ideality" by endowing the poetic Wallenstein with "a certain soaring of ideas." Yet deviating from his earlier method of compensating for the "missing truth" by "beautiful ideality," he offers to take the "unknown" or at least "untried path" of accomplishing it by "mere truth." In his remarks about the difference between "embellishing" and "idealizing" a character where the artist focuses on the "generic" rather than on the "specific" characteristics, Schiller stresses the fact that such a portrait will match the original "in none of its particulars completely," but will be "the truer to it in its entirety."[10] His theories about the complementary nature of realism and idealism, as prosaic derivatives of naive and sentimental poetry,[11] suggest that the "mere truth" meant to compensate for the missing ideality of Wallenstein would be the truth of nature aimed at in the transformation of historical into poetic truth.[12]

Schiller's notion of the art of semblance as not only extending the realm of beauty, but even preserving the boundaries of truth, provides the guidelines for this transformation:

> Da alles wirkliche Dasein von der Natur, als einer fremden Macht, aller Schein aber ursprünglich von dem Menschen, als vorstellendem Subjekte, sich herschreibt, so bedient er sich bloß seines absoluten Eigentumsrechts, wenn er den Schein von dem Wesen zurück nimmt und mit demselben nach eignen Gesetzen schaltet. Mit ungebundener Freiheit kann er, was die Natur trennte, zusammenfügen, sobald er es nur irgend zusammen denken kann, und trennen, was die Natur verknüpfte, sobald er es nur in seinem Verstande absondern kann.

Asked to take the material for his work from the present, but the form from a nobler time, the poet necessarily will separate what nature connected and connect what nature separated.[13] "Representing the species through an individual and exhibiting a universal concept in a particular case," the poetic imagination, in its "striving for totality of determination," exercises its "right to complete, to enliven, to transform the given image at pleasure and to follow it in all its connections and transformations."[14] In his attempt to reduce empirical to aesthetic forms, Schiller comments on his own task in connection with the way the Greeks dealt with tragedy:

> Die alten Muster, sowohl im Poetischen als im Plastischen, scheinen mir vorzüglich *den* Nutzen zu leisten, daß sie eine empirische Natur, die bereits auf eine aesthetische reduziert ist, aufstellen, und daß sie, nach einem tiefen Studium, über das Geschäft jener Reduktion selbst Winke geben können.[15]

Referring to Schiller's *Wallenstein* and the *Prolog*'s remarks about the transformative powers of art, Goethe considers it the "duty of an aesthetic observer" to pay close attention to the "means" for transforming a historical into a poetic figure.[16] Using parallels to archetypal characters and plots from Greek epic and tragic poetry as means towards the symbolic stylization of his modern historical drama, Schiller utilizes art forms which, through their aesthetic reduction of empirical nature, give him access to a nature lost in the course of history.

Taking the material for *Wallenstein* from the history of the Thirty Years' War, but the form from a subtle suffusion of Greek archetypal patterns into the texture of his highly modern poetic fabric, Schiller fulfills his own requirements for a poetic work:

> *erstlich*: notwendige Beziehung auf seinen Gegenstand (objektive Wahrheit); *zweitens*: notwendige Beziehung dieses Gegenstandes, oder doch der Schilderung desselben, auf das Empfindungsvermögen (subjektive Allgemeinheit).[17]

By abstracting from the brutal and monstrous aspects of the historical character, Schiller makes it possible for Wallenstein to become a tragic hero. By surrounding the poetic figure with a mythical horizon of Homeric and Euripidean overtones, Schiller makes it possible for his tragic hero to both retain the modern characteristic of being an individual and regain the Greek characteristic of being "eine idealische Maske."[18] Schiller's sense that, compared with the artful form of *Wallenstein*, its content hardly counts, obliges the "aesthetic observer" not only to pay attention to the fact, but also to the mode of Schiller's dramatic stylization.[19]

Exercising his "right to complete, to enliven, to transform the given image at pleasure and to follow it in all its connections and transformations," Schiller strikes parallels between *Wallenstein* and both Homer's *Iliad* and Euripides's *Iphigenia in Aulis*. Such multiple parallels are the more significant as they create a maze of cross-references between the epic and tragic archetypes behind the characters and plots of Schiller's modern historical drama. Compared to Homer's Achilles, the archetype of the natural hero, and to Euripides's Agamemnon, the archetype of the conventional ruler, Schiller's Wallenstein (with the other characters in the trilogy following suit) is infinitely more complex. Blending naturally opposed characters from artistically complementary forms of poetry, Schiller's characters reflect more than they act and express their reflections in abstract rather than concrete language. Supportive of this increased differentiation in the characters' expression of themselves, staggered parallels between the plots of Schiller's *Wallenstein* and those of Homer's *Iliad* and Euripides's *Iphigenia in Aulis* exhibit the problematic complexity of the modern world. Against the background of the ancient archetypal patterns, this complexity seems to point to the fragmentation of man in modern times as well as to his striving for a new totality of human nature made possible through history.[20]

Schiller's advice to the modern artist about taking the material for his work from the present, but the form from a nobler time, ends with a qualification about the ultimate source of the work of art lying "beyond all time." With the "absolute unchangeable unity" of the artist's being as the touchstone for his work, Schiller's formulation about connecting what nature separated and separating what nature connected loses some of its arbitrariness. Nurtured at the source of nature, the poet, in spirit, has both the privilege and the duty to live as a contemporary of all ages.

Extending the horizon of his modern historical drama into the mythical regions of Greek epic and tragic poetry, Schiller effects a transformation of historical into poetic truth. Whether this extension is only an artistic device, or essentially connects with his theories on aesthetic education,[21] is a difficult question to decide. Schiller's prognosis that the "imitation of nature" preserved in Greek works of art will become instrumental in restoring the lost dignity of mankind seems to imply that the "presentation of the ideal" recognized as the modern poet's task is more than merely a regulative assumption. Schiller's later omission of the passage contemplating a union of naive and sentimental poetry as the highest peak of all art might be his own answer to the question.[22] That the transformation of the historical into the poetic Wallenstein, however, utilizes the first and last great works of Greek poetry and thus, in Schiller's eyes, effects a union of nature and art, seems to me to be highly significant. In order to judge the function that Schiller's aesthetic theories have within his poetic practice, one might consider the effect of the Greek overtones on the poetic conception of the modern historical figure of Wallenstein.

Without being aware of the intricate parallels to Greek poetry, Otto Ludwig criticizes Schiller for presenting the Wallenstein of his fifth act in "ancient-Greek costume," playing the role of a "sentimental Socrates": "Aber es war dem Dichter ja um eine Gestalt zu tun, die das Resultat seiner tragischen Studien illustrieren sollte. So haben wir denn in seinem Wallenstein ein Bild, wie es ein Landschafter machen würde, der verschiedene Gesichtspunkte in einem vereinigen wollte." Notwithstanding the wrongheadedness of this criticism and its misconstruction of Schiller's artistic intentions,[23] Schiller himself probably would have appreciated Ludwig's keen sense of the indeterminacy of Wallenstein's character. An expression of poetic universality, this indeterminacy of character has been connected with Schiller's notion of infinite potentiality synonymous with the freedom of the aesthetic state. Focusing on this notion of infinite potentiality, Wolfgang Binder, Oskar Seidlin, Gerhard Kaiser, and Ilse Graham interpret the indecision of Wallenstein, and of Schiller's tragic heroes in general, as the tendency to persist in the freedom of the aesthetic state.[24]

Schiller himself explains that certain characters, "welche ihren Genuß mehr in das Gefühl des *ganzen Vermögens* als einer *einzelnen* Handlung desselben setzen," are bound to try to extend the aesthetic state. With the crucial qualification, "vorausgesetzt, daß sie mit diesem Vermögen zugleich Realität vereinigen," Schiller claims that such characters are born "fürs Ganze und zu großen Rollen." Striving to extend his "potentiality" without the concomitant ability to extend his "reality," Wallenstein takes on the "great role" of a tragic hero.[25] In his aspiration to unite "absolute potentiality" with "absolute reality," which, for Schiller, is the most authentic mark of the divine, Wallenstein transgresses the boundaries of historical existence.[26] As if to verify Schiller's dictum that "even with historical characters it is not their existence, but the potentiality revealed through their existence which is poetic," Wallenstein treats history as if it were governed by aesthetic rather than physical and moral laws.[27]

Interpreting Wallenstein's attitude as an expression of the tragic hero's striving for an ideal order of the world, Gert Sautermeister calls attention to the conflict between dramatic and idyllic elements in Schiller's dramatic work. Gerhard Kaiser's criticism, "Es ließe sich darüber rechten, ob Wallenstein handelt um einer Idee willen oder ob ihm noch die Idee Mittel zum Zweck ist, sich einen archimedischen Punkt unbedingten Handelns zu gewinnen," seems to imply that the two positions exclude each other. Yet the convergence of time and timelessness effected by the symbolic extension of Wallenstein's historical world into a mythical horizon of Greek epic and tragic overtones might rather suggest a collapse of the two positions into one.[28] Striving for an ideal order of the world, Wallenstein avoids all commitments to the real world. Playing with the political powers as if they were forces to be fashioned into a living work of art, he seems to follow Schiller's maxim about man being "fully man only where he plays."[29] Contrary to his premise that man ought to play "only with beauty," Schiller speaks of a time when this maxim, applied to the "double seriousness of duty and fate," shall not only sustain aesthetic art but the art of life as well. Referring back to Greek life and art, Schiller takes the Olympian gods as examples of a freedom which, expressing a higher concept of necessity, transcends the necessity of both natural and moral law.[30] Schiller's vision of a time when the historical development of human nature will encompass the necessity of the physical and moral states in the freedom of the aesthetic state implies that history will lead man to an existence comparable to the life of the Olympian gods. Very much aware of the utopian aura of this vision, Schiller, nevertheless, has his tragic heroes live and die in the glow of it. Intensified by the presence of archetypal characters and plots from Greek epic and tragic poetry, Wallenstein's Olympian usurpation of history is an example of the tragic hero's "Übertritt in den Gott."[31]

That this "extinction of time in timelessness,"[32] characteristic of the hybris of the tragic hero, evokes overtones of the mythical past as well as of the historical future seems to imply what Werner Keller calls "Gegenwartskritik im Medium der Vergangenheit und der Zukunft."[33] Deeply appreciative of the Kantian connection between time and consciousness, however, Schiller also uses this "gegenstrebige Doppelbewegung" between myth and history to reinterpret both past and future in the light of the present. The consummation of Olympian humanity in the tragic hero's death points, therefore, to the importance of time as much as of timelessness.[34] With his death spanning the gap between mortality and immortality, the tragic hero makes it possible for life to become the material for art. As a sign of this gap, a comma rather than a conjunction stands between the two halves of the *Prolog*'s final line, "Ernst ist das Leben, heiter ist die Kunst." By constructing that line in two consecutive parallel units, Schiller emphasizes the separateness of life and art as much as their inherent connection. Claiming "Ernst" and "Spiel" as constitutive elements of the aesthetic, the former grounded in the content, the latter in the form of a work of art, Schiller at the same time acknowledges the priority of life and the superiority of art.[35] In the light of Schiller's symbolism involving the numbers eleven and twelve, the completion of the last and eleventh act of *Wallenstein* in twelve scenes (with the *Prolog* rounding out the number of acts to twelve) points to the serenity of art as an aesthetic transfiguration of the seriousness of life.

IX. "I Am and Remain Merely a Poet"

In his evaluation of Schiller's poetic genius, Wilhelm von Humboldt speaks of an "intellectuality which, fathoming everything, wants to split it, and connecting everything, wants to unite it in a whole." Considering *Wallenstein* the one poetic work of Schiller's that exhibits all these traits in a heightened form, Humboldt marvels about the degree to which it, nevertheless, presents itself as nature:

> Wahrlich nicht das Machen, aber das Walten des Kunstgeists
> ist unverkennbar in Ihrem Werk; aber man erstaunt nur mit
> doppelter Bewunderung, da Sie nun hervortreten und es sich
> selbst überlassen, zu sehen, in welchem Grade es Natur ist.[1]

Schiller's own view about his poetic powers varies only slightly over the years. Even though his historical studies might persuade him that he is closer to Montesquieu than to Sophocles, he thanks heaven for every poetic line he did not mind the trouble of making.[2] In his conversations with Eckermann, Goethe reminisces about Schiller's having been a born poet, but having let history and philosophy interfere with the purely poetic success of his work.[3] Early in his correspondence with Goethe, Schiller deems his fellow poet's mind the "more intuitive" and his own the "more symbolizing"; he also confesses that the poetic spirit usually overtakes him when he ought to philosophize and that the philosophical spirit seizes him when he wants to write poetry.[4] Shortly thereafter, with a shift from "wo ich philosophieren sollte" to "wo ich philosophieren will," Schiller reports to Körner that he is writing his treatise about the Naive and, at the same time, thinking about the plan for *Wallenstein*:

> Vor dieser Arbeit ist mir ordentlich angst und bange, denn ich
> glaube mit jedem Tag mehr zu finden, daß ich eigentlich nichts
> weniger vorstellen kann als einen Dichter, und daß höchstens da,
> wo ich philosophieren will, der poetische Geist mich überrascht.[5]

Depending on whether one connects "weniger" with "vorstellen" or with "nichts," Schiller sounds more or less pessimistic about his being a poet. The opening and closing of the sentence seem to me to favor the more pessimistic reading.

Full of impatience for something poetic, his pen "itching especially for *Wallenstein*," Schiller reflects on his engaging in poetic theory for the sake of poetic practice.[6] Though aware of the damaging effect of critical philosophy on his creative powers, he expects the intermediate stage of self-conscious artistry to lead to a new and higher form of nature:

> Soviel habe ich nun aus gewisser Erfahrung, daß nur strenge Bestimmtheit der Gedanken zu einer Leichtigkeit verhilft. Sonst glaubte ich das Gegenteil und fürchtete Härte und Steifigkeit. Ich bin jetzt in der Tat froh, daß ich es mir nicht habe verdrießen lassen, einen sauren Weg einzuschlagen, den ich oft für die poetisierende Einbildungskraft verderblich hielt. Aber freilich spannt diese Tätigkeit sehr an, denn wenn der Philosoph seine Einbildungskraft und der Dichter seine Abstraktionskraft ruhen lassen darf, so muß ich, bei dieser Art von Produktionen, diese beiden Kräfte immer in gleicher Anspannung erhalten, und nur durch eine ewige Bewegung in mir kann ich die zwei heterogenen Elemente in einer Art von Solution erhalten.[7]

Schiller's conviction of having written better poetry during and after his speculative period than before that time[8] helps in explicating his later evaluation of *Wallenstein*, in November 1796: "Keins meiner alten Stücke hat soviel Zweck und Form, als der *Wallenstein* jetzt schon hat; aber ich weiß jetzt zu genau, was ich will und was ich soll, als daß ich mir das Geschäft so leicht machen könnte."[9] Judging from a letter to Goethe of the same date, which uses the formulation "was ich will und was ich soll" even more elaborately, Schiller's term "Zweck" seems to refer to the connection between poetic material and poetic form and, therefore, ultimately to the transformation of historical into poetic truth. In his admiration for the rigorous intellectual unity of Schiller's poetry, Wilhelm von Humboldt distinguishes between two aspects:

> Er forderte von der Dichtung einen tieferen Anteil des Gedankens, und unterwarf sie strenger einer geistigen Einheit, letzteres auf zweifache Weise, indem er sie an eine festere Kunstform band, und indem er jede Dichtung so behandelte, daß ihr Stoff unwillkürlich und von selbst seine Individualität zum Ganzen einer Idee erweiterte.[10]

Considering the suggestion of even minor changes in the plot of *Wallenstein* an intrusion upon its integrity, Schiller insists that in a "living work" of art "everything hangs together with everything" and "nothing can be moved without dislocating everything."[11]

Correlation of everything with everything can be found throughout Schiller's *Wallenstein*: The polarity of the characters sustains the symmetry of the plots which, in concentric circles of scenes and acts, form the whole of the trilogy. Corresponding to the three parts of the *Prolog*, the three plays of *Wallenstein* explore the relationship between nature and art, portrayed in the life of individuals representative of the life of mankind. Schiller's integration of characters and plots from Greek epic and tragic poetry into his modern historical drama contributes to the symbolic nature of his poetic figures and raises the question of the relationship between Ancients and Moderns, a dominant theme of his philosophical writings. The correspondence between dramatic characters and aesthetic principles ties together life and art by interpreting them in terms of history understood in the light of nature.

Speaking of *Wallenstein* as a "small universe," Schiller rejoices in a new and hard-won balance of his speculative and creative powers.[12] In the spirit of his letter to Schiller concerning *Wallenstein*, written in September 1800, Wilhelm von Humboldt later marvels at the complementary intensity of those powers. Considering Schiller naive in a higher degree than the decided disposition towards the sentimental seems to allow for, Humboldt concludes:

> Seine sich selbst überlassene Natur führte ihn mehr der höheren Idee zu, in welcher sich der Unterschied zwischen jenen Gattungen wieder von selbst verliert, als sie ihn in eine von beiden verschloß, und wenn er dieses Vorrecht mit einigen der größesten Dichtergenies teilte, so gesellte sich dazu noch in ihm, daß er schon in die Idee selbst die Forderung absoluter Freiheit des sich idealisch bildenden Sinnenstoffs legte.[13]

True to his early conviction about being and remaining merely a poet,[14] Schiller claims in 1795:

> Von jeher war Poesie die höchste Angelegenheit meiner Seele, und ich trennte mich eine Zeit lang bloß von ihr, um reicher und würdiger zu ihr zurückzukehren. In der Poesie endigen alle Bahnen des menschlichen Geistes und desto schlimmer für ihn, wenn er sie nicht bis zu diesem Ziele zu führen den Mut hat.[15]

This statement, which expresses Schiller's feelings after the completion of his elegy "Der Spaziergang," at the same time mirrors the movement of that poem. With Schiller's philosophy of history providing the perspectives, nature, in "Der Spaziergang," encompasses the manifestations of human nature throughout the course of history. By striving to give human nature its fullest expression possible, poetry, in Schiller's view, appears as a fulfillment of history and philosophy and, as such, as a human representation of nature in all its comprehensiveness.

Comparative Panorama

Nebenher entwerfe ich ein detailliertes Szenarium des ganzen Wallensteins, um mir die Übersicht der Momente und des Zusammenhangs auch durch die Augen mechanisch zu erleichtern.

(To Goethe, April 4, 1797)

HOMER *The Iliad*	SCHILLER *Wallenstein* *Prolog*	EURIPIDES *Iphigenia in Aulis*
I, 1–5 Wrath of Achilles	*1–69* *History and art*	I, 1–47 Tragic condition of man
I, 5 Will of Zeus	*70–110* *Historical personality*	I, 48–132 Fateful past
I, 6–7 Cause of wrath	*111–38* *Nature and art*	I,133–77 Tragic conflict
II, 484–93 Muse to list leaders	*133–38* *Muse to transform* *life to art*	

	Wallensteins Lager	1st Choral Interlude
II, 211–70 Uproar about Thersites	*Scenes 1–2 (cf. 10–11)* *Uproar about Peasants* *(dice)*	I, 178–237 Heroes: Ajax (dice)— Achilles (leader)
II, 278–440 Odysseus, Nestor, Agamemnon (leaders)	*Sc. 6* *Sergeant and Soldiers* *(mock leaders)*	I, 238–95 Ships: Achilles— Ajax
II, 494–785 Catalogue of Heroes and Ships	*Sc. 11* *Panorama of* *whole camp*	

HOMER	*SCHILLER* *Die Piccolomini*	EURIPIDES
	I, 1 *Attempt to detain* *Buttler*	II, 1 Slave detained
IX, 185–655 Odysseus, Phoinix, Ajax (discussion of Achilles's claim to leadership)	I, 2 *(cf. II, 7)* *Octavio, Questenberg* *(discussion of* *Wallenstein's claim* *to leadership)*	II, 2 Menelaus, Agamemnon (discussion of Agamemnon's claim to leadership)
	I, 2 *Arrival signal* *(Thekla)*	II, 3 Arrival signal (Iphigenia)
IX, 656–713 Agamemnon, Odysseus (discussion of Achilles's arrogance)	I, 3 *Questenberg, Octavio* *(discussion of* *Wallenstein's arrogance)*	
	I, 4 *Defense of idea* *of peace*	II, 4 Defense of life of Iphigenia
	I, 5 *Curse over Max's trip*	2nd Choral Interlude Curse over Paris's trip
	II, 1 *Scheme to avoid* *evil omen*	III, 1 Hope to avoid evil omen
	II, 2 *Pretext of* *marriage*	III, 2 Anticipation of marriage
	II, 3 *Father/Daughter*	III, 3 Father/Daughter
	II, 4 *Max's virtues*	III, 4 Achilles's virtues
	III, 1 *Terzky/Illo, annoyance* *with Wallenstein*	IV, 1 Achilles, annoyance with Agamemnon
	III, 2 *Suspicions about* *marriage*	IV, 2–3 Discovery of fraud about marriage

HOMER	*SCHILLER*	EURIPIDES
VI, 237–502 Hector/Andromache (Family) Remembrance of past— vision of future	*III, 3–5* *Max/Thekla (Individuals)* *Remembrance of past—* *vision of future*	
	III, 4 *Thekla adorned as if* *for sacrifice*	IV, 3, 1110–1217 Vision of Iphigenia as bride adorned for sacrifice
	III, 5 *Defying custom* *in embrace*	IV, 3, 1218–89 Respect for custom— no embrace
	III, 8 *Friedland: acquired nobility* *Piccolomini: born nobility* *Importance of Self even in* *sacrifice*	4. Choral Interlude IV, 1290–1343 Praise of Achilles's mortal and immortal ancestors (wedding of Peleus and Thetis)
	III, 9 *No place for love,* *Thekla's premonition* *of doom*	Epode, IV, 1344–65 Iphigenia's sacrifice, in place of her wedding, as a sign of doom
XVIII, 478–607 Shield of Achilles (Nature)	*IV, 5* *Chalice (History)*	
	IV, 1–7 *Oath, chalice* *30 signatures,* *3 crosses, kiss, sword*	*New Testament* Judas's betrayal of Jesus
SOPHOCLES *Philoctetes* Odysseus, Neoptolemos Philoctetes's bow	*V, 1–3* *Octavio, Max* *Wallenstein's army*	

HOMER *The Iliad*	SCHILLER *Wallensteins Tod*	EURIPIDES *Iphigenia in Aulis*
I, Second Half Achilles's meeting with Thetis, and her visit to Zeus on Olympus	I, 1 *Wallenstein's starwatch* *(conjunction between the* *planets Venus and Jupiter)*	I, 1–177 Agamemnon's starwatch
	I, 2 *Capture of Sesina*	II, 1 Capture of Slave
	I, 3 *Terzky/Illo: annoyance* *with Wallenstein's* *indecision*	II, 2 Menelaus: annoyance with Agamemnon's change of decision
IX, 185–91 Achilles's song about heroic deeds of men	I, 4 *Wallenstein's reflection* *on freedom and necessity* *in human nature*	II, 4 Agamemnon's despair over necessity
IX, 622–57 Ajax	I, 5 (cf. 4, 139–58) *Wrangel*	
IX, 432–619 Phoinix	I, 6 (cf. 4, 159–91) *Terzky/Illo*	
IX, 222–429 Odysseus	I, 7 (cf. 4, 192–222) *Countess* *Wallenstein's acceptance* *of necessity*	II, 4 (cf. III, 780–82) Agamemnon's succumbing to necessity
XVI, 1–100 (cf. XV, 390–405) (cf. XI, 597–848) Patroclos's critique of Achilles	II, 2 (cf. I, 7, 474–81) *Max's critique* *of Wallenstein*	IV, 1–3 Achilles's critique of Agamemnon
XVI, 220–56 Achilles's prayer to Zeus	II, 3, 891–960 (cf. 4, 970) *Wallenstein's communion* *with the World Spirit*	

HOMER	*SCHILLER*	EURIPIDES
	III, 3 *Duchess's account* *of her marriage*	V, 3 Clytemnestra's account of her marriage
	III, 4 *Thekla in tears* *No song*	V, 3 Iphigenia in tears No enchantment
I, 234–46 Achilles's scepter without branches and foliage	*III, 13* *Wallenstein's likening* *himself to a treetrunk* *without branches and foliage*	
XVI, 155–220 Achilles's success in arming the Myrmidons	*III, 15–16* *Wallenstein's failure* *to convince Max's troops*	
XVI, 33–35 Achilles's hard heart	*III, 18, 2088–93* *Wallenstein's hard heart*	
	III, 18, 2135–41 *Max's rejection of* *involvement*	V, 3, 1541–46 Iphigenia's rejection of involvement
IX, 485–98 Phoinix's fatherly services to Achilles	*III, 18, 2142–85* *Wallenstein's fatherly* *services to Max*	
XVI, 97–100 Vision of Achilles and Patroclos fighting side by side	*III, 20, 2235 (cf. IV, 7,* *2768–69, 2773–75)* *Threat of Wallenstein and* *Max fighting on opposite sides*	
XVIII, 203–38 Achilles in blaze of fire at wall	*III, 20, 2260–66* *Wallenstein no longer* *"Sun in Battle"*	

(XI, 786–89 Patroclos—the Older)	*(IV, 2, 2546* *Gordon—for Max—* *the Older)*	
XVI, 777 Sunset—Onset of Assault	*IV, 4, 2649; 8, 2847–62* *Sunset—Onset* *of Assault*	

HOMER	SCHILLER
XXII, 460–67 Andromache, swooning at sight of Hector being dragged on the battlefield	*IV, 9* *Thekla, swooning at* *news of Max's death*
XVI, 682 ff. Patroclos's attack on Troy	*IV, 10, 3029–51* *Max's attack on* *the Swedes*
XXII Achilles's fight against Hector in his old armor	*IV (cf. II, 3, 926–31)* *Max's death in the* *image of Wallenstein's* *dream before Lützen*
XXIII, 1–256 Patroclos's funeral	*IV, 10, 3063–72* *Max's funeral*
XXIII, 59–107 Call of Patroclos's ghost	*IV, 12, 3155* *Call of Max's* *ghost*

XVIII, 3–4 Achilles in thought	*V, 3, 3393/94* *Wallenstein in thought*
XVIII, 22–35 Achilles's reaction to Patroclos's death	*V, 3, 3406–30* *Wallenstein's reaction* *to Max's death*
XVIII, 203–6 Achilles like a blaze of fire	*V, 3, 3400–3401* *Wallenstein reminded* *to be like the sun*
XVIII, 73–77 Thetis's sympathy with Achilles's mourning	*V, 3, 3398–99, 3435–37* *Countess's attempt to* *dispel Wallenstein's* *mourning*
XVIII, 80–82 No more happiness after friend's death	*V, 4, 3589–92* *No more happiness* *after friend's death*
XIX, 268–74 Achilles's sharing of responsibility	*V, 5, 3657–61* *Wallenstein's full acceptance* *of responsibility*

Notes

Schiller's works are quoted, as much as possible, from *Schillers Werke*, Nationalausgabe, ed. Lieselotte Blumenthal and Benno von Wiese (Weimar: Böhlau, 1943 ff.). Where the volumes of the Nationalausgabe do not exist yet, as in the case of later versions of poems or later poems, or in the case of Schiller's translations from Euripides, references are to Friedrich Schiller, *Sämtliche Werke*, ed. Gerhard Fricke and Herbert Göpfert, 5th ed. (München: Hanser, 1975). In all German texts orthography, interpunctuation, and capitalization have been adapted to modern usage.

Schiller's personal letters are identified by date. The plays, except for a first reference to the Nationalausgabe and an occasional look at variant readings or the commentary, are cited by act, scene, and line numbers.

The Homeric quotes are taken from the translation by Johann Heinrich Voß, reprinted in Homer, *Ilias* (München: Goldmann, 1957).

The titles of frequently cited texts, editions, and publications are abbreviated as follows:

Pr.	*Prolog* to *Wallenstein*
WL	*Wallensteins Lager*
DP	*Die Piccolomini*
WT	*Wallensteins Tod*
Il.	*The Iliad*
IA	*Iphigenia in Aulis*
NA	Nationalausgabe of *Schillers Werke*
SW	Schiller, *Sämtliche Werke*, ed. Fricke and Göpfert
JDSG	*Jahrbuch der deutschen Schillergesellschaft*
WdF	Wege der Forschung

Introduction

1. Letter 6, NA XX, 321–28.
2. NA XX, 432, 436–38, 473–76.
3. NA XXI, 287–88.
4. NA XX, note to 473; cf. letter to Wilhelm von Humboldt, Dec. 25, 1795. See also Peter Szondi, "Das Naive ist das Sentimentalische: Zur Begriffsdialektik in Schillers Abhandlung," *Euphorion*, 66 (1972), 190–204; idem, "Antike und Moderne in der Aesthetik der Goethezeit," in *Poetik und Geschichtsphilosophie* I, 3rd ed. (1974; rpt. Frankfurt am Main: Suhrkamp, 1980), pp. 172–75.
5. To Körner, May 25, 1792.

6. To Körner, Sept. 12, 1794; to Humboldt, Dec. 25, 1795.

7. To Körner, Sept. 4, 1794.

8. NA VIII, *Pr.* 50–56.

9. *Pr.* 61–69.

10. To Körner, Oct. 20, 1788; *Pr.* 126–27.

11. To Goethe, Aug. 24, 1798.

12. *Über die aesthetische Erziehung des Menschen*, Letter 9, NA XX, 333–34.

13. I am not sure whether this means that the form of Greek art, because of its imitation of nature, can no longer be considered form, but only content, form being reserved for the presentation of the ideal. Cf. Wolfgang Düsing, "Aesthetische Form als Darstellung der Subjektivität," in *Friedrich Schiller: Zur Geschichtlichkeit seines Werkes*, ed. Klaus L. Berghahn (Kronberg: Scriptor, 1975), p. 205, with a quote from Schiller's *Kalliasbriefe* (to Körner, Jan. 25, 1793): "Ich bin wenigstens überzeugt, daß die Schönheit nur die Form einer Form ist, und daß das was man ihren Stoff nennt schlechterdings ein geformter Stoff sein muß. Die Vollkommenheit ist die Form eines Stoffes, die Schönheit hingegen ist die Form dieser Vollkommenheit; die sich also gegen die Schönheit wie der Stoff zu der Form verhält."

14. NA XXI, 288.

15. To Körner, Nov. 28, 1796.

16. To Ernst von Schimmelmann, July 13, 1793.

17. To Charlotte von Schimmelmann, Nov. 4, 1795. Cf. Wolfgang Binder, "Aesthetik und Dichtung in Schillers Werk," in *Schiller: Zur Theorie und Praxis der Dramen*, ed. Klaus L. Berghahn and Reinhold Grimm, WdF, 323 (Darmstadt: Wissenschaftliche Buchgesellschaft, 1972), pp. 206–32.

18. *Hebbels Werke*, ed. Friedrich Brandes (Leipzig: Reclam, 1912), I, 260; cf. Wilhelm von Humboldt, "Über Schiller und den Gang seiner Geistesentwicklung," *Werke*, ed. Andreas Flitner and Klaus Giel (Darmstadt: Wissenschaftliche Buchgesellschaft, 1969), II, 385: ". . . war er nicht bloß Schöpfer, sondern auch Richter, und forderte Rechenschaft von dem poetischen Wirken auf dem Gebiete des Denkens."

19. To Körner, Nov. 28, 1796.

20. To Goethe, Dec. 29, 1797.

21. NA XX, 218; XXI, 193–94.

22. *Pr.* 102–7.

23. *Über die aesthetische Erziehung des Menschen*, Letter 9, NA XX, 334.

24. To Körner, Aug. 20, Oct. 20, Dec. 12, 1788; March 10, 1789; Nov. 26, 1790; Nov. 24, 1791; July 16, 1803.

I. *History of the Thirty Years' War* and *The Iliad*

1. To Körner, Nov. 28, 1791.

2. To Körner, March 10, 1789.

3. Golo Mann, *Wallenstein: Sein Leben erzählt* (Frankfurt am Main: Fischer,

1974), p. 732; cf. p. 719: "Wenn der Dichter den Schwergekränkten sagen läßt: 'Tod und Teufel! Ich hatte, was ihm Freiheit schaffen konnte!' so ist das bloß ein Dichterwort"; p. 775: "Dürstete Wallenstein nach Genugtuung für die Regensburger Schmach, was ja doch nur eine Sage ist: konnte er noch Kläglicheres wollen?"; p. 792: "Man sagt, er habe sich verändert seit dem Regensburger Fürstentag; loyal bis dahin; einsamer, von Rachedurst gepeinigter Verräter von da ab. Die Zeitgenossen glaubten es, die Späteren schleppten es weiter. Wir werfen es ab."

4. Leopold von Ranke, *Geschichte Wallensteins* (Düsseldorf: Droste, 1967), p. 22.

5. *Geschichte des dreißigjährigen Krieges*, NA XVIII, 132 in 113–34; cf. *Il.* I. (Though the epic character of passages throughout Schiller's *Geschichte des dreißigjährigen Krieges* convinces me of his attunement to Homer, it would have been misleading to use actual quotes from the *Iliad* for comparison with Schiller's texts. The translations he must have been familiar with at the time are not within my reach. Johann Heinrich Voß's *Iliad* translation, which Schiller seized on immediately, appeared only in 1793, half a year after the completion of Schiller's *Geschichte des dreißigjährigen Krieges*.)

6. NA XVIII, 132–33; cf. *Il.* I, 318–48.

7. NA XVIII, 133–34; cf. *Il.* I, 488–92, and II, 686–94, 768–79.

8. NA XVIII, 141–42; cf. *Il.* VI, 237–502. For Schiller's thinking in terms akin to Greek poetry, see NA XVIII, 265: "Wie liebenswürdig zeigt sich uns Gustav, eh er auf ewig von uns Abschied nimmt! So weigert sich der Agamemnon des Griechischen Trauerspiels, auf den Purpur zu treten, den die Ehrfurcht zu seinen Füßen ausbreitet." It is interesting to note that Schiller, like Homer, follows the technique of interspersing the antagonist's story between the earlier and later parts of the protagonist's story.

9. NA XVIII, 134, 235 (185–222); cf. *Il.* IX (VIII–XV).

10. NA XVIII, 233–34, 190, 238–46; cf. *Il.* IX.

11. NA XVIII, 268–80 (cf. Conrad Ferdinand Meyer, *Gustav Adolfs Page*, V, where the dying page murmurs, "Der König . . . im Nebel . . . die Kugel des Lauenburgers . . ."); cf. *Il.* XVI, 682–865.

12. NA XVIII, 273; cf. *Il.* XVII; about the fall of Magdeburg, see NA XVIII, 163: "Der kaiserliche General durchritt die Straßen, um als Augenzeuge seinem Herrn berichten zu können, daß seit Trojas und Jerusalems Zerstörung kein solcher Sieg gesehen worden sei"; about the siege at Altenberg, see NA XVIII, 257: "Tiefe Gräben umschlossen unersteigliche Schanzen, dichte Verhacke und stachelige Pallisaden verrammelten die Zugänge zu dem steil anlaufenden Berge, von dessen Gipfel Wallenstein, ruhig und sicher wie ein Gott, durch schwarze Rauchwolken seine Blitze versendete."

13. NA XVIII, 274; cf. *Il.* XVI, 777–90.

14. NA XVIII, 277; cf. *Il.* XXII, XXIV.

15. NA XVIII, 9–88; cf. Herodotus, *Histories*, II, 113–20 (I, 1–5).

16. NA XVIII, 143; cf. Euripides, *Iphigenia in Aulis*, translated by Schiller in 1788, SW III, 283–355.

17. Hellmut Diwald, *Friedrich Schiller, Wallenstein: Geschichte und Legende* (Frankfurt am Main: Ullstein, 1972), pp. 39–40. Ibid., p. 41, concerning "Schillers unerhörtes historisches Gespür": "Er hatte damit etwas zur Hand, was nur höchst wenig Historiografen so ausgeprägt besessen haben—den unbestechlichen Blick für das Wesentliche, für die treibenden Kräfte, für die bewegenden Motive, für die Interessenlage und -verteilung innerhalb der Konflikte, für das Gewicht der Gewalten, die den Ausgang der Kämpfe schließlich bestimmen und für die Nachwirkungen. Daraus entspringt auch die Meisterschaft seiner Charakteristiken der geschichtlichen Akteure. Sie verlieren selbst dort kaum an Imposanz, wo sie falsch sind und stehen immer noch weit über den Hervorbringungen derjenigen Historiker, die sich mit mikroskopischer Zuverlässigkeit bei jedem einzelnen Baum auskennen, vom Wald dagegen nichts wissen."

18. To Caroline von Beulwitz, Dec. 10, 1788; cf. to Körner, Jan. 7, 1788: "Deine Geringschätzung der Geschichte kommt mir unbillig vor. Allerdings ist sie willkürlich, voll Lücken und sehr oft unfruchtbar, aber eben das Willkürliche in ihr könnte einen philosophischen Geist reizen, sie zu *beherrschen*; das Leere und Unfruchtbare einen schöpferischen Kopf herausfordern, sie zu befruchten und auf dieses Gerippe Nerven und Muskeln zu tragen."

19. Humboldt, "Über Schiller," pp. 381–82.

20. To Körner, July 16, 1803.

21. NA XVIII, 327–28; cf. Walter Hinderer, *Der Mensch in der Geschichte: Ein Versuch über Schillers Wallenstein* (Königstein/Taunus: Athenäum, 1980), p. 28: "Am Schluß des vierten Buches errichtet Schiller sogar für Wallenstein eine Art Epitaph."

22. *Il.* I, 7.

23. For the reciprocity between past and present in the historical drama's interpretation of historical—or for that matter, mythical—sources, see Werner Keller, "Drama und Geschichte," in *Beiträge zur Poetik des Dramas*, ed. Werner Keller (Darmstadt: Wissenschaftliche Buchgesellschaft, 1976), pp. 298–339.

24. *Pr.* 102–7.

25. To Körner, March 10, 1789.

26. To Körner, Oct. 20, 1788.

27. To Körner, Nov. 28, 1791.

28. To Körner, May 25, 1792.

29. *Über das Pathetische*, NA XX, 218; *Über die notwendigen Grenzen beim Gebrauch schöner Formen*, NA XXI, 9–10; letter to Goethe, April 4, 1797. Cf. Friedrich Wilhelm Wentzlaff-Eggebert, "Die poetische Wahrheit in Schillers 'Wallenstein'," in *Germanistik in Forschung und Lehre* (Berlin: Schmidt, 1965), pp. 135–42; Benno von Wiese, "Geschichte und Drama," in *Geschichtsdrama*, ed. Elfriede Neubuhr, WdF, 485 (Darmstadt: Wissenschaftliche Buchgesellschaft, 1980), pp. 396–98.

30. Caroline von Wolzogen, *Schillers Leben* (Stuttgart/Tübingen: Cotta, 1851), p. 126. In this regard one should also consider Schiller's admiration

for Homer in his inclusion of Homer's image in the four cameos (Lyre, Psyche, Apollo, Homer) that he ordered from Goeschen; cf. Helmut Rehder, "The Four Seals of Schiller," in *A Schiller Symposium*, ed. A. Leslie Willson (Austin: University of Texas, Department of Germanic Languages, 1960), pp. 11–27. What Eliza Marian Butler has to say in *The Tyranny of Greece over Germany* (Boston: Beacon, 1958), p. 163, needs no further comment: "He was acquainted with Homer . . . but Homer, whilst occasionally supplementing his knowledge of Virgil's and Ovid's gods and heroes, in no way nourished his genius, either in his plays or in his poems."

31. To Körner, June 3, 1797. Cf. Aristotle, *Poetics*, IX, 1451a36–1451b10; Gotthold Ephraim Lessing, *Hamburgische Dramaturgie*, 19, in *Gesammelte Werke* (Berlin: Aufbau, 1954), VI, 101 2; Hartmut Reinhardt, "Schillers 'Wallenstein' und Aristoteles," *JDSG*, 20 (1976), 278–337.

32. *Pr.* 79–80; cf. *Il.* II, 134, 295, 328–29.

33. *Pr.* 91–110; cf. *Il.* I, 1–7.

34. *WL* as compared to *Il.* II, 484–779. See also the letter to Goethe, Dec. 1, 1797.

35. *DP* III, 4 and 5; cf. *Il.* VI, 237–502.

36. *DP* IV, 5 (cf. *Geschichte des dreißigjährigen Krieges*, I, NA XVIII, 9–88); cf. *Il.* XVIII, 478–607.

37. *WT* I, 1; cf. *Il.* I, 348–427, 488–533.

38. *WL* 11, 1036–38; *DP* I, 4; *DP* II, 4; *DP* V; *WT* II, 2; *WT* V, 3; cf. *Il.* I, IX, XVI, XVIII, XXIII.

II. *Wallenstein* and *The Iliad*

1. Gero von Wilpert, *Schiller-Chronik* (Stuttgart: Kröner, 1958), pp. 15, 19, 23.

2. *Die Räuber*, II, 2, SW I, 528–29; *Die Räuber*, IV, 4, SW I, 584–85. Cf. *Il.* VI, 392–502. See also Dieter Borchmeyer, "Hektors Abschied: Schillers Aneignung einer homerischen Szene," *JDSG*, 16 (1972), 277–98.

3. *Die Räuber*, IV, 3, SW I, 577–80; cf. *Odyssey*, XIX, 357–494.

4. *Don Carlos*, I, 4, 512–16, NA VII, i, 385; cf. *Odyssey*, I, 1–5; this Homeric touch, however, occurs only in the final edition of 1805. The editions of 1787 (NA VI, 33; NA VII, i, 27), i.e., before Schiller's extensive reading of Voß's translations of Homer, have: "Sie haben viele Höfe / besucht auf Ihren Reisen, Chevalier; / den halben Norden, les' ich, durchgereist— / In London waren Sie sehr lang'."

5. *Die Verschwörung des Fiesco zu Genua*, III, 5, SW I, 706; cf. *Il.* XXI, 107. See also "Das Siegesfest," 79–80, SW I, 426, "Denn Patroklus liegt begraben, und Thersites kommt zurück."

6. *Die Jungfrau von Orléans*, II, 7, NA IX, 228–31. Cf. NA XLII, 334: "Die Szene mit dem Walliser Montgomery ist eine Lieblingsepisode des Dichters, die er ganz im Geiste homerischer Dichtung nach der Art bildete, wie dort

in der Ilias Lykaon das Leben von Achilles erfleht"; and Gerhard Storz, *Der Dichter Friedrich Schiller* (Stuttgart: Klett, 1959), pp. 354–57.

7. *Die Jungfrau von Orléans*, III, 10, NA IX, 263–67; cf. *Il.* VI, 119–236. Schiller's transformation of this Homeric scene illustrates his reflections on the difference between naive and sentimental poetry, *Über naive und sentimentalische Dichtung*, NA XX, 433–35. The fact that the *Prolog* to *Die Jungfrau von Orléans* echoes Vergil's *Eclogues*, while the body of the play abounds with allusions to Homer's *Iliad*, demonstrates the play's inherent tension between idyllic and heroic sentiments.

8. Keller, "Drama und Geschichte," p. 317.

9. To Körner, Aug. 20, 1788: "Du wirst finden, daß mir ein vertrauter Umgang mit den Alten äußerst wohltun—vielleicht Klassizität geben wird. Ich werde sie in guten Übersetzungen studieren—und dann—wenn ich sie fast auswendig weiß, die griechischen Originale lesen. Auf diese Art getraue ich mir spielend griechische Sprache zu studieren"; cf. NA XLII, 153 (1792), "Schon in der Militärakademie hatte er diesen Dichter [Vergil], wie den Homer, den er damals im Originale las, liebgewonnen."

10. Cf. Emil Staiger, *Friedrich Schiller* (Zürich: Atlantis, 1967), pp. 187–88.

11. "Die Künstler," 232–34, NA I, 207.

12. To Körner, April 30, 1789.

13. NA XLII, 172; cf. ibid., 168, "Da wir von den Sternen sprachen, fiel ihm eine Stelle aus der Odyssee ein, welche er (nach Vossens Übersetzung) rezitierte. Sie handelt vom *Ulysses*, der, einsam in seinem Schiff fahrend, nach dem Wagen, und Orion sieht."

14. *Pr.* 1–69, 70–110, 111–38; cf. *Il.* I, 1–5, 5, 6–7.

15. Cf. Hinderer, *Der Mensch in der Geschichte*, pp. 25–34.

16. *Il.* II, 484–93; *Pr.* 133–38, cf. 50–69, 104–7.

17. To Goethe, Aug. 24, 1798.

18. *Pr.* 121–23, 114, 67–69.

19. *Il.* II, 771–79. Garlieb Merkel's critique (Jan. 27, 1801, quoted in *Friedrich Schiller, Wallenstein: Erläuterungen und Dokumente*, ed. Kurt Rothmann [Stuttgart: Reclam, 1977], p. 237) of *Wallensteins Lager* as "ein noch viel müßigeres Hors d'oeuvre, als das Schiffsverzeichnis in der Iliade" at least recognizes the similarity. For the poetic significance of Homer's Catalogue of Ships, see Kenneth John Atchity, *Homer's Iliad, The Shield of Memory* (Carbondale: Southern Illinois University Press, 1978), pp. 276–84, "Catalogues, Invocations, and Miniatures."

20. To Körner, March 10, 1789.

21. Cf. Caroline von Wolzogen's impression (quoted in Reinhard Buchwald, *Schiller: Leben und Werk* [Wiesbaden: Insel, 1959], p. 713) of the dress rehearsal of *Wallensteins Lager:* ". . . Der Wallone (d. h. der 1. Kürassier) erschien uns wie eine beinahe homerische Gestalt, die das Edle des neuen Kriegslebens plastisch darstellte."

22. *WL* 7, 421–37; cf. *Il.* II, 100–109, 185–87, 198–282. For the importance of the scepter in the Homeric context, see Atchity, *Homer's Iliad*, pp. 119–33, "The Scepters of Argos."

23. *WL* 8; cf. *Il.* II, 211–70.

24. *Über naive und sentimentalische Dichtung*, NA XX, 446. For a comprehensive interpretation of *Wallensteins Lager*, see Gerhard Kaiser, "Wallensteins Lager: Schiller als Dichter und Theoretiker der Komödie," in *Schillers Wallenstein*, ed. Fritz Heuer and Werner Keller, WdF, 420 (Darmstadt: Wissenschaftliche Buchgesellschaft, 1977), pp. 333–63.

25. *DP* I, 4, 479–80; cf. 405–62 and 463–78; NA XVIII, 327–28. Cf. *Il.* I, 7; I, 277–81; IX, 37–39. Schiller's remark to Goethe after the completion of *Wallenstein* (March 19, 1799) is relevant here: "Neigung und Bedürfnis ziehen mich zu einem frei phantasierten, nicht historischen, und zu einem bloß leidenschaftlichen und menschlichen Stoff, denn Soldaten, Helden und Herrscher habe ich vor jetzt herzlich satt."

26. For Schiller's change in the date of Piccolomini's promotion to "Fürst" (1634 instead of 1639) in order for it to coincide with the murder of Wallenstein, see Rothmann, *Wallenstein: Erläuterungen*, p. 83; for the complexity of the figure of Octavio, see Wolfgang Wittkowski, "Octavio Piccolomini: Zur Schaffensweise des 'Wallenstein'-Dichters," in *Schiller*, ed. Berghahn and Grimm, pp. 407–65, esp. 457, 462; for the impact of the last line of *Wallenstein*, see Herbert Singer, "Dem *Fürsten* Piccolomini," in *Schillers Wallenstein*, ed. Heuer and Keller, pp. 180–212.

27. Harold Jantz, "William Tell and the American Revolution," in *A Schiller Symposium*, ed. Willson, p. 74.

28. *DP* I, 2, 94–97. Cf. *Il.* V, 519; XIII, 46–82, 701–9; XXIII, 706–9, 753–55; II, 527–30; XVIII, 157–58. Voß's preferred epithet "schnell" for Ajax, the son of Oileus, may have had some influence on Schiller's change from "Es ist die Stärke und Geschwindigkeit" to "Es ist die Stärke, Freund, und Schnelligkeit"; cf. NA VIII, 424, to *DP* I, 2, 82–97.

29. *WT* II, 5; II, 6. Cf. *Il.* XXIII, 700–739, 740–84. For Schiller's sentiment about Book XXIII of the *Iliad*, see Caroline von Beulwitz's remark of 1788 (*Schillers Gespräche*, ed. Julius Petersen [Leipzig: Insel, 1911], Nr. 121): "Schiller sagte einst in einer schwermütigen Stimmung: 'Wenn man auch nur gelebt hätte, um den dreiundzwanzigsten Gesang der Ilias zu lesen, so könnte man sich nicht über sein Dasein beschweren.' "

30. *DP* I, 2; II, 7. Cf. *Il.* IX.

31. To Goethe, Dec. 1, 1797; cf. Storz, *Dichter*, pp. 308–11.

32. To Goethe, Aug. 24, 1798; cf. Walter Müller-Seidel, "Episches im Theater der deutschen Klassik: Eine Betrachtung über Schiller's *Wallenstein*," JDSG, 20 (1976), 338–86.

33. For an intriguing view of such "supernumeraries," see Keller, "Drama und Geschichte," pp. 316–17; this does not mean, however (Walter Silz, "Chorus and Choral Function in Schiller," in *Schiller 1759/1959: Commemorative American Studies*, ed. John R. Frey [Urbana: University of Illinois Press, 1959], pp. 158–61), that Max and Thekla, like choral figures, have no "tragic conflict in them"; on the contrary.

34. *Il.* XVI, 20, 585, 690, 742, 786, 810, 841. Consider the letters to Goethe, to Körner, Nov. 28, 1796, and the fact that the actor portraying Max also

spoke the poet's *Prolog* (Wilpert, *Schiller-Chronik*, p. 225).

35. *DP* I, 1, 23–39 between 22 and 40. Cf. *Il.* XI, 780–803; I, 304–7, 329–48; IX, 185–668; XI, 599–848.

36. *DP* II, 4, 782–89 between the stage direction at 774/775 and line 795; *DP* II, 4 between 3 and 5.

37. *DP* I, 4 (cf. I, 2). Cf. *Il.* IX, 182–653 (cf. I, 1–7, 274–81; IX, 37–39, 157–61).

38. This, of course, does not mean that there are no examples of great initiative in Homer's *Iliad*. Yet the otherwise comparable elements emphasize the difference between Max and Patroclos

39. *DP* III; cf. *Il.* VI, 237–502. See also Fritz Martini, "Schillers Abschieds-szenen," in *Über Literatur und Geschichte: Festschrift für Gerhard Storz*, ed. Bernd Hüppauf and Dolf Sternberger (Frankfurt am Main: Athenäum, 1973), pp. 159–62, 176–78; Martini's statement on p. 177, "Die Erinnerung an Hektors Abschied stellt sich ein . . .," though possibly nothing more than a reference to Schiller's poem, strikes a welcome supportive chord.

40. Cf. Borchmeyer, "Hektors Abschied," p. 289: "Aus der Sicht des 'klassischen' Schiller müßte demnach die Übertragung einer Szene der *Ilias* in einen lyrischen Wechselgesang einer Übertragung des Naiven ins Sentimentalische gleichkommen."

41. To Goethe, Nov. 9, 1798. It certainly is no accident that these central scenes of *Die Piccolomini*, more than any other part of the *Wallenstein* trilogy, echo the key terms of the *Prolog*: "heiter" (*Pr.* 6, 134, 138; *DP* III, 4, 1547, 1566, 1627, 1645, 1663), "Spiel" (*Pr.* 1, 124, 131, 135; *DP* III, 4, 1566), "Bühne" (*Pr.* 4, 51, 67, 69, 111, 127; *DP* III, 4, 1556), "Bild" (*Pr.* 114, 122 "Gemälde"; *DP* III, 4, 1557, 1599), "Leben" (*Pr.* 53, 69, 116, 138; *DP* III, 4, 1558, 1562, 1564, 1566, 1626), "Wahrheit" (*Pr.* 134, 137; *DP* III, 4, 1558, 1626).

42. *Il.* VI, 429–32; *DP* III, 8, 1849–53.

43. *DP* III, 9, 1889–91; cf. Klaus L. Berghahn, " 'Doch eine Sprache braucht das Herz': Beobachtungen zu den Liebesdialogen in Schillers 'Wallenstein'," in *Schillers Wallenstein*, ed. Heuer and Keller, pp. 386–95. One might add that the change of address from "Sie" in scene 4 to "Du" in scene 5 conveys an "Intimität des Sprechens" which, indeed, marks the "heart" of the trilogy.

44. Cf. John Neubauer, "Die Geschichtsauffassung in Schillers 'Wallenstein'," in *Geschichtsdrama*, ed. Neubuhr, p. 177: "Indem Kant auf die Sterne über uns und das moralische Gesetz in uns verwies, postulierte er zwei verschiedene Gesetze im Universum, ein natürliches und ein moralisches. Obwohl die Parallele zu glatt aufgeht, um die komplexen Gegebenheiten des Dramas zu erklären, könnte man als allgemeine Orientierung darauf hinweisen, daß Max auf sein Herz hört, in der Hoffnung, dort das moralische Gesetz der Geschichte zu finden, während Wallenstein ganz wörtlich nach den Sternen greift, um das Geheimnis der geschichtlichen Welt zu enträtseln."

45. *DP* III, 4, 1561–65; *DP* III, 5, 1716–20.

46. *DP* IV, 5 (cf. *Geschichte des dreißigjährigen Krieges*, I, NA XVIII, 9–88); cf.

Il. XVIII, 478–607 (cf. Atchity, *Homer's Iliad*, pp. 158–87, "The Great Shield"). For Schiller's fondness for using the story of Achilles in his works, see "Das Glück," 43–48, NA I, 410; "Nänie," 7–10, SW I, 242; *Über die aesthetische Erziehung des Menschen*, Letter 8, NA XX, 330; "Die vier Weltalter," SW I, 417–18; "Achilles," SW I, 294 (an almost verbatim rendering of Johann Heinrich Voß's translation of Homer's *Odyssey* XI, 484–86).

47. To Goethe, April 4, 1797.

48. *DP* V; cf. *Philoctetes*, 1–200. Wilhelm Süvern, *Über Schillers Wallenstein in Hinsicht auf griechische Tragödie* (Berlin: Buchhandlung der Königlichen Realschule, 1800), p. 88, mentions the parallel between Octavio in Schiller's *Wallenstein* and Odysseus in Sophocles's *Philoctetes* without discussing its implications.

49. *DP* V, 1; 3; cf. *DP* I, 4, 561–82; *DP* II, 5; 7, 1180–83; *DP* III, 4, 1654–76; *WT* III, 15, 1948–68; *WT* V, 1, 3217–18; and *Geschichte des dreißigjährigen Krieges*, IV, NA XVIII, 329: "Noch hat sich das Dokument nicht gefunden, das uns die geheimen Triebfedern seines Handelns mit historischer Zuverlässigkeit aufdeckte, und unter seinen [Wallensteins] öffentlichen allgemein beglaubigten Taten ist keine, die nicht endlich aus einer unschuldigen Quelle könnte geflossen sein. Viele seiner getadeltsten Schritte beweisen bloß seine ernstliche Neigung zum Frieden."

50. *DP* V–*WT* III; *DP* V, 1–3 (*Philoctetes*, 1–200); *WT* I, 7 and II, 2 (*Phil.* 201–465); *WT* II, 4 (*Phil.* 543–626); *WT* II, 7 (*Phil.* 974–1080); *WT* III, 9, 13, 18, 21, 23 (*Phil.* 465–541, 627–1081); *WT* III, 15 (*Phil.* 1081–221); *WT* IV, 3–7, 9, 10 (*Phil.* 1222–472); *WT* V, end, "Dem *Fürsten* Piccolomini" (*Phil.* 1408–71, deus ex machina).

51. *DP* III, 5; cf. Wallenstein's brutal contempt for Max's hopes of marrying Thekla (*WT* III, 4; cf. *DP* II, 3 and 4) and Achilles's spiteful refusal to marry a daughter of Agamemnon's (*Il.* IX, 388–416).

52. *WT* IV, 10; cf. *WT* II, 3.

53. *DP* V, 3, 2639–46. I do not have the sense of a "choral ode" (Silz, "Chorus," p. 159) as much as of a Homeric simile.

54. *Il.* XI, 597–848; XV, 390–405; XVI, 1 ff. Cf. Benno von Wiese, *Die deutsche Tragödie von Lessing bis Hebbel*, 8th ed. (Hamburg: Hoffmann und Campe, 1973), p. 227.

55. To Körner, Sept. 30, 1798; cf. Goethe to Schiller, March 18, 1799: "Freilich hat das letzte Stück den großen Vorzug, daß alles aufhört politisch zu sein und bloß menschlich wird, ja das Historische selbst ist nur ein leichter Schleier, wodurch das Reinmenschliche durchblickt."

56. *WT* I, 1; cf. *Il.* I, 348–430, 493–533. Cf. the letter to Goethe, March 19, 1799: "Wie beneide ich Sie um Ihre jetzige nächste Tätigkeit [*Achilleis*]. Sie stehen auf dem reinsten und höchsten poetischen Boden, in der schönsten Welt bestimmter Gestalten, wo alles gemacht ist und alles wieder zu machen ist. Sie wohnen gleichsam im Hause der Poesie, wo Sie von Göttern bedient werden. Ich habe in diesen Tagen wieder den Homer vorgehabt und den Besuch der Thetis beim Vulkan mit unendlichem Vergnügen gelesen. In der anmutigen Schilderung eines Hausbesuchs, wie man ihn alle Tage erfahren

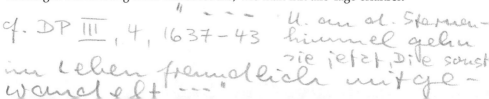

cf. DP III, 4, 1637–43 "u. an d. Sternen-
im Leben freundlich mitge-
wandelt ..." himmel gehn
sie jetzt, die sonst

kann, in der Beschreibung eines handwerksmäßigen Geschäfts ist ein Unendliches in Stoff und Form enthalten, und das Naive hat den ganzen Gehalt des Göttlichen."

57. Cf. Gert Sautermeister, *Idyllik und Dramatik im Werk Friedrich Schillers: Zum geschichtlichen Ort seiner klassischen Dramen*, Studien zur Poetik und Geschichte der Literatur, 17 (Stuttgart: Kohlhammer, 1971), pp. 72–73, 134–35.

58. *WT* I, 3, lines 92, 98, 136–37; cf. *WT* II, 3, 943; *DP* I, 3, 355–72.

59. *WT* I, 4; cf. *Il.* IX, 185–91; and Sautermeister, *Idyllik und Dramatik*, pp. 67–70, 130–33. The stage directions at *WT* I, 4, 158/159, 179/180, 191/192 (cf. *DP* II, 6, 985/986), visibly portray the difference between man moved by deliberate choice and heavenly bodies depending in their continuous regular motion on laws of nature.

60. *WT* I, 4; cf. *Il.* IX, 185–91; *WT* I, 5 (cf. 4, 139–58), cf. *Il.* IX, 622–57; *WT* I, 6 (cf. 4, 159–91), cf. *Il.* IX, 432–619; *WT* I, 7 (cf. 4, 192–222), cf. *Il.* IX, 222–429.

61. *WT* II, 2; cf. *Il.* XVI.

62. *WT* I, 7, 474–81; cf. *Il.* XV, 390–405 (cf. XI, 597–848); and a "Homeric" variant to *WT* I, 7, 626, NA VIII, 444: "Jetzt ist sie da, sie naht mit schnellen Rossen. / Drum rasch dich in den Wagensitz geschwungen, / Mit sicher, fester Hand von Zaum und Zügel / Besitz genommen, eh der Gegner dir / Zuvorkommt und den leeren Sitz erobert."

63. *WT* II, 2; cf. *Il.* XVI. Book XVI, after two transitional episodes in books XI and XV, continues the Homeric Achilles line.

64. *WT* II, 2, 756–61; cf. *Il.* XVI, 30–32.

65. *WT* II, 2, 813–43; cf. *Il.* XVI, 38–45, 64–100, 124–29; XI, 796–803.

66. *WT* II, 3, 891–960 (cf. I, 3, 92, 98, 136–37); 4, 970 (cf. *DP* I, 3, 354–72); *WT* III, 10; cf. *Il.* XVI, 220–56.

67. *WT* III, 10, 1740–48; *WT* III, 13, 1791–94.

68. NA VIII, 429.

69. NA VIII, 432.

70. *Il.* I, 234–46; cf. Atchity, *Homer's Iliad*, pp. 129–33.

71. Cf. Immanuel Kant, *Kritik der praktischen Vernunft*, Akademieausgabe (Berlin: de Gruyter, 1968), V, 47–50: "Von der Deduction der Grundsätze der reinen praktischen Vernunft," 94–98: "Kritische Beleuchtung der Analytik der reinen praktischen Vernunft"; Schiller, *Über die aesthetische Erziehung des Menschen*, Letters 11–22, NA XX, 341–83; Eugen Kühnemann, *Die Kantischen Studien Schillers und die Komposition des Wallenstein* (Marburg: Ehrhardt's Universitätsbuchhandlung, 1889); Binder, "Aesthetik," pp. 231–32; Ilse Graham, *Schiller's Drama: Talent and Integrity* (London: Methuen, 1974), pp. 280–83. For Schiller's combination of Kantian philosophy and Greek spirit, see Theodor Meyer, "Der Griechentraum Schillers und seine philosophische Begründung," *Jahrbuch des freien deutschen Hochstifts*, 27 (1928), 126: "So erhob sich für Schiller eine doppelte Aufgabe: von der Anschauung der Griechen aus das Bild der echten Sittlichkeit, Kultur und Poesie zu entwickeln und mit diesem Bild die Kantische Philosophie zu bereichern oder, wo sie nicht fähig schien, es mit ihren Begriffen zu umfassen und zu verste-

hen, diese umzubilden und zu berichtigen und andererseits das Wesen der Griechen mit den gegebenen oder weitergebildeten Begriffen der Kantischen Philosophie zu deuten und scharf zu umreißen."

72. *DP* I, 3, 362–66.

73. *WT* II, 3, 897–903.

74. Cf. *DP* II, 1, 626–29, "Wie der Mensch aus Gutem / Und Bösem ist gemischt," a remark that immediately precedes Wallenstein's first appearance.

75. *WT* II, 3, 953–60; cf. 932–38.

76. *WT* III, 13, 1813–14; *WT* III, 15 and 16; cf. *Il.* XVI, 155–220.

77. *WT* III, 15, 1844–51.

78. *WT* III, 18–23; cf. *Il.* XVI, 1–100; cf. Martini, "Schillers Abschiedsszenen," pp. 178–84.

79. *WT* III, 18, 2058, 2062–65; cf. *DP* V, 1, 2430–31; *WT* V, 11, 3777–78, Octavio: "Es darf nicht sein! Es ist nicht möglich! Buttler! / Gordon! Ich wills nicht glauben. Saget nein!"

80. *WT* III, 18, 2088–93; cf. *Il.* XVI, 33–35; cf. IX, 628–32: "Aber Achilleus / Trägt ein Herz voll Stolzes und Ungestüms in dem Busen! / Grausamer! Nichts bewegt ihn die Freundschaft seiner Genossen, / Die wir stets bei den Schiffen ihn hochgeehrt vor den andern! / Unbarmherziger Mann!" and 636–38: "Allein dir gaben ein hartes, / Unversöhnliches Herz die Unsterblichen wegen des einen / Mägdleins!" This agreement between Patroclos and Ajax, in their criticism of Achilles, throws an interesting light on the shift from an initial agreement to a later disagreement between Max and Buttler with respect to Wallenstein's treason.

81. *WT* III, 18, 2135–36. Cf. Hellmut Diwald's critique of Max, *Schiller, Wallenstein*, p. 84: "Mit seiner 'reinen Idee', seinem Wunsch, von der 'Doppelschuld und Freveltat' unbehelligt zu bleiben, schert er einfach aus der Unauflöslichkeit, dem fundamentalen Wertekonflikt aus. Er bekennt nicht Farbe, deshalb deklassiert er sich als Schwärmer." That should be tempered with Schiller's discussion of "realism" and "idealism" in *Über naive und sentimentalische Dichtung* (NA XX, 491–503).

82. *WT* III, 18, 2186–91; cf. NA XVIII, 234.

83. *DP* I, 4, 416–20; *WT* III, 3, 1380–84. For Schiller's "fire" images, see Ilse Graham, "Die Struktur der Persönlichkeit in Schillers dramatischer Dichtung," in *Schiller*, ed. Berghahn and Grimm, pp. 330–38.

84. *WT* III, 18; cf. II, 2; cf. I, 4 (5, 6, 7). Cf. *Il.* XVI, 1–100; cf. IX; cf. I, 53–307.

85. *Il.* IX, 485–95, 496–98.

86. *WT* III, 18, 2142–62, 2183–85.

87. *WT* III, 20, 2235; *Il.* XVI, 97–100.

88. *WT* III, 20, 2246–48.

89. *WT* IV; cf. Max Kommerell, "Schiller als Gestalter des handelnden Menschen," in *Geist und Buchstabe der Dichtung* (Frankfurt am Main: Klostermann, 1962), pp. 148–50.

90. *WT* III, 20, 2260–66 (cf. 22, 2362, 2364; 23, 2387–88); cf. *Il.* XVIII, 203–38.

91. *WT* III, scenes 20, 22 between scenes 18, 21, 23; 23, 24‑27 (cf. *WL*, 11, 1052–107); *WT* IV, scenes 3, 4, 5, 6, 7, 9, 10 between scenes 1, 2, 6, 8; cf. Gerhard Storz, "Die Bauform der Wallensteintrilogie," *Zeitschrift für deutsche Bildung*, 16 (1940), 18, note 1, pointing to the "Gleichzeitigkeit" of the report on Max's death with the recruiting of Wallenstein's murderers; Hans Schwerte, "Simultaneität und Differenz des Wortes in Schillers 'Wallenstein'," in *Schillers Wallenstein*, ed. Heuer and Keller, pp. 247–89.

92. *WT* II, 3, 926–31; cf. Ilse Graham, *Schiller: Ein Meister der tragischen Form* (Darmstadt: Wissenschaftliche Buchgesellschaft, 1974), pp. 156–57; cf. *Il.* XVI, 682–865 (the death of Patroclos) and its anticipation in 467–69 (the death of Pedasos, cf. 145–54) and 479–502 (the death of Sarpedon).

93. *WT* IV, 4, 2649 (cf. 10, 3020); 8, 2847–62; cf. *Il.* XVI, 777; and the description of the death of Gustavus Adolphus in Schiller's *Geschichte des dreißigjährigen Krieges*, NA XVIII, 268–77, esp. 274: "Die Sonne neigt sich eben zum Untergang, indem beide Schlachtordnungen aufeinander treffen." (See above, p. 15.)

94. *WT* IV, 7, 2768–69, 2773–75; cf. *Il.* XVI, 1–100.

95. *Il.* XVI, 781–94 (cf. 696–709).

96. *WT* IV, 10, 3029–51. Without elaborating on the implications of such a reference, Gerhard Storz ("Bauform," p. 22) refers to Max's fate as "geradezu eine Aristeia." As in the context of Schiller's *Geschichte des dreißigjährigen Krieges*, this passage evokes a flashback to Hector's attempt to break through the wall built around the Greek ships, *Il.* XII, 49–57: "So im Gewühl ging Hektor umhergewandt und ermahnte / Über den Graben zu springen die Seinigen. Aber nicht wagten's / Ihm die Rosse, geflügelten Laufs; sie wieherten laut auf, / Stehend am äußersten Bord; denn zurück sie schreckte des Grabens / Breite, zum Sprung hinüber nicht schmal genug, noch zum Durchgang / Leichtgebahnt; denn ein jäh abhängiges Ufer erhob sich / Rings an jeglicher Seit', auch war mit spitzigen Pfählen / Obenher er bepflanzt, die Achaias Söhne gerammt, / Dichtgereiht und mächtig, zur Abwehr feindlicher Männer." For Schiller's invention of the encounter between the Swedes and the forces of the Emperor at that time, see Rothmann, *Wallenstein: Erläuterungen*, p. 79.

97. *WT* IV, 10, 3062–72. Cf. *Il.* XXIII, 175–76 in 163–232; XVIII, 336–37; XXI, 26–27. For the significance of the number twelve in Schiller's *Wallenstein*, see below, pp. 64–65.

98. *Il.* XIX, 297–300 in 282–302.

99. *Il.* XXII, 460–67 in 437–515; cf. XXIV, 719–46.

100. *WT* IV, 9, 2915–23.

101. *WT* IV, 12, 3180; cf. Oskar Seidlin, "Wallenstein: Sein und Zeit," in *Schillers Wallenstein*, ed. Heuer and Keller, pp. 243–44.

102. *SW* I, 242, 7–14; cf. Goethe, *Achilleis*, 362–66: "Aber wie er den Freund mit gewaltiger Neigung umfaßte, / Also halt ich auch ihn; und so wie er jenen bejammert, / Werd ich, wenn er nun fällt, den Sterblichen klagen, die Göttin. / Ach! daß schon so frühe das schöne Bildnis der Erde / Fehlen soll! die weit und breit am Gemeinen sich freut," and Staiger, *Schiller*, pp. 221–

24. The final date for Goethe's *Achilleis* as well as Schiller's *Wallensteins Tod* and "Nänie" (cf. to Schiller, Dec. 23, 1797; May 12, 16, 1798; to Goethe, May 18, 1798; March 19, 1799) is 1799.

103. *Il.* XVIII, 52–62 (cf. 35–62).

104. *WT* IV, 12, 3155; cf. *Il.* XXIII, 59–107; *WT* IV, 14, 3194–96; cf. V, 5, 3677–79, and Schiller's poem "Thekla," SW I, 460–61.

105. *Il.* XVIII, 3–4; *WT* V, 3, 3393/3394; *Il.* XVIII, 22–35.

106. *WT* V, 3, 3404, 3406–13.

107. *Il.* XVIII, 203–6 in 203–27; cf. *WT* V, 3, 3400–3401.

108. *Il.* XVIII, 73–77; cf. *WT* V, 3, 3398–99, 3435–37.

109. *WT* II, 2, 751–53; *WT* V, 3, 3423–25.

110. *DP* III, 4, 1560; *WT* V, 3, 3446; cf. Seidlin, "Wallenstein," pp. 246–47. For Wallenstein's "Todesklage" in connection with Schiller's understanding of elegiac poetry in *Über naive und sentimentalische Dichtung*, cf. Sautermeister, *Idyllik und Dramatik*, pp. 155–58.

111. *WT* V, 4, 3589–92; cf. 3, 3452–55; cf. *Il.* XVIII, 80–82; cf. XXIII, 46–47.

112. *WT* V, 5, 3657–61; cf. *Il.* XIX, 268–74; cf. 55–66; XVIII, 12–14, 107–13.

113. *WT* I, 7, 600–602, 654–56; *DP* III, 8, 1839–40.

114. *DP* I, 1, 80–81, Buttler: "Ich fürchte, / Wir gehn nicht von hier, wie wir kamen," and *DP* I, 5, 596, Octavio about Max: "Er kommt mir nicht zurück, wie er gegangen"; *DP* I, 2 (Buttler) and 4 (Max); *DP* II, 7, 1207–9, Max's "Nach des Gesetzes Wort—den Tod!" and Buttler's "Den Tod nach Kriegsrecht!", interspersed between Illo's and Isolani's "Den Tod!", setting Max and Buttler apart from Illo and Isolani. Yet the placement of "des Gesetzes Wort" and "Kriegsrecht," with respect to "Tod," also sets Max apart from Buttler. Max's "Mein General!", repeated after Wallenstein's informing him of his intended treason (*WT* II, 2, 685, 711), echoes in Buttler's "Mein General—" after Octavio's betrayal of Wallenstein (*WT* III, 10, 1692). Wallenstein's acceptance of Buttler and rejection of Max, both against his inner voice (*WT* III, 4), are reconfirmed in Buttler's refusal of Max's hand (*WT* III, 23, 2399–403); cf. Walter Silz, "Charakter und Funktion von Buttler in Schillers 'Wallenstein'," in *Schillers Wallenstein*, ed. Heuer and Keller, pp. 254–73.

115. *WT* IV, 2, 2546; cf. *Il.* XI, 786–89.

116. *DP* I, 2, 94–97, and above, I, 2, 31; cf. Homer, *Odyssey* XI, 541–64; Ovid, *Metamorphoses*, XIII, 1–392; and Singer, "Dem *Fürsten* Piccolomini," pp. 180–212.

III. "No *Iliad* Possible Any More after *The Iliad*"

1. *Pr.* 65–66, 53–56, 70–110, 126–27.

2. To Humboldt, Oct. 26, 1795.

3. Cf. Melitta Gerhard, *Schiller und die griechische Tragödie* (Weimar: Duncker, 1919), p. 70.

4. To Körner, April 7, 1797.

5. To Goethe, Oct. 20, 1797. Cf. Goethe's elegy "Hermann und Dorothea,"

30, "Doch Homeride zu sein, auch nur als letzter, ist schön," and Walter Rehm, *Griechentum und Goethezeit*, 4th ed. (Leipzig: Dietrich, 1938; rpt. Bern/ München: Francke, 1968), ch. V, "Goethe, Sehnsucht und Fülle," pp. 114– 90; Butler, *The Tyranny of Greece over Germany*, ch. IV, "Goethe, The Homeride," pp. 121–35; Wolfgang Schadewaldt, "Goethe und Homer," *Trivium*, 7 (1949), 200–232, esp. 201–2: "Das Eigene und das andere 'begegnen' sich in einem ihnen beiden von Grund auf Gemeinsamen. Es ist nicht eine unio mystica (denn hier ist nichts Mystisches), doch wirkliche Vermählung aus vorgängiger Wahlverwandtschaft, wo man sich in einer schwer ausdrück- baren Mischung von Selbsthingabe und Selbstbehauptung im Andern wie- derfindet und das andere wie ein Stück von einem selber wird."

6. *Il.* XVIII, 478–616; cf. to Goethe, Sept. 22, 1797: "Indessen zweifle ich garnicht, daß Ihr Hermann schlechterdings über alle diese Subjektivitäten triumphieren wird, und dieses durch die schönste Eigenschaft bei einem poetischen Werk, nämlich durch sein Ganzes, durch die reine Klarheit sei- ner Form und durch den völlig erschöpften Kreis menschlicher Gefühle."

7. To Goethe, March 19, 1799: "Wie beneide ich Sie um Ihre jetzige nächste Tätigkeit. Sie stehen auf dem reinsten und höchsten poetischen Bo- den, in der schönsten Welt bestimmter Gestalten, wo alles gemacht ist und alles wieder zu machen ist. Sie wohnen gleichsam im Hause der Poesie, wo Sie von Göttern bedient werden."

8. To Goethe, May 18, 1798; cf. Goethe to Schiller, May 12: "Soll mir ein Gedicht gelingen, das sich an die Ilias einigermaßen anschließt, so muß ich den Alten auch darinne folgen, worin sie getadelt werden, ja ich muß mir zu eigen machen, was mir selbst nicht behagt; dann nur werde ich einiger- maßen sicher sein Sinn und Ton nicht ganz zu verfehlen"; to Goethe, May 15, 1798: "Das, was Ihnen im Homer mißfällt, werden Sie wohl nicht ab- sichtlich nachahmen, aber es wird, wenn es sich in Ihre Arbeit einmischt, für die Vollständigkeit der Versetzung in das Homerische Wesen und für die Echtheit Ihrer Stimmung beweisend sein." For the problematic nature of Schiller's relationship to Homer, see Rehm, *Griechentum und Goethezeit*, ch. VI, "Schiller, Höhe und Kampf," pp. 191–228; Gerhard Storz, *Klassik und Ro- mantik* (Mannheim: Bibliographisches Institut, 1972), p. 77.

9. To Goethe, April 27, 1798: "Dafür lese ich in diesen Tagen den Homer mit einem ganz neuen Vergnügen, wozu die Winke, die Sie mir darüber ge- geben, nicht wenig beitragen. Man schwimmt ordentlich in einem poe- tischen Meere, aus dieser Stimmung fällt man auch in keinem einzigen Punkte und alles ist ideal bei der sinnlichsten Wahrheit."

10. To Humboldt, Dec. 25, 1795.

11. To Humboldt, Oct. 26, 1795.

12. To Schiller, Sept. 27, 1795.

13. To Schiller, April 19, 1798.

14. Luke 5:37–38: "And no man putteth new wine into old bottles; else the new wine will burst the bottles, and be spilled, and the bottles shall perish / But new wine must be put into new bottles; and both are preserved."

15. Luke 5:39; cf. to Humboldt, Nov. 9, 1795: "Wir haben dieser Tage auch

viel über griechische Literatur und Kunst gesprochen, und ich habe mich bei dieser Gelegenheit ernstlich zu etwas entschlossen, was mir längst schon im Sinne lag, nämlich das Griechische zu treiben. . . . In Absicht auf die zu lesenden Autoren würde ich den Homer gleich vornehmen. . . . Langsam freilich wird diese Arbeit gehen, da ich nur wenige Zeit darauf verwenden kann, aber ich will sie so wenig als möglich unterbrechen, und dabei ausharren. Neben meinem Schauspiel ist sie mir leichter möglich, und sie hilft mir zugleich das Moderne vergessen."

16. To Schiller, Nov. 6, 1795.

17. "Blau" and "Grün," like a theme with variations, permeate the whole poem.

18. Cf. *Über naive und sentimentalische Dichtung*, NA XX, 436–38.

19. To Körner, April 7, 1797.

20. Humboldt, "Über Schiller," p. 379; cf. Emil Staiger, "Dialektik der Begriffe Nachahmung und Originalität," in *Tradition und Ursprünglichkeit*, Akten des III. Internationalen Germanistenkongresses 1965 in Amsterdam, ed. Werner Kohlschmitt and Herman Meyer (Bern/München: Francke, 1966), pp. 29–38.

IV. Dramatic versus Epic Poetry

1. To Körner, April 7, 1797; to Goethe, Nov. 24, 1797.

2. To Goethe, April 25, 1797; Aug. 24, 1798.

3. Goethe to Schiller, Dec. 23, and the response to Goethe, Dec. 26, 1797; cf. NA XXI, 336–40, and Müller-Seidel, "Episches im Theater der deutschen Klassik."

4. Cf. *Über die aesthetische Erziehung des Menschen*, Letter 19, NA XX, 369: "Ehe wir im Raum einen Ort bestimmen, gibt es überhaupt keinen Raum für uns; aber ohne den absoluten Raum würden wir nimmermehr einen Ort bestimmen. Eben so mit der Zeit. Ehe wir den Augenblick haben, gibt es überhaupt keine Zeit für uns; aber ohne die ewige Zeit würden wir nie eine Vorstellung des Augenblicks haben. Wir gelangen also freilich nur durch den Teil zum Ganzen, nur durch die Grenze zum Unbegrenzten; aber wir gelangen auch nur durch das Ganze zum Teil, nur durch das Unbegrenzte zur Grenze"; Letter 11, NA XX, 343: "Nur indem er sich verändert, *existiert er*; nur indem er unveränderlich bleibt, existiert *er*. Der Mensch, vorgestellt in seiner Vollendung, wäre demnach die beharrliche Einheit, die in den Fluten der Veränderung ewig dieselbe bleibt."

5. To Goethe, Dec. 26, 1797.

6. To Goethe, July 21, 1797.

7. To Körner, Aug. 20, Oct. 20, Dec. 12, 1788; to Caroline von Beulwitz and Charlotte von Lengefeld, Dec. 4, 1788 and Nov. 15, 1789; to Körner, Oct. 24, 1791.

8. To Körner, March 9, 1789; cf. to Humboldt, Dec. 25, 1795: "Um endlich auch die Erfahrung zu befragen, so werden Sie mir eingestehen, daß kein

griechisches Trauerspiel dem *Gehalt nach* sich mit demjenigen messen kann, was in dieser Rücksicht von Neuern geleistet werden *kann.* Eine gewisse Armut und Leerheit wird man immer daran zu tadeln finden, wenigstens ist dies mein, immer gleichförmig wiederkehrendes Gefühl."

9. Wolzogen, *Schillers Leben*, p. 126.

10. To Goethe, May 4, 1798.

11. Cf. Aristotle's notion of tragedy as being superior to epic poetry, *Poetics*, V, 1449b9–20, and XXVI, 1461b26–1462b15; and to Goethe, May 5, 1797; to Körner, Nov. 26, 1790.

12. Cf. to Goethe, March 18, 1796; April 4, 1797.

13. For the influence of Euripides's *Iphigenia in Aulis* on Schiller's *Die Malteser*, see Butler, *The Tyranny of Greece over Germany*, p. 189.

14. NA XLII, 193; cf. 265. For Schiller's familiarity with what he calls "Euripidische Methode," see his letter to Goethe, April 26, 1799, which seems to disprove Florian Prader's remark in *Schiller und Sophokles* (Zürich: Atlantis, 1954), p. 111: ". . . und wir möchten sie vielleicht schon eher mit den euripideischen Gestalten vergleichen, ohne indessen bei Schiller einen Hinweis darauf zu finden."

15. *Über naive und sentimentalische Dichtung*, NA XX, 432; cf. Staiger, *Schiller*, p. 189: "Sogar als Übersetzer befaßt sich Schiller keineswegs mit der erfüllten Gegenwart Homers, obwohl eine Ilias in Versen noch zu leisten gewesen wäre und ein solches Unternehmen die epischen Pläne, die er damals hegte, hätte fördern können. Er wendet sich den Tragikern zu, und zwar Euripides, dem am meisten problematischen, reflektierten."

16. This comparison will provide ample ground to disprove Melitta Gerhard's claim (*Schiller und die griechische Tragödie*, p. 38): "Die Art des Einflusses der griechischen Tragödie auf Schillers eigene Dramatik ist also aus seinen Übersetzungen des Euripides nicht zu erkennen."

17. *Über die aesthetische Erziehung des Menschen*, Letter 15, NA XX, 355–59.

18. Cf. Hegel's later formulation: "Es kommt nach meiner Einsicht, welche sich nur durch die Darstellung des Systems selbst rechtfertigen muß, alles darauf an, das Wahre nicht als *Substanz*, sondern eben so sehr als *Subjekt* aufzufassen und auszudrücken" (Vorrede zur *Phänomenologie des Geistes*, ed. Johannes Hoffmeister, 6th ed. [Hamburg: Meiner, 1952], p. 19; cf. pp. 20, 24; 558–64). Hegel's choice of a slightly altered quotation from Schiller's poem "Die Freundschaft" for the finale of his *Phänomenologie des Geistes* is tacit acknowledgment of their affinity of thought.

V. *Wallenstein* and *Iphigenia in Aulis*

1. SW III, 348; cf. to Körner, Dec. 12, 1788.

2. SW III, 349.

3. *Pr.* 1; 138; cf. *Über die aesthetische Erziehung des Menschen*, Letter 15, NA XX, 357: "indem es mit Ideen in Gemeinschaft kommt, verliert alles Wirk-

liche seinen Ernst, weil es *klein* wird, und indem es mit der Empfindung zusammen trifft, legt das Notwendige den seinigen ab, weil es *leicht* wird."

4. *Pr.* 1–69 (art), 70–110 (life), 111–38 (art).

5. *Pr.* 1–138: 1–69, 70–110, 111–38; 1–69: 1–49, 50–60, 61–69; 70–110: 70–78, 79–90, 91–110; 111–38: 111–18, 119–29, 129–38.

6. *Pr.* 1–49 in 1–69; 1–9, cf. 1–69; 10–30, cf. 70–110; 31–49, cf. 111–38. Cf. Graham, *Schiller's Drama*, pp. 257–62.

7. *IA* (SW III, 284–355), 1–177: 1–47, 48–132, 133–77. For the authenticity of the Euripidean text, as Schiller had it, see Bernard M. W. Knox, "Euripides' *Iphigeneia in Aulide* 1–163 (in that order)," *Yale Classical Studies*, 22 (1968), 239–61.

8. *WL*; cf. *IA*, 1st choral interlude.

9. To Goethe, April 7, 1797; NA XLII, 229.

10. Cf. *DP* II, 2: Wallenstein's first appearance, not with his army, but with his family. For the importance of playing at dice, see Seidlin, "Wallenstein," pp. 247–50; O. J. Matthijs Jolles, "Die Sprache des 'Spiels' und 'Antispiels' in den frühen Dramen Schillers," *Modern Philology*, 58 (1961), 246–54.

11. *WL* 9, 636, 637 (my emphasis).

12. Cf. *DP* I, 1, 10–14.

13. Kaiser, "Wallensteins Lager," p. 346.

14. For the "aesthetic associations" of this chorus, and their thematic significance in *Wallenstein*, see Graham, *Schiller, Ein Meister*, pp. 103–9; Kaiser, "Wallensteins Lager," pp. 342–44; for the importance of the fact that this chorus, the finale of scene eleven, is at the same time the finale of the only act in *Wallenstein* with eleven scenes, see below, pp. 64–65.

15. *IA* 178–295: 178–237, 238–95.

16. *WL* 6; cf. *IA* I, 222–47; cf. Seidlin, "Wallenstein," pp. 248–49.

17. Even though the words of the chorus anticipate the sacrifice of Iphigenia (*IA* I, 198–201), the women are unaware of that. For the question of man's unity with nature, cf. *Über naive und sentimentalische Dichtung*, NA XX, 436–37.

18. *Pr.* 112–14.

19. *DP* I, 1, 22, 40–51 and *DP* I, 2; *WT* II, 6 and *WT* IV–V. Cf. *IA* II, 1; II, 2; IV, 3.

20. *DP* I, 2; cf. *IA* II, 2.

21. *DP* I, 2, 267–71; cf. *IA* II, 3 (*WT* IV, 10; *WT* II, 3; cf. Aeschylus, *Oresteia*).

22. *DP* I, 4, 534–58; cf. *IA* II, 4, 533–39.

23. *DP* I, 5. Cf. *IA* II, 4, 676–98; and *Über die aesthetische Erziehung des Menschen*, Letter 6, NA XX, 321–28.

24. *DP* II, 1; cf. *IA* III, 1.

25. *Pr.* 118.

26. *DP:* I = 5 scenes; II = 7 scenes; III = 9 = 7(+2) scenes; IV = 7 scenes; V = 3 = 5(−2) scenes.

27. *WT:* I = 7 scenes; II = 7 scenes; III = 23 = 11+1+11 scenes; IV = 14 = 7+7 scenes; V = 12 = 11+1 scenes.

28. *WT* III, 15.

29. *WT* V, 2, 3352; 3, 3462. For Schiller's changing the time of the murder from eight in the evening to eleven/twelve at night, see Rothmann, *Wallenstein: Erläuterungen*, p. 151; Mann (*Wallenstein*, 1124) mentions the time as being between ten and eleven. It might not be uninteresting to note that the planet Jupiter takes between eleven and twelve earth years for one complete revolution.

30. This interpretation of the poetic form of *Wallenstein* seems to harmonize with what Neubauer ("Geschichtsauffassung," pp. 184–85) calls "ästhetische Unvermeidlichkcit"; cf. Müller-Seidel, "Episches im Theater der deutschen Klassik," p. 352, "Die Schlußverse des *Prologs* von der Heiterkeit der Kunst beziehen sich auf das Ganze der Trilogie. Damit ist die künstlerische Form gemeint, die Darstellung—nicht das dargestellte Leben selbst, wie wir es als Zuschauer überblicken."

31. *DP* II, 1, 626–29. Notice the tension between poetic content and poetic form which seems to express the problematic mixture of good and evil in man's soul. The fact that line 627, "Des Menschen Seele. Wie der Mensch aus Gutem," withholds "aus Gutem" from line 628, "Und Bösem ist gemischt," leaves that element of the human soul hovering over an abyss. The necessity of completing the thought, however, points to man's conscious involvement in crossing the threshold between good and evil. The most striking example of this is *WT* I, 4, 220–22, the moment before Wallenstein's pact with Wrangel: (*Wallenstein hat den Blick nachdenkend auf die Türe geheftet*) "Noch ist sie rein—noch! Das Verbrechen kam / Nicht über diese Schwelle noch—So schmal ist / Die Grenze, die zwei Lebenspfade scheidet!" Despite Wallenstein's claim that crime has not yet crossed the threshold, the tension between "kam" at the end of the previous line and "nicht" at the beginning of the following line, reaching on to "noch" in the middle of that line, is almost unbearable. Wallenstein's monologue preceding these lines struggles with exactly this problem: the part thought plays in the consummation of the deed.

32. *DP* II, 2 (cf. *WL* 2, 57–58; *DP* I, 1, 31–35; *DP* I, 2, 270–71; *DP* I, 5); cf. *IA* III, 2 (cf. I, 110–20; II, 2, 393–96; 3, 501–4; 4, 525–43).

33. *IA* II, 3, 501–3; cf. *DP* II, 2, 639–42; cf. *WL* 2, 57–58: "Die Herzogin kommt ja heute herein / Mit dem fürstlichen Fräulein—Das ist nur der Schein."

34. *IA* III, 2, 715–18; cf. *DP* II, 3, 722–23; *DP* II, 4, 786–87.

35. *DP* II, 3, after 753.

36. *DP* III, 3–5; cf. *IA* III, 3.

37. *IA* IV, 1, 991–92; cf. *DP* III, 1; cf. *DP* II, 5, 871.

38. *DP* III, 2, 1392–97; cf. *IA* IV, 2; *IA* IV, 3, 1090–91: "Und diese vorgegebene Vermählung, / Die mich von Argos rief—Wozu denn die?"

39. *DP* III, 3; cf. *IA* IV, 3, 1041–109.

40. *IA* IV, 3, 1123–26; cf. *DP* III, 4, 1530–44; cf. *IA* IV, 3, 1110–217.

41. *DP* III, 5—notice the change of address from "Sie" in scene 4 to "Du" in scene 5; cf. *IA* IV, 3, 1218–89. Compare also *DP* III, 5, 1699–1700: "Ich

werfe mich zu deines Vaters Füßen, / Er soll mein Glück entscheiden, er ist wahrhaft" with *IA* IV, 3, 1267–69: "Fall ihm zu Füßen! Fleh ihn an, daß er / Sein Kind nicht töte! Bleibt er unerbittlich, / Dann komm zu mir!"

42. *DP* III, 1 (Terzky, Illo), cf. *IA* IV, 1 (Achilles); *DP* III, 3 (Max), cf. *IA* IV, 3, 1041–109 (Slave); *DP* III, 3 (Max), cf. *IA* IV, 3, 1110–289 (Achilles).

43. *DP* III, 4, 1561; cf. Seidlin, "Wallenstein," pp. 242–46. For the idyllic landscape as symbol in Schiller's dramatic poetry, cf. Binder, "Aesthetik," pp. 226–27: "Die Sphäre der nicht-idealen Wirklichkeit und des nicht-wirklichen Ideals ist die Sphäre der Zeit; im Zusammenfall beider hebt sich die Zeit auf. Jene idyllischen Bilder beziehen sich aber auf reale Personen in der Zeit. Den Widerspruch löst die Beobachtung, daß diese Zustände stets nur erinnert oder antizipiert oder—in Landschaften—symbolisiert, aber niemals gegenwärtig dargestellt werden."

44. *IA* IV, 3, 1351–56; cf. *DP* III, 8, 1834, 1838, 1885.

45. *DP* III, 8, 1811–20; cf. *DP* III, 9, 1895–98: "Das ist kein Schauplatz, wo die Hoffnung wohnt, / Nur dumpfes Kriegsgetöse rasselt hier, / Und selbst die Liebe, wie in Stahl gerüstet, / Zum Todeskampf gegürtet, tritt sie auf."

46. *IA* IV, 3, 1363–65; cf. *DP* III, 9, 1907–12.

47. To Goethe, Nov. 9, 1798, and Dec. 12, 1797; cf. O. J. Matthijs Jolles, "Das Bild des Weges und die Sprache des Herzens: Zur strukturellen Funktion der sprachlichen Bilder in Schillers *Wallenstein*," *Deutsche Beiträge zur geistigen Überlieferung*, 5 (1965), 109–42; Sautermeister, *Idyllik und Dramatik*, pp. 77–81.

48. *NA* X, 15.

49. *DP* IV, 1; cf. Romans 2:28–29; Matthew 5:17; *DP* IV, 2; IV, 4; IV, 7.

50. *DP* IV, 5; cf. Matthew 26:27–28 (Schiller's "Kelch," cf. Luther's Bible translation). For the stage direction after *DP* IV, 5, 2061: "Kellermeister mit Kopfschütteln, indem er den Pokal hervorholt und ausspült," cf. *IA* IV, 3, 1305–8: "Unter den Freuden des festlichen Mahls / Schöpfte des Nektars himmlische Gabe / Jovis Liebling, der phrygische Knabe, / In die Bäuche des goldnen Pokals."

51. *DP* IV, 6, 2192 (cf. *DP* I, 1, 15: "Von dreißig Regimentern haben sich / Die Obersten zusammen schon gefunden"); *WT* I, 5, 366–68: "Nein! wir haben / Um Judas' Lohn, um klingend Gold und Silber, / Den König auf der Walstatt nicht gelassen"; cf. Matthew 26:14–16. The symbolic meaning of the numbers twelve and eleven in Schiller's *Wallenstein* (see above, pp. 64–65) is verified here in the number of disciples before and after Judas's betrayal of Jesus.

52. *WT* V, 2, 3265–66.

53. *DP* IV, 6, 2193–95; cf. Matthew 27:37–38.

54. *DP* IV, 7, 2201–8, cf. Matthew 26:47–50; *DP* IV, 7, 2236, cf. Matthew 12:30; *DP* IV, 7, 2260–61, cf. Matthew 26:51–52 (cf. John 18:10–11).

55. *WL* 6; *WL* 8, 622–23; *WL* 11; *DP* I, 4, 567–77; *DP* II, 5; *DP* II, 7; *DP* III, 4, 1654–76; *DP* V, 1, 2330–40; cf. Matthew 5–7.

56. *WT* V, 1, 3217–18 (cf. *DP* III, 4, 1656–57: "Er wird den Ölzweig in den Lorbeer flechten, / Und der erfreuten Welt den Frieden schenken").

57. *DP* I, 2, 208; II, 5, 801–2: "Des Kaisers Söhnlein, der ist jetzt ihr Heiland, / Das neu aufgehende Gestirn!"

58. *WL* 2; 6; 7; 11. Cf. Kaiser, "Wallensteins Lager," pp. 334–35; cf. *DP* V, 1, 2528; *WT* IV, 3, 2603–10; Matthew 9, 10, 12–17, 21, 23, 26–28. The thematic connection between Wallenstein and the doctrine of the New Testament is prefigured in the chorus of the soldiers at the end of *Wallensteins Lager*: "Und setzet ihr nicht das Leben ein, / Nie wird euch das Leben gewonnen sein."

59. Cf. the story of the sacrifice of Iphigenia as an example of the horrors perpetrated by religion, in Lucretius, *De rerum natura*, I, 80–101; cf. *IA* I, 23–26.

60. *WT* I, 1; cf. *IA* I, 1; cf. Seidlin, "Wallenstein," pp. 240–42.

61. *DP* II, 6, 960–65.

62. *WT* I, 2; cf. *IA* II, 1.

63. *WT* I, 3; cf. *IA* II, 2; cf. Graham, *Schiller's Drama*, ch. VI, "Wallenstein's Poodle: An Essay in Elusion and Commitment," pp. 125–45 (cf. 63–66).

64. *WT* I, 4, 139; cf. *IA* II, 4, 513. Concerning the conflict between "Sollen und Vollbringen" in the Ancients, but "Wollen und Vollbringen" in the Moderns, see Reinhardt, "Schillers Wallenstein und Aristoteles," pp. 316–18.

65. *IA* II, 4, 515–17, 633–34.

66. *WT* I, 3, 112–14, 136–37, cf. 92, 98. Cf. Oskar Seidlin, "Schiller: Poet of Politics," in *A Schiller Symposium*, ed. Willson, pp. 41–42: "It is in the *Wallenstein* trilogy that Schiller drives the problem of political man to its last and extreme consequence, to the point where the man of action can no longer act, because in order to act freely—and only if he acts freely can he make history instead of being made by it—he must be able to choose freely, to keep all avenues open so that at no time will the direction of his course be dictated to him. Seen in this light, the freedom to act, which is the premise upon which the existence of political man rests, is transmuted into a freedom from action."

67. *IA* II, 4, 512–46, 547–96, 597–614; cf. II, 3.

68. *WT* I, 5 (cf. 3; cf. 4, 139–58); 6 (cf. 2; cf. 4, 159–91); 7 (cf. 1; cf. 4, 192–222).

69. *WT* I, 7; cf. *IA* III, 4.

70. *IA* II, 4, 597–99; III, 3, 780–82; cf. 4, 904–12; cf. *WT* I, 7, 600–602, 654–56.

71. *WT* I, 7, 474–80; *IA* IV, 1; 2; 3.

72. *WT* II, 2, 685–86, 711; cf. *DP* II, 4, 759, "Mein General" and 763, "Mein Fürst" framing Wallenstein's acknowledgment, "Heut hast du / Den Vater dir, den glücklichen, verpflichtet," as prelude to, and *WT* III, 10, 1692, Buttler's "Mein General," as postlude to *WT* II, 2. The latter has to be seen in the light of the polarity between Max and Buttler throughout *Wallenstein*.

73. *WT* II, 2, 756–61; cf. *IA* IV, 3, 1110–215.

74. *WT* II, 2, 833–35; cf. *WT* I, 7, 654–56; cf. *IA* V, 3, 1566–67.

75. *WT* II, 2; 3; I, 7; *WT* II, 4, 970.

76. *WT* II, 4, 970; cf. I, 4.

77. To Körner, March 24, 1800. For "Entsprechungen als Kennzeichen der Struktur," see Gerhard Storz, "Zur Gestalt von Schillers 'Wallenstein'," in *Schillers Wallenstein*, ed. Heuer and Keller, p. 173: "Wie glitzernde Refraktionen erhellen sie für Augenblicke die Zwischenräume des Ungesagten und Verborgenen, lassen das jetzt so bestimmt Gesagte hernach ins Fragwürdige gleiten und vertiefen dadurch das Dunkel des Rätselhaften und Ironischen. Zugleich verstärken sie wie Verzahnungen oder Klammern den Zusammenhalt der Teile innerhalb des ausgedehnten, weitverzweigten Baues."

78. *WT* III, 3; cf. *IA* V, 3, 1425–505.

79. *WT* III, 4, 1469–85 (cf. 3, 1414, 1417); cf. *IA* V, 3, 1509–14 (cf. Aeschylus, *Agamemnon*, 245).

80. *WT* III, 4, 1486–91. It is in keeping with the Countess's philosophy of life that here as well as in *WT* I, 7, 474–80 she mistakes Max's and Thekla's more noble motives.

81. *WT* III, 4, 1490–534; cf. *IA* V, 4, 1590; cf. *DP* III, 4, 1539–44.

82. *IA* V, 3, 1541–46; cf. *WT* III, 18, 2135–41; cf. III, 21, 2352: "Doch wir gehören nicht zu unserm Hause"; *WT* III, 23, 2386–89.

83. *DP* III, 6, 1738; *WT* III, 23, 2377; cf. *IA* V, 6, 1850–51 (cf. *IA* IV, 3, 1323–24: "Heil dir! Heil dem schönen Sterne, / Der aus deinem Schoß ersteht!"); cf. *DP* II, 4, 754–58; *WT* IV, 10, 3072 (cf. *WT* IV, 5, 2675: "Sie will sterben!"). For references to Max as star, cf. *DP* I, 4, 397; *WT* V, 3, 3414–55; and Seidlin, "Wallenstein," pp. 242–48.

84. *WT* IV, 12. For an interpretation of this ending as a removal into a "mythische Region," see Storz, *Dichter*, pp. 292–97, "Der Tod der Liebenden." It might be interesting to note that in Schiller's poems published in 1800 the 4th choral interlude from his translation of Euripides's *Iphigenia in Aulis* followed upon his poem "Nänie" (reported in SW I, 886), which was written at the time of *Wallensteins Tod*.

85. See Schiller's note (SW III, 347): "Hier schließt sich die dramatische Handlung. Was noch folgt, ist die Erzählung von Iphigeniens Betragen beim Opfer und ihrer wunderbaren Errettung"; cf. Hans-Martin Schreiber, *Iphigeniens Opfertod: Ein Beitrag zum Verständnis des Tragikers Euripides* (Diss., Frankfurt am Main, 1963), pp. 57–60, 83, 92–99.

86. To Körner, Dec. 12, 1788, and Oct. 24, 1791. Cf. Süvern, *Über Schillers Wallenstein*, p. 151: ". . . durch die grausenvolle Stille tönt kurzes Waffengeklirr, und des Herzogs, wie dort Agamemnons, Todesruf"; Eugen Kühnemann, *Schiller*, 2nd ed. (München: Beck, 1914), p. 490: "Das Verhältnis zur griechischen Tragödie wäre Schiller in seinem Bewußtsein wohl das wichtigste gewesen. Sprechen wir von Einzelheiten, so scheint für den letzten Akt Agamemnon das Vorbild gegeben zu haben. Wie der Stier zum Opfer, so gehen Agamemnon und Wallenstein beide gleichermaßen ahnungslos in den Tod. Sogar der rote Teppich, in dem man Wallensteins Leiche bringt, stammt daher." The last statement is incorrect to the extent that Schiller's main historical source, Christian Murr, already mentions the red carpet (cf.

Rothmann, *Wallenstein: Erläuterungen*, p. 154). In spirit, however, Kühnemann's observation seems to me to be correct.

87. Concerning the complexities of poetic structure in *Wallenstein*, see Schwerte, *Simultaneität und Differenz*, pp. 274–89.

88. *Über die aesthetische Erziehung des Menschen*, Letters 18, 20–24, NA XX, 365–68, 373–93; *WL*, 6; *DP* III, 5; *WT* III, 12.

89. *DP* II, 1, 626–29.

90. *Pr.* 102–10.

91. *Über naive und sentimentalische Dichtung*, NA XX, 437; XXI, 287–88.

VI. *Wallenstein*—"Not a Greek Tragedy"

1. To Körner, Jan. 8, 1798.

2. To Süvern, July 26, 1800.

3. Georg Wilhelm Friedrich Hegel, "Über Wallenstein," in *Schillers Wallenstein*, ed. Heuer and Keller, pp. 15–16. For a refutation of Hegel on the basis of Schiller's correspondence between "Formgefüge" and "Sinngefüge," see Schwerte, *Simultaneität und Differenz*, pp. 277, 282: "Nur in solcher simultanen Konstellation hält Schiller sein Drama im Gleichgewicht des Ertragbaren, das, wie auch er verlangte, Furcht und Mitleid erregen sollte. Nur so vermochte er, seiner Absicht nach, die moderne, neuzeitliche Variation der antiken Tragödie zu geben, allerdings indem er entschieden das Zeitelement auf neue, moderne Weise handelnd in den Aufbau seiner Tragödie einfügte und poetisch gegenwärtig machte. . . . Schillers Drama gibt nicht Verklärung . . . Schillers Drama gibt Aufklärung." Pp. 287–88: "Aber Hegel sah falsch, vielmehr: zu wenig. Er übersah die Simultaneität der inneren Szenerie, das simultane Gegengewicht . . . das Aufblitzen einer der Freiheit des Menschen allein möglichen Gegenwelt im 'Schönen', die aber in der Welt der Geschichtsmächte und deren Wortdifferenz existenziell unhaltbar ist, nur als 'Idee', oder wahrscheinlich genauer: nur als poetische Potentialität aufleuchtet. Schiller wollte keine erleichterte Brust. Er wollte als Dichter zeigen, wie es zugeht. Das war seine Art der poetischen Aufklärung."

4. NA I, 349; cf. Staiger, *Schiller*, pp. 356–57.

5. *Poetics*, VI, 1449b24–28; cf. Laurence Berns, "Aristotle's *Poetics*," in *Ancients and Moderns: Essays on the Tradition of Political Philosophy in Honor of Leo Strauss*, ed. Joseph Cropsey (New York/London: Basic Books, 1964), pp. 70–87.

6. To Körner, June 3, 1797. With reference to the ending of Schiller's *Die Braut von Messina*, see Wolfgang Schadewaldt, "Antikes und Modernes in Schillers 'Braut von Messina'," *JDSG*, 13 (1969), 304: "Für Schiller ist weder die Aischyleische noch die Sophokleische Form der Katharsis möglich. Doch ist das Große an ihm, daß er aus den Bedingungen der modernen Welt, die, anders als die griechische, durch den Subjektivismus geprägt ist, eine neue, eigene Form der Katharsis gefunden hat. Sie vollzieht sich am Ende des Stückes durch den Akt der absoluten Freiheit, mit der Don Cesar in seinem Freitod sich selber richtet."

7. Cf. Immanuel Kant, *Grundlegung zur Metaphysik der Sitten*, III, Akademieausgabe, IV, 446–47, "Der Begriff der Freiheit ist der Schlüssel zur Erklärung der Autonomie des Willens," 445–59, "Von der äußersten Grenze aller praktischen Philosophie"; *Kritik der reinen Vernunft*, Akademieausgabe, III, Vorrede, B XXVII–XXX, B 560–86, "Auflösung der kosmologischen Ideen von der Totalität der Ableitung der Weltbegebenheiten aus ihren Ursachen"; *Kritik der praktischen Vernunft*, Akademieausgabe, V, 47–50, "Von der Deduction der Grundsätze der reinen praktischen Vernunft," 94–98, "Kritische Beleuchtung der Analytik der reinen praktischen Vernunft." See above, p. 120, note 71.

8. Humboldt to Schiller, Sept. 1800; cf. Humboldt to Schiller, Nov. 6, 1795, and Feb. 17, 1803; cf. Rehder, "The Four Seals of Schiller," p. 12: "Just as Aeschylus or Euripides dramatized for their time the myth of antiquity, Schiller dramatized a significant aspect of the myth of Western, occidental civilization in that he substituted Wilhelm Tell for Prometheus, Maria Stuart for Helen of Troy, and the archetype of modern diplomacy, Wallenstein, for the patriarchal ruler of the Hellenic tribes, Agamemnon."

9. Hinderer, *Der Mensch in der Geschichte*, p. 4.

10. Cf. Reinhardt, "Schillers Wallenstein und Aristoteles," p. 313: "Ein Versuch, die neuere Tragödie über einzelne, seit Humboldt immer wieder vermerkte Bezüge hinaus im Hinblick auf die dramatische Struktur in die Nähe der griechischen zu rücken, kann daher nicht in Betracht kommen"; in a note (n. 147), Reinhardt comments: ". . . Dieser Vergleich ist vom Text her durchaus beglaubigt . . ., darf aber nicht überstrapaziert werden."

11. Storz, *Dichter*, p. 376.

12. Prader, *Schiller und Sophokles*, pp. 94–96, 98, 138–41.

13. The abstract nature of Schiller's language asserts itself even in his translation of Euripides, where a word like "Sittlichkeit" as a translation of *arete* (IA II, 4, 666; cf. Euripides, IA 563–67) certainly seems out of place.

14. Hugo von Hofmannsthal, *Ausgewählte Werke in zwei Bänden* (Frankfurt am Main: Fischer, 1957), II, 407–11, 409.

15. Staiger, *Schiller*, p. 368.

16. Schadewaldt, "Antikes und Modernes," pp. 290, 294–98, 306; cf. idem, "Der Weg Schillers zu den Griechen," *JDSG*, 4 (1960), 95: "Ob Schillers Griechentum ein 'Urerlebnis', ob es ein 'Bildungserlebnis' war?—Das Unzureichende dieses Begriffspaars erweist sich, wenn irgendwo, der Art Schillers gegenüber, das Griechentum ebenso vielfältig wie grundsätzlich neu zu denken, jedoch es so groß und lebensmächtig umfassend zu denken, daß das Gedachte dem Erlebten gleichkam und, immer unter der Bedingung des modernen Primats der Subjektivität, die Substanz des griechischen Wesens schöpferisch anverwandelt wurde."

17. Schadewaldt, "Antikes und Modernes," pp. 290–92.

18. Jantz, "William Tell," pp. 69, 74 (Schiller, *Wilhelm Tell*, III, 3, 1770–813; cf. Aeschylus, *Persians*, 230–45); cf. idem, "Kontrafaktur, Montage, Parodie: Tradition und symbolische Erweiterung," in *Tradition und Ursprünglichkeit*, ed. Kohlschmitt and Meyer, p. 64.

19. Jantz, "Kontrafaktur," p. 54.

20. Cf. Dieter Borchmeyer, "Hektors Abschied."

21. Cf. Helmut Koopmann, "Joseph und sein Vater. Zu den biblischen Anspielungen in Schillers *Räubern*," in *Herkommen und Erneuerung: Essays für Oskar Seidlin*, ed. Gerald Gillespie and Edgar Lohner (Tübingen: Niemeyer, 1976), pp. 150–67.

22. Others include the Bible, Sophocles, and Shakespeare; cf. Staiger, *Schiller*, pp. 369–70: "Er verneigt sich vor Shakespeare und deutet in die Romantik und in die Antike hinüber, um seine Verbundenheit mit dem Genius anderer Zeiten und ihre Verwandtschaft im Ewig-Menschlichen zu bezeugen und durch die Erinnerung an vorgeformte Stile den Kunstcharakter dessen, was auf der Bühne geschieht, uns noch entschiedener einzuprägen. . . . Daß er darüber jemals seinen eigenen Ton einbüßen würde, brauchte Schiller nicht zu befürchten. Gerade weil er sich stets behauptet und weil die Anspielungen niemals unwillkürlich, sondern mit Willen an passenden Stellen eingesetzt sind, überhört man sie leicht oder meint wohl gar, seinen eigenen Ohren nicht glauben zu dürfen."

23. To Humboldt, March 21, 1796.

24. To Goethe, April 26, 1799; to Körner, Nov. 15, 1802.

25. "Selbstbesprechung im 'Wirtembergischen Repertorium'," SW I, 624.

26. Cf. *Schiller-Lexikon: Erläuterndes Wörterbuch zu Schillers Dichterwerken*, ed. Ludwig Rudolph and Karl Goldbeck (Berlin: Nicolai, 1869), "Homer," I, 416, with many other interesting references, 414–19.

27. To Goethe, April 4; to Körner, April 7, 1797, and Jan. 8, 1798; cf. Gerhard Storz, *Das Drama Friedrich Schillers* (Frankfurt am Main: Societäts Verlag, 1938), p. 138: ". . . die dramatische Architektur, aufgeführt über dem Grundstein des Paradoxons, ist um so vieles reicher, verwickelter, ausgreifender, als es die eines jeden antiken Dramas ist und sein konnte, eines Dramas, das hinter der einen Orchestra, vor der steten Palastfront, um den einen Altar die schmale Begebenheit des allen- und altbekannten Mythos spielte."

28. To Caroline von Beulwitz and Charlotte von Lengefeld, Dec. 4, 1788.

29. Cf. Staiger, *Schiller*, p. 420: "Schiller spielt auf Homer, auf Shakespeare, auf die attischen Tragiker und romantischen Stilelemente an, um sich und uns von der im Wandelbaren verborgenen Einheitlichkeit des Menschenwesens zu überzeugen; das heißt, er vollbringt damit einen Akt der menschlichen Solidarität."

30. NA X, 12.

31. The fact that Schiller's *Prolog* and *Wallensteins Lager* relate as much to the early parts of Homer's *Iliad* as to the early parts of Euripides's *Iphigenia in Aulis*, while *Die Piccolomini* relates more to *Iphigenia in Aulis* and *Wallensteins Tod* more to the *Iliad*, might have something to do with the difference between drama and tragedy. Schiller's notion of *Die Piccolomini* as a drama, but of *Wallensteins Tod* as a tragedy seems to be underscored by the latter's lasting parallel to Homer, the "foremost of the tragedians," as Socrates calls him (Plato, *Theaetetus*, 152 e; cf. Aristotle, *Poetics*, IV, 1448b34–36; VIII, 1451a22–24; XV, 1454b8–15; XXIII, 1459a30–37, 1459b2–4; XXIV, 1459b8–17, 1460a5–8).

32. This, of course, does not mean that Euripides never speaks of ideas. Yet the comparison accentuates the difference.

33. Helmut Koopmann, "Schillers *Wallenstein*: Antiker Mythos und moderne Geschichte," in *Teilnahme und Spiegelung: Festschrift für Horst Rüdiger*, ed. Beda Allemann and Erwin Koppen (Berlin/New York: de Gruyter, 1975), pp. 263–74, 272.

34. Euripides, *IA* 55, 366, 443, 453, 489, 511, 657, 719, 745, 864, 1009, 1136, 1202, 1257–58, 1280, 1336–37, 1403. This affinity between Schiller and Euripides could be shown throughout their dramatic work.

35. Cf. Storz, *Drama*, p. 163: "Das griechische Musterbild gleicht, geprüft an dem im 'Wallenstein' Geleisteten, der 'Arbeitshypothese' in den Naturwissenschaften."

36. Cf. Keller, "Drama und Geschichte," pp. 331–33; and Helmut Koopmann, "Dantons Tod und die antike Welt," in *Geschichtsdrama*, ed. Neubuhr, p. 237: "um am antiken Vorbild nachzuweisen, was die Gegenwart oder die Gegenwart allein nicht zeigen konnte"; cf. pp. 246, 248–50. Interestingly enough, Büchner, in *Dantons Tod*, reverts to the method (long abandoned by Schiller) of having his characters name and even parody their ancient models.

VII. Philosophical Poems and Aesthetic Writings

1. To Körner, March 9, 1789, and Feb. 3, 1794; cf. Staiger, *Schiller*, pp. 154–55; "Die Künstler," 1–12, NA I, 201; "Die Künstler," 270–73, NA I, 208; *Über die aesthetische Erziehung des Menschen*, Letter 2, NA XX, 311.

2. "Die Künstler," 443–45, cf. 393–96: "Mit euch, des Frühlings erster Pflanze, / Begann die seelenbildende Natur, / Mit euch, dem freudgen Erntekranze, / Schließt die vollendende Natur" (later version), SW I, 186, cf. 184–85.

3. *Über die aesthetische Erziehung des Menschen*, Letter 6, NA XX, 321–28; cf. *Über das Pathetische*, NA XX, 197–99, and NA XXI, 189–90; cf. Hans Robert Jauss, "Fr. Schlegels und Fr. Schillers Replik auf die 'Querelle des anciens et des modernes'," in *Europäische Aufklärung*, ed. Hugo Friedrich and Fritz Schalk (München: Fink, 1967), pp. 117–40.

4. "Der Genius," 29–34, SW I, 239; cf. "Die Sänger der Vorwelt," 16: "Die der Neuere kaum, kaum noch im Herzen vernimmt," SW I, 228.

5. Cf. *Über Anmut und Würde*, NA XX, 254–55.

6. *Über die aesthetische Erziehung des Menschen*, Letter 6, NA XX, 326–28.

7. "Die Sänger der Vorwelt," 15, SW I, 228; "Der Genius," SW I, 238–39; "Die Götter Griechenlands," 112, 121–28 (later version), SW I, 172–73.

8. "Die Sänger der Vorwelt," 15–16, SW I, 228; "Der Genius," 33–34, SW I, 239; "Der Antritt des neuen Jahrhunderts," 33–36, SW I, 459: "In des Herzens heilig stille Räume / Mußt du fliehen aus des Lebens Drang, / Freiheit ist nur in dem Reich der Träume, / Und das Schöne blüht nur im Gesang."

9. "Die drei Alter der Natur," SW I, 256; cf. "Die Künstler," 270–73, NA I,

208; *Über die aesthetische Erziehung des Menschen,* Letter 6, NA XX, 321; *Über naive und sentimentalische Dichtung,* NA XX, 414.

10. NA XX, 436, 427, 424; 428–29.

11. NA XX, 432; cf. 430–31: "Bei diesen artete die Kultur nicht so weit aus, daß die Natur darüber verlassen wurde"; cf. 431–32: "So wie nach und nach die Natur anfing, aus dem menschlichen Leben als *Erfahrung* und als das (handelnde und empfindende) *Subjekt* zu verschwinden, so sehen wir sie in der Dichterwelt als *Idee* und als *Gegenstand* aufgehen."

12. NA XX, 437; cf. XXI, 291–93, 297–99; NA XX, 473–74, 476; cf. Düsing, "Aesthetische Form," pp. 198, 207, 219, 225–28.

13. NA XX, 438, 470. Imitation of nature as a "finite goal," of course, will have to be understood not in a quantitative but in a qualitative sense.

14. Humboldt to Schiller, Dec. 18, and Schiller's response to Humboldt, Dec. 25, 1795; for Schiller's use of the terms "naive" and "sentimental," see Szondi, "Das Naive," pp. 191–92: "Insofern sind *naiv* und *sentimentalisch* bei Schiller immer schon mehr als Epochenbegriffe. Sie bezeichnen Dichtungs- und Empfindungsweisen, deren Zuordnung zu den Epochen Antike und Moderne nur auf Grund einer geschichtsphilosophisch konzipierten Poetik möglich ist, nach der jeweils eine dieser Dichtungsweisen und eine oder mehrere ihnen jeweils entsprechende poetische Gattungen in der bestimmten Epoche den Ton angeben."

15. I even doubt whether such a summary term can have any meaning.

16. NA XX, 414: "Sie *sind,* was wir *waren;* sie sind, was wir wieder *werden sollen.* Wir waren Natur wie sie, und unsere Kultur soll uns, auf dem Wege der Vernunft und der Freiheit, zur Natur zurückführen. Sie sind also zugleich Darstellung unserer verlornen Kindheit, die uns ewig das Teuerste bleibt; daher sie uns mit einer gewissen Wehmut erfüllen. Zugleich sind sie Darstellungen unserer höchsten Vollendung im Ideale, daher sie uns in eine erhabene Rührung versetzen. Aber ihre Vollkommenheit ist nicht ihr Verdienst, weil sie nicht das Werk ihrer Wahl ist." See Humboldt to Schiller, Nov. 6; Dec. 18, 1795; cf. Meyer, "Der Griechentraum Schillers," pp. 126, 149.

17. Meyer, "Der Griechentraum Schillers," p. 144: "Es war Griechenromantik, wenn Schiller in den Griechen der klassischen Zeit, die die Einheitlichkeit ihrer Kultur ihrer einseitigen Naturhaftigkeit und dem gebundenen mythologischen Denken verdankten, Totalmenschen glaubte entdecken zu können und daher eine Rückkehr zu ihnen auf höherer Stufe verlangte, es war Griechenromantik, wenn er an ihrer Kultur nur die Schönheit, nicht auch die tiefen Schatten bemerkte, und wenn er aus ihnen ein allgemeines Ideal des Menschentums glaubte ableiten zu können, das doch nur eine sehr beschränkte Gültigkeit für eine besondere Klasse von Menschen besitzt." The most striking example of this, in my opinion, is Schiller's idealization of Achilles throughout his work.

18. *Über naive und sentimentalische Dichtung,* NA XX, 450–51; cf. Rehm, *Griechentum und Goethezeit,* pp. 19, 205.

19. *Über naive und sentimentalische Dichtung,* NA XX, 448.

20. It is important to note that the walk begins and ends not in a Greek, but in a definitely German landscape. For an interpretation of the elegy as a whole, see both Storz, *Dichter*, pp. 220–25, and Staiger, *Schiller*, pp. 190–94.

21. Lines 87–98, SW I, 231; lines 186–88, SW I, 234; lines 1–38, 173–200, SW I, 228–29, 233–34.

22. Gerhard Kaiser, *Wanderer und Idylle: Goethe und die Phänomenologie der Natur in der deutschen Dichtung von Geßner bis Gottfried Keller* (Göttingen: Vandenhoeck und Ruprecht, 1977), ch. III, "Schiller und Goethe," p. 91.

23. To Caroline von Beulwitz and Charlotte von Lengefeld, Sept. 10, 1789; cf. NA XLII, 152: "Ach man muß doch das Schöne in die Natur erst hineintragen."

24. "Die Künstler," 270–73, NA I, 208.

25. Preface to *Die Braut von Messina*, NA X, 10; cf. *Über naive und sentimentalische Dichtung*, NA XX, 450: "Der Inhalt der dichterischen Klage kann also niemals ein äußrer, jederzeit nur ein innerer idealischer Gegenstand sein; selbst wenn sie einen Verlust in der Wirklichkeit betrauert, muß sie ihn erst zu einem idealischen umschaffen. In dieser Reduktion des Beschränkten auf ein Unendliches besteht eigentlich die poetische Behandlung. Der äußere Stoff ist daher an sich selbst immer gleichgültig, weil ihn die Dichtung niemals so brauchen kann, wie sie ihn findet, sondern nur durch das, was sie selbst daraus macht, ihm die poetische Würde gibt."

VIII. Theory in Practice: Art and Nature in Schiller's Presentation of the Ideal

1. Preface to *Die Braut von Messina*, NA X, 9–10; cf. letter to Herzog Friedrich Christian von Augustenburg, July 13, 1793; cf. Humboldt, "Über Schiller," p. 392: "Was er unter einer solchen Behandlung eines dramatischen Stoffes verstand, zeigte er gleich an dem schwierigsten in dieser Hinsicht, am *Wallenstein*. Alles Einzelne in der großen, so unendlich Vieles umfassenden Begebenheit sollte der Wirklichkeit entrissen, und durch dichterische Notwendigkeit verbunden erscheinen."

2. To Goethe, Aug. 24, 1798, and Dec. 29, 1797; cf. Diwald, *Schiller, Wallenstein*, pp. 93–98.

3. *Über die aesthetische Erziehung des Menschen*, Letter 9, NA XX, 333; cf. NA XXI, 258–59.

4. Letter 2, NA XX, 311; cf. *On the Aesthetic Education of Man*, ed. Elizabeth M. Wilkinson and L. A. Willoughby (Oxford: Clarendon, 1967), p. 224; cf. Schiller's letters to Herder, Nov. 4, 1795, and to Humboldt, Nov. 9, 1795, where Schiller's report about wanting to relearn Greek and to read as first authors Homer and Xenophon ends with the remark, "Neben meinem Schauspiel [*Wallenstein*] ist sie [diese Arbeit] mir leichter möglich, und sie hilft mir zugleich das Moderne vergessen"; cf. Goethe to Schiller, Nov. 25, 1797: "auf alle Fälle sind wir genötigt, unser Jahrhundert zu vergessen, wenn wir nach unserer Überzeugung arbeiten wollen."

5. Cf. *Über naive und sentimentalische Dichtung*, NA XX, 432.

6. To Goethe, Nov. 24, 1797; *Über die aesthetische Erziehung des Menschen*, Letter 22, NA XX, 382; cf. *On the Aesthetic Education of Man*, ed. Wilkinson and Willoughby, p. 267; Jolles, "Das Bild des Weges," p. 141, note 2: "Was Schiller hier unter *Stoff* und *Form* versteht, weicht erheblich von dem üblichen Sprachgebrauch ab. Wenn er von *Stoff* redet, so meint er damit nicht nur die Realität des dargestellten Gegenstandes, sondern auch die Sprache, das Medium der Darstellung. Was man gewöhnlich als die Form eines Gedichtes bezeichnet, z. B. die 'Form' der Worte, Laute, Reime, die 'Form' der Sätze und Reimverbindungen, all dies ist für Schiller Stoff oder Rohmaterial, das ganz in dem, was er nun seinerseits als *Form* bezeichnet, aufgehen muß. *Form* in seinem Sinne ist die *Idee* des dargestellten Gegenstandes, die sinnliche Erscheinung oder das Symbol des Gegenstandes."

7. *Über die aesthetische Erziehung des Menschen*, Letter 9, NA XX, 333–34. Concerning "aufbewahrt in bedeutenden Steinen," cf. Schiller's elegy, "Der Spaziergang," 87, "heilige Steine!" 98, "der rührende Stein," 124, "der fühlende Stein," and his letter to Herzog Friedrich Christian von Augustenburg, July 13, 1793, "So wandelt noch jetzt der griechische Geist in seinen wenigen Überresten durch die Nacht unsers nordischen Zeitalters, und sein elektrischer Schlag weckt manche verwandte Seele zum Gefühl ihrer Größe auf."

8. *Über naive und sentimentalische Dichtung*, NA XX, 437; NA XXI, 287–88; NA XX, 414–15, 428–29, 436. Cf. Johannes Haupt, "Geschichtsperspektive und Griechenverständnis im ästhetischen Programm Schillers," *JDSG*, 18 (1974), 420–23; and Benno von Wiese, "Das Problem der ästhetischen Versöhnung bei Schiller und Hegel," *JDSG*, 9 (1965), 180–81.

9. To Körner, Sept. 12, 1794. Cf. to Körner, Sept. 4, 1794; NA XXI, 278–86; and Wolzogen, *Schillers Leben*, p. 239: ". . . indes schrieb er doch fast täglich, meistens in der Nacht, einige Stunden an seinem *Wallenstein*, der damals seine Hauptbeschäftigung war. Die Stunden, wo er sich weniger dazu aufgelegt fühlte, widmete er seinen Briefen an den Herzog von Augustenburg über die aesthetische Erziehung des Menschen."

10. To Böttiger, March 19, 1799; to Humboldt, March 21, 1796; to Körner, Sept. 4, 1794; to Herzog Friedrich Christian von Augustenburg, Nov. 11, 1793. Cf. Keller, "Drama und Geschichte," p. 324: "Das Theater, das auf Erhellung des Vergangenen zur Bewußtmachung des Gegenwärtigen zielt, bedarf eines Verstehenshorizonts, vor dem das Zufällige den Charakter des Notwendigen und Typischen erhält, der Ausschnitt 'Ganzheit' beanspruchen kann und das Irrationale rational durchschaut ist."

11. *Über naive und sentimentalische Dichtung*, NA XX, 492–503; NA XXI, 311–14; to Humboldt, Jan. 9, 1796. Cf. Wolfgang Binder, "Die Begriffe 'Naiv' und 'Sentimentalisch' und Schillers Drama," *JDSG*, 4 (1960), 155.

12. Cf. *Über die tragische Kunst*, NA XX, 166–67; *Über Matthissons Gedichte*, NA XXII, 269; Preface to *Die Braut von Messina*, NA X, 9: "Und eben darum weil die wahre Kunst etwas Reelles und Objektives will, so kann sie sich nicht bloß mit dem Schein der Wahrheit begnügen; auf der Wahrheit selbst,

auf dem festen und tiefen Grunde der Natur errichtet sie ihr ideales Gebäude."

13. *Über die aesthetische Erziehung des Menschen*, Letter 26, NA XX, 401; XXI, 274–75. For the aesthetic phenomenon of "Schein," cf. Staiger, *Schiller*, pp. 194–99; cf. Binder, "Aesthetik," p. 221: "Poesie und Historie können sich de facto verbinden, müssen aber de iure getrennt bleiben. Ob sich das Verhältnis von Aesthetik und Dichtung nach diesem Muster bestimmen läßt, wäre jetzt die Frage. Allerdings müßte man die Formel dann wohl umkehren: de iure verbunden und de facto getrennt."

14. *Über die notwendigen Grenzen beim Gebrauch schöner Formen*, NA XXI, 10.

15. To Goethe, Sept. 14, 1797. See also letter to Goethe, April 4, 1797. Cf. Schiller's poem "Ilias," NA I, 259: "Immer zerreißt den Kranz des Homer, und zählet die Väter / Des vollendeten ewigen Werks! / Hat es doch Eine Mutter nur und die Züge der Mutter, / Deine unsterblichen Züge, Natur." Cf. Binder, "Aesthetik," p. 219: "Über eine derart vermittelnde Stufe gelangte man von der 'Metaphysik' zur 'Physik' der Kunst, d. h. zu den praktischen Verfahrensregeln des Dichters. Wie eine solche Mittelstufe auszusehen hätte, sagt Schiller nicht. Sie vertritt jedoch die systematische Stelle, die in Kants 'Kritik der reinen Vernunft' der sogenannte Schematismus innehat. Wie die Vernunft die reinen Verstandesbegriffe durch Schemata an die sinnliche Anschauung vermittelt, so müßten zwischen die reinen ästhetischen Begriffe und die konkreten dichterischen Phänomene Schemata eingeschoben werden, die mit jenen die Allgemeinheit und mit diesen die Anschaulichkeit teilten" (cf. p. 225).

16. "Piccolomini, Wallensteins erster Teil," in *Schillers Wallenstein*, ed. Heuer and Keller, p. 3.

17. *Über Matthissons Gedichte*, NA XXII, 269; cf. Düsing, "Aesthetische Form," pp. 219–20.

18. To Goethe, April 4, 1797. See also letter to Körner, Nov. 28, 1796; *Über die aesthetische Erziehung des Menschen*, Letter 22, NA XX, 382. Cf. Neubauer, "Geschichtsauffassung," p. 185: "Die Rolle der Idee übernimmt im 'Wallenstein' eine nicht greifbare Beschaffenheit der Form und der Gestaltung, die nicht dem Material, sondern allein dem schöpferischen Willen eigen ist. Der 'Wallenstein' ist so das einzige Drama Schillers, das die Forderung der Briefe 'Über die ästhetische Erziehung des Menschen', daß nämlich die Form alles leisten solle, erfüllt; und das in hervorragender Weise. Im 'Wallenstein' gelang es Schiller, das historische Schicksal durch ästhetische Absicht und den historischen oder 'höheren' Sinn durch künstlerische Gestaltung zu ersetzen. Obwohl sich die Charaktere in einer historischen Welt bewegen, in der das Chaos eine begrenzte Freiheit erlaubt, sind sie in einem dichten Netz ästhetischer Unvermeidlichkeit gefangen."

19. To be sure, my concentration on Greek archetypes in Schiller's *Wallenstein* does not deny traces of Shakespearean characters as well. My claim, however, is that the Greek archetypes pervade the poetic structure of the trilogy as a whole.

20. This, I think, adds to Ilse Graham's understanding of Schiller's tech-

nique of "Veräußerung" (*Schiller: Ein Meister*, pp. 213–14; "Struktur der Persönlichkeit," pp. 351, 365). What it adds is a variation on the same theme: in addition to unity out of fragmentation a unity out of wholeness, but on a more complex level.

21. To Humboldt, June 27, 1798: "Sie müssen sich nicht wundern, lieber Freund, wenn ich mir die Wissenschaft und die Kunst jetzt in einer größern Entfernung und Entgegensetzung denke, als ich vor einigen Jahren vielleicht geneigt gewesen bin. Meine ganze Tätigkeit hat sich gerade jetzt der Ausübung zugewendet, ich erfahre täglich, wie wenig der Poet durch *allgemeine reine* Begriffe bei der Ausübung gefördert wird, und wäre in dieser Stimmung zuweilen unphilosophisch genug, alles was ich selbst und andere von der Elementarästhetik wissen, für einen einzigen empirischen Vorteil, für einen Kunstgriff des Handwerks hinzugeben." Cf. to Goethe, Dec. 29, 1797; and Graham, *Schiller: Ein Meister*, pp. 172–73.

22. *Über die aesthetische Erziehung des Menschen*, Letter 9, NA XX, 334; *Über naive und sentimentalische Dichtung*, NA XX, 436–37, 473 note 1; NA XXI, 286; cf. Koopmann, "Schillers *Wallenstein*," p. 274.

23. Otto Ludwig, "Schillers Wallenstein," in *Schillers Wallenstein*, ed. Heuer and Keller, p. 50; cf. Binder, "Die Begriffe," pp. 146–47: "Schiller hat diese Gestalten selbstverständlich nicht nach seinem Begriff entworfen, aber er hat sie im Horizont derselben Seinsweise konzipiert, die er einst rein spekulativ in einem aesthetischen Begriff zu fassen gesucht hatte. Begriff und dramatische Gestalt sind nicht dasselbe, und sowenig jener den faktischen Reichtum der Gestalt erschöpft, sowenig erreicht diese die transzendentale Bestimmtheit des Begriffs. Aber wenn man beiderseits vom tatsächlichen Befund auf die ihn prägende Struktur, d. h. von der seienden Gestalt auf die sie bestimmende Seinsweise und vom gedachten Begriff auf die ihn bestimmende Denkform zurückgeht, dann dürfte sich eine legitime und notwendige Beziehung erkennen lassen."

24. For example, Binder, "Aesthetik," p. 229: "Diesen Zustand des totalen Vermögens ohne Fixierung auf Bestimmtes kennen wir. Es ist der in ganz anderen Zusammenhängen entworfene, aber bis in den Wortlaut mit Wallensteins Situation identische 'aesthetische Zustand' einer unbegrenzten Potentialität vor aller Selbstbegrenzung in einem bestimmten Tun. Sobald man den verborgenen theologischen Kern des Gedankens erkennt, befremdet dieser Vergleich nicht mehr. Der aesthetische Zustand ist nämlich nichts anderes als die menschlich-endliche Analogie der ewigen Existenz Gottes vor der Schöpfung der Welt. Da sich der Mensch aber in einer vorhandenen Welt befindet, darf er Gottes metaphysisches Allvermögen nur aesthetisch, d. h. nach innen nachahmen. Nur über die Kräfte seines Subjekts darf er in analoger Weise gebieten, und er muß es sogar, wenn er Mensch werden will. Wallenstein aber dehnt sein Subjekt in die Welt hinein aus. Identisch mit seinem Werk glaubt er, über eine Welt gebieten zu können; und wirklich herrscht er eine Zeitlang über alle, vom einfachen Soldaten bis hinauf zum Kaiser. Darin liegt aber der Keim seiner 'superbia' und seines Falles. Indem er im Glauben an seine Auserwähltheit, die ihm die Sterne bezeugen, die-

sen Moment um ein weniges überdehnt, versäumt er die politische Stunde und stürzt.

"Wallensteins Zögern auf der Höhe seiner Macht zeigt also die volle Struktur des aesthetischen Zustandes, aber nicht nach innen, sondern nach außen. Er versucht dem politischen Zustand, der Entscheidung und damit Begrenzung verlangt, die Form des aesthetischen und seiner Freiheit zu geben, nicht über sich selbst, sondern über eine Welt total zu verfügen, die er gleichsam nur für die Außensphäre seines Ichs hält. Es ist die Tragödie des großen Menschen, den seine Größe verlockt, die Grenze seiner Menschheit zu überschreiten."

25. *Über die aesthetische Erziehung des Menschen*, Letter 21, note 1, NA XX, 378. Cf. Graham, *Schiller's Drama*, pp. 63–66; idem, *Schiller, Ein Meister*, pp. 254, 259–63.

26. *Über die aesthetische Erziehung des Menschen*, Letter 11, NA XX, 343. Cf. Kaiser, "Vergötterung und Tod: Die thematische Einheit von Schillers Werk," in *Von Arkadien nach Elysium: Schiller-Studien* (Göttingen: Vandenhoeck und Ruprecht, 1978)," pp. 16–17; idem, "Wallensteins Lager," p. 345; idem, "Von Arkadien nach Elysium. Eine Rezension," in *Von Arkadien nach Elysium*, p. 209.

27. *Über das Pathetische*, NA XX, 218; NA XXI, 260–63, 268–70. Cf. Binder, "Aesthetik," p. 218.

28. Sautermeister, *Idyllik und Dramatik*, pp. 67–84, 174–76, 201–5; Kaiser, "Von Arkadien," p. 212; idem, "Wallensteins Lager," pp. 357–63.

29. Cf. NA XXI, 274–76; *Über die aesthetische Erziehung des Menschen*, Letter 15, NA XX, 359; NA XXI, 265; cf. Graham, *Schiller's Drama*, p. 126.

30. Cf. Kaiser, "Vergötterung," pp. 25–31, 35, 42–43, note 97.

31. NA XXI, 276; cf. Dieter Borchmeyer, *Tragödie und Öffentlichkeit: Schillers Dramaturgie im Zusammenhang seiner aesthetisch-politischen Theorie und die rhetorische Tradition* (München: Fink, 1973), pp. 139–40, 146–47, 249–50; Kaiser, "Von Arkadien," p. 209.

32. Seidlin, "Wallenstein," pp. 238–42.

33. Keller, "Drama und Geschichte," pp. 331–33; cf. Graham, "Struktur," p. 352: "Ich glaube, daß die Auffassung, eine Idee sei der eigentliche Held der Schillerschen Dramen, eine unanfechtbare Wahrheit enthält. Nur ist es nicht die Idee des Übersinnlichen, vielmehr ist es die Idee eines erneuerten aesthetischen, in Wahrheit organischen Menschentums, die als unsichtbarer tragischer Held durch Schillers Dichtung wandelt; ein Held, der immer wieder beschworen und von Zeit zu Zeit aus der Ferne gesichtet wird, der am Ende aber doch nicht in die Wirklichkeit gebannt zu werden vermag."

34. Cf. Kaiser, "Die Idee der Idylle in der 'Braut von Messina'," in *Von Arkadien nach Elysium*, pp. 164–66; Graham, *Schiller's Drama*, pp. 257–62.

35. Consider, on the other hand, the last line of Schiller's *Die Jungfrau von Orléans*, NA IX, 315: "Kurz ist der Schmerz und ewig ist die Freude!" Cf. letter to Goethe, Aug. 17, 1797. For Schiller's understanding of "Form" and "Stoff," see Wilkinson and Willoughby, eds., *On the Aesthetic Education of Man*, pp. 308–10, 317–20.

IX. "I Am and Remain Merely a Poet"

1. Humboldt, "Über Schiller," p. 360, 392; letter to Schiller, Sept. 1800.
2. To Körner, Feb. 12, 1788.
3. Johann Peter Eckermann, *Gespräche mit Goethe*, July 23, 1827; cf. Wolfgang Paulsen, "Goethes Kritik am Wallenstein, Zum Problem des Geschichtsdramas in der deutschen Klassik," *Deutsche Vierteljahresschrift für Literaturwissenschaft und Geistesgeschichte*, 28 (1954), 61–83.
4. To Goethe, Aug. 31, 1794; cf. to Herzog Friedrich Christian von Augustenburg, July 13, 1793: "Meine Philosophie wird ihren Ursprung nicht verleugnen, und, wenn sie je verunglücken sollte, eher in den Untiefen und in den Strudeln der poetisierenden Einbildungskraft untersinken, als an den kahlen Sandbänken trockener Abstraktion scheitern."
5. To Körner, Sept. 4, 1794.
6. Cf. to Goethe, Dec. 17, 1795: ". . . es ist hohe Zeit, daß ich für eine Weile die philosophische Bude schließe. Das Herz schmachtet nach einem betastlichen Objekt."
7. To Goethe, Oct. 16, 1795. Earlier letters to Körner reflect this concern of Schiller's as well—e.g., the letter dated May 25, 1792; and the one dated Feb. 25, 1789: "Aber ich habe mir eigentlich ein eigenes Drama nach meinen Talenten gebildet, welches mir eine gewisse Exzellence darin gibt, eben weil es mein eigen ist. Will ich in das natürliche Drama einlenken, so fühl ich die Superiorität, die er [Goethe] und viele andere Dichter aus der vorigen Zeit über mich haben, sehr lebhaft."
8. To August Wilhelm Schlegel, Jan. 9, 1796. I cannot agree with Gerhard Storz's arbitrary disqualification of this passage (*Dichter*, p. 226, note 75).
9. To Körner, Nov. 28, 1796.
10. Humboldt, "Über Schiller," p. 360.
11. To Körner, March 24, 1800.
12. To Körner, Jan. 8, 1798; cf. Körner to Schiller, Jan. 16, 1800: "Gäbe es für uns noch Feste der Kunst, wie bei den Griechen, so ließe sich denken, daß alle drei Teile des Wallenstein an *einem* Tage aufgeführt würden. Die Totalwirkung in einem solchen Falle kann derjenige ahnen, der sich das Privatfest gemacht hat, das ganze Werk ohne Unterbrechung von Anfang bis Ende durchzulesen. Aber ein solcher Genuß wird selbst dem echten Freunde der Kunst jetzt selten zuteil, und es fragt sich also zuvörderst, ob Dein Gemälde *für unsere Zimmer* nicht zu groß ist."
13. Humboldt, "Über Schiller," pp. 385–86, 392: ". . . im höheren Sinne Natur." Cf. Schiller to Körner, May 25, 1792: "Bin ich aber erst soweit, daß mir *Kunstmäßigkeit* zur *Natur* wird. . . ."
14. To Körner, Feb. 27, 1792; cf. to Goethe, Jan. 7, 1795: "Soviel ist indes gewiß, der Dichter ist der einzige wahre *Mensch*, und der beste Philosoph ist nur eine Karikatur gegen ihn."
15. To Charlotte von Schimmelmann, Nov. 4, 1795; cf. Wiese, "Das Problem der aesthetischen Versöhnung," p. 171: "Das wahrhaft Wirkliche, das zugleich das Vernünftige und damit das Wahre ist, findet im poetischen

Kunstwerk als einem unendlichen Organismus, der zu keinem anderen Lebensgebiet in einem Verhältnis der Abhängigkeit steht, seine ihm durchaus entsprechende sinnlich-geistige Gestalt. Die Form der Entsprechung ist die der Analogie."

Bibliography

Included are works of secondary literature relating to Schiller.

Berghahn, Klaus L. " 'Das Pathetischerhabene': Schillers Dramentheorie." In *Schiller: Zur Theorie und Praxis der Dramen*. Ed. Klaus L. Berghahn and Reinhold Grimm. WdF, 323. Darmstadt: Wissenschaftliche Buchgesellschaft, 1972, pp. 485–522.

————. " 'Doch eine Sprache braucht das Herz': Beobachtungen zu den Liebesdialogen in Schillers 'Wallenstein'." In *Schillers Wallenstein*. Ed. Fritz Heuer and Werner Keller. WdF, 420. Darmstadt: Wissenschaftliche Buchgesellschaft, 1977, pp. 386–95.

Binder, Wolfgang. "Die Begriffe 'Naiv' und 'Sentimentalisch' und Schillers Drama." *JDSG*, 4 (1960), 140–57.

————. "Aesthetik und Dichtung in Schillers Werk." In *Schiller: Zur Theorie und Praxis der Dramen*. Ed. Klaus L. Berghahn and Reinhold Grimm. WdF, 323. Darmstadt: Wissenschaftliche Buchgesellschaft, 1972, pp. 206–32.

Böckmann, Paul. "Gedanke, Wort und Tat in Schillers Dramen." In *Schiller: Zur Theorie und Praxis der Dramen*. Ed. Klaus L. Berghahn and Reinhold Grimm. WdF, 323. Darmstadt: Wissenschaftliche Buchgesellschaft, 1972, pp. 274–324.

Borchmeyer, Dieter. "Hektors Abschied: Schillers Aneignung einer homerischen Szene." *JDSG*, 16 (1972), 277–98.

————. *Tragödie und Öffentlichkeit: Schillers Dramaturgie im Zusammenhang seiner aesthetisch-politischen Theorie und die rhetorische Tradition*. München: Fink, 1973.

Buchwald, Reinhard. *Schiller: Leben und Werk*. 3rd ed. Wiesbaden: Insel, 1959.

Burschell, Friedrich. *Friedrich Schiller: In Selbstzeugnissen und Bilddokumenten*. Hamburg: Rowohlt, 1976.

Butler, Eliza Marian. *The Tyranny of Greece over Germany*. Boston: Beacon, 1958.

Diwald, Hellmut. *Friedrich Schiller, Wallenstein: Geschichte und Legende*. Frankfurt am Main: Ullstein, 1972.

Düsing, Wolfgang. "Aesthetische Form als Darstellung der Subjektivität." In *Friedrich Schiller: Zur Geschichtlichkeit seines Werkes*. Ed. Klaus L. Berghahn. Monographien Literaturwissenschaft, 21. Kronberg: Scriptor, 1975.

Gerhard, Melitta. *Schiller und die griechische Tragödie*. Weimar: Duncker, 1919.

Graham, Ilse. "Die Struktur der Persönlichkeit in Schillers dramatischer Dichtung." In *Schiller: Zur Theorie und Praxis der Dramen*. Ed. Klaus L.

Berghahn and Reinhold Grimm. WdF, 323. Darmstadt: Wissenschaftliche Buchgesellschaft, 1972, pp. 325–67.

_____. *Schiller: Ein Meister der tragischen Form: Die Theorie in der Praxis.* Darmstadt: Wissenschaftliche Buchgesellschaft, 1974. (Original English version: *Schiller, A Master of the Tragic Form: His Theory in His Practice.* Pittsburgh: Duquesne, 1973.)

_____. *Schiller's Drama: Talent and Integrity.* London: Methuen, 1974.

Haupt, Johannes. "Geschichtsperspektive und Griechenverständnis im aesthetischen Programm Schillers." *JDSG,* 18 (1974), 407–30.

Hettner, Hermann. "Schillers Wallenstein." In *Schillers Wallenstein.* Ed. Fritz Heuer and Werner Keller. WdF, 420. Darmstadt: Wissenschaftliche Buchgesellschaft, 1977, pp. 58–73.

Hinderer, Walter. *Der Mensch in der Geschichte: Ein Versuch über Schillers Wallenstein.* Königstein/Taunus: Athenäum, 1980.

Humboldt, Wilhelm von. "Über Schiller und den Gang seiner Geistesentwicklung." *Werke.* Ed. Andreas Flitner and Klaus Giel. Darmstadt: Wissenschaftliche Buchgesellschaft, 1969, II, pp. 357–94.

Jantz, Harold. "William Tell and the American Revolution." In *A Schiller Symposium.* Ed. A. Leslie Willson. Austin: University of Texas, Department of Germanic Languages, 1960, pp. 65–81.

_____. "Kontrafaktur, Montage, Parodie: Tradition und symbolische Erweiterung." In *Tradition und Ursprünglichkeit,* Akten des III. Internationalen Germanistenkongresses 1965 in Amsterdam. Ed. Werner Kohlschmitt and Herman Meyer. Bern/München: Francke, 1966, pp. 53–65.

Jauss, Hans Robert. "Fr. Schlegels und Fr. Schillers Replik auf die 'Querelle des anciens et des modernes'." In *Europäische Aufklärung.* Ed. Hugo Friedrich and Fritz Schalk. München: Fink, 1967, pp. 117–40.

Jolles, O. J. Matthijs. "Die Sprache des 'Spiels' und 'Antispiels' in den frühen Dramen Schillers." *Modern Philology,* 58 (1961), 246–54.

_____. "Das Bild des Weges und die Sprache des Herzens: Zur strukturellen Funktion der sprachlichen Bilder in Schillers *Wallenstein.*" *Deutsche Beiträge zur geistigen Überlieferung,* 5 (1965), 109–42.

Kaiser, Gerhard. "Wallensteins Lager: Schiller als Dichter und Theoretiker der Komödie." In *Schillers Wallenstein.* Ed. Fritz Heuer and Werner Keller. WdF, 420. Darmstadt: Wissenschaftliche Buchgesellschaft, 1977, pp. 333–63.

_____. *Wanderer und Idylle: Goethe und die Phänomenologie der Natur in der deutschen Dichtung von Geßner bis Gottfried Keller.* Göttingen: Vandenhoeck und Ruprecht, 1977, ch. III, "Schiller und Goethe," pp. 82–106.

_____. *Von Arkadien nach Elysium: Schiller-Studien.* Göttingen: Vandenhoeck und Ruprecht, 1978.

Keller, Werner. "Drama und Geschichte." In *Beiträge zur Poetik des Dramas.* Ed. Werner Keller. Darmstadt: Wissenschaftliche Buchgesellschaft, 1976, pp. 298–339.

Kommerell, Max. "Schiller als Gestalter des handelnden Menschen." In

Geist und Buchstabe der Dichtung. Frankfurt am Main: Klostermann, 1962, pp. 132–74.

Koopmann, Helmut. "Schiller und die Komödie." *JDSG*, 13 (1969), 272–85.

————. "Schillers *Wallenstein*: Antiker Mythos und moderne Geschichte: Zur Begründung der klassischen Tragödie um 1800." In *Teilnahme und Spiegelung: Festschrift für Horst Rüdiger*. Ed. Beda Allemann and Erwin Koppen. Berlin/New York: de Gruyter, 1975, pp. 263–74.

————. "Joseph und sein Vater: Zu den biblischen Anspielungen in Schillers *Räubern*." In *Herkommen und Erneuerung: Essays für Oskar Seidlin*. Ed. Gerald Gillespie and Edgar Lohner. Tübingen: Niemeyer, 1976, pp. 150–67.

————. *Friedrich Schiller*. 2nd ed. Stuttgart: Metzler, 1977.

————. "Dantons Tod und die antike Welt: Zur Geschichtsphilosophie Georg Büchners." In *Geschichtsdrama*. Ed. Elfriede Neubuhr. WdF, 485. Darmstadt: Wissenschaftliche Buchgesellschaft, 1980, pp. 233–55.

Kühnemann, Eugen. *Die Kantischen Studien Schillers und die Komposition des Wallenstein*. Marburg: Ehrhardt's Universitätsbuchhandlung, 1889.

————. *Schiller*. 2nd ed. München: Beck, 1914.

Lange, Barbara. *Die Sprache von Schillers "Wallenstein"*. Quellen und Forschungen zur Sprach- und Kulturgeschichte der germanischen Völker. Berlin/New York: de Gruyter, 1973.

Leitzmann, Albert. *Die Hauptquellen zu Schillers Wallenstein*. Halle an der Saale: Niemeyer, 1915.

Ludwig, Otto. "Schillers Wallenstein." In *Schillers Wallenstein*. Ed. Fritz Heuer and Werner Keller. WdF, 420. Darmstadt: Wissenschaftliche Buchgesellschaft, 1977, pp. 47–52.

Mann, Golo. *Wallenstein: Sein Leben erzählt*. Frankfurt am Main: Fischer, 1974.

Mann, Thomas. *Versuch über Schiller*. Frankfurt am Main: Fischer, 1955.

Martini, Fritz. "Schillers Abschiedsszenen." In *Über Literatur und Geschichte: Festschrift für Gerhard Storz*. Ed. Bernd Hüppauf and Dolf Sternberger. Frankfurt am Main: Athenäum, 1973, pp. 151–84.

May, Kurt. *Friedrich Schiller: Idee und Wirklichkeit im Drama*. Göttingen: Vandenhoeck und Ruprecht, 1948.

————. "Schillers Wallenstein." In *Form und Bedeutung: Interpretationen deutscher Dichtung des 18. und 19. Jahrhunderts*. Stuttgart: Klett, 1957, pp. 178–242.

Meyer, Theodor. "Der Griechentraum Schillers und seine philosophische Begründung." *Jahrbuch des freien deutschen Hochstifts*, 27 (1928), 125–53.

Müller-Seidel, Walter. "Episches im Theater der deutschen Klassik: Eine Betrachtung über Schillers 'Wallenstein'." *JDSG*, 20 (1976), 338–86.

Neubauer, John. "Die Geschichtsauffassung in Schillers 'Wallenstein'." In *Geschichtsdrama*. Ed. Elfriede Neubuhr. WdF, 485. Darmstadt: Wissenschaftliche Buchgesellschaft, 1980, pp. 171–88.

Paulsen, Wolfgang. "Goethes Kritik am Wallenstein: Zum Problem des Geschichtsdramas in der deutschen Klassik." *Deutsche Vierteljahresschrift für Literaturwissenschaft und Geistesgeschichte*, 28 (1954), 61–83.

Petersen, Julius. *Schillers Gespräche*. Leipzig: Insel, 1911.

Prader, Florian. *Schiller und Sophokles*. Zürcher Beiträge zur deutschen Literatur- und Geistesgeschichte, 7. Zürich: Atlantis, 1954.

Ranke, Leopold von. *Geschichte Wallensteins*. Düsseldorf: Droste, 1967.

Rehder, Helmut. "The Four Seals of Schiller." In *A Schiller Symposium*. Ed. A. Leslie Willson. Austin: University of Texas, Department of Germanic Languages, 1960, pp. 11–27.

Rehm, Walter. *Griechentum und Goethezeit*. 4th ed. Leipzig: Dietrich, 1938; rpt. Bern/München: Francke, 1968.

Reinhardt, Hartmut. "Schillers Wallenstein und Aristoteles." *JDSG*, 20 (1976), 278–337.

Rothmann, Kurt. *Friedrich Schiller, Wallenstein: Erläuterungen und Dokumente*. Stuttgart: Reclam, 1977.

Rudolph, Ludwig, and Goldbeck, Karl. *Schiller-Lexikon: Erläuterndes Wörterbuch zu Schillers Dichterwerken*. Berlin: Nicolai, 1869.

Sautermeister, Gert. *Idyllik und Dramatik im Werk Friedrich Schillers: Zum geschichtlichen Ort seiner klassischen Dramen*. Studien zur Poetik und Geschichte der Literatur, 17. Stuttgart: Kohlhammer, 1971.

Schadewaldt, Wolfgang. "Goethe und Homer." *Trivium*, 7 (1949), 200–232.

⸺. "Der Weg Schillers zu den Griechen." *JDSG*, 4 (1960), 90–97.

⸺. "Antikes und Modernes in Schillers 'Braut von Messina'." *JDSG*, 13 (1969), 286–307.

Schatz, Rudolf. *Schiller und die Mythologie*. Diss., Zürich, 1955.

Schwerte, Hans. "Simultaneität und Differenz des Wortes in Schillers 'Wallenstein'." In *Schillers Wallenstein*. Ed. Fritz Heuer and Werner Keller. WdF, 420. Darmstadt: Wissenschaftliche Buchgesellschaft, 1977, 274–89.

Seidlin, Oskar. "Schiller: Poet of Politics." In *A Schiller Symposium*. Ed. A. Leslie Willson. Austin: University of Texas, Department of Germanic Languages, 1960, pp. 31–48.

⸺. "Wallenstein: Sein und Zeit." In *Schillers Wallenstein*. Ed. Fritz Heuer and Werner Keller. WdF, 420. Darmstadt: Wissenschaftliche Buchgesellschaft, 1977, 237–53.

Silz, Walter. "Chorus and Choral Function in Schiller." In *Schiller 1759/1959: Commemorative American Studies*. Ed. John R. Frey. Urbana: University of Illinois Press, 1959, pp. 147–70.

⸺. "Charakter und Funktion von Buttler in Schillers 'Wallenstein'." In *Schillers Wallenstein*. Ed. Fritz Heuer and Werner Keller. WdF, 420. Darmstadt: Wissenschaftliche Buchgesellschaft, 1977, pp. 254–73.

Singer, Herbert. "Dem *Fürsten* Piccolomini." In *Schillers Wallenstein*. Ed. Fritz Heuer and Werner Keller. WdF, 420. Darmstadt: Wissenschaftliche Buchgesellschaft, 1977, pp. 180–212.

Staiger, Emil. "Dialektik der Begriffe Nachahmung und Originalität." In *Tradition und Ursprünglichkeit*, Akten des III. Internationalen Germanistenkongresses 1965 in Amsterdam. Ed. Werner Kohlschmitt and Herman Meyer. Bern/München: Francke, 1966, pp. 29–38.

⸺. *Friedrich Schiller*. Zürich: Atlantis, 1967.

Storz, Gerhard. *Das Drama Friedrich Schillers*. Frankfurt am Main: Societäts Verlag, 1938.

————. "Die Bauform der Wallensteintrilogie." *Zeitschrift für deutsche Bildung*, 16 (1940), 17–25.

————. *Der Dichter Friedrich Schiller*. Stuttgart: Klett, 1959.

————. "Schiller und die Antike." *JDSG*, 10 (1966), 189–204.

————. *Klassik und Romantik*. Mannheim: Bibliographisches Institut, 1972.

————. "Zur Gestalt von Schillers 'Wallenstein'." In *Schillers Wallenstein*. Ed. Fritz Heuer and Werner Keller. WdF, 420. Darmstadt: Wissenschaftliche Buchgesellschaft, 1977, pp. 157–79.

Süvern, Wilhelm. *Über Schillers Wallenstein in Hinsicht auf griechische Tragödie*. Berlin: Buchhandlung der Königlichen Realschule, 1800.

Szondi, Peter. "Das Naive ist das Sentimentalische: Zur Begriffsdialektik in Schillers Abhandlung." *Euphorion*, 66 (1972), 174–206.

————. "Antike und Moderne in der Aesthetik der Goethezeit." In *Poetik und Geschichtsphilosophie I*. 3rd ed. 1974; rpt. Frankfurt am Main: Suhrkamp, 1980, pp. 11–265.

Wallenstein, Paul Robert. *Die dichterische Gestaltung der historischen Persönlichkeit, gezeigt an der Wallensteinfigur*. Würzburg: Triltsch, 1934.

Wentzlaff-Eggebert, Friedrich Wilhelm. "Schiller und die Antike." In *Schiller: Reden im Gedenkjahr*. Stuttgart: Klett, 1955, pp. 317–33.

————. "Die poetische Wahrheit in Schillers 'Wallenstein'." In *Germanistik in Forschung und Lehre*. Berlin: Schmidt, 1965, pp. 135–42.

Wiese, Benno von. "Das Problem der aesthetischen Versöhnung bei Schiller und Hegel." *JDSG*, 9 (1965), 167–88.

————. *Die deutsche Tragödie von Lessing bis Hebbel*. 8th ed. Hamburg: Hoffmann und Campe, 1973.

————. "Geschichte und Drama." In *Geschichtsdrama*. Ed. Elfriede Neubuhr. WdF, 485. Darmstadt: Wissenschaftliche Buchgesellschaft, 1980, pp. 381–403.

Wilkinson, Elizabeth M., and Willoughby, L. A., eds. *Friedrich Schiller: On the Aesthetic Education of Man*. Oxford: Clarendon, 1967.

Wilpert, Gero von. *Schiller-Chronik: Sein Leben und Schaffen*. Stuttgart: Kröner, 1958.

Wittkowski, Wolfgang. "Octavio Piccolomini: Zur Schaffensweise des 'Wallenstein'-Dichters." In *Schiller: Zur Theorie und Praxis der Dramen*. Ed. Klaus L. Berghahn and Reinhold Grimm. WdF, 323. Darmstadt: Wissenschaftliche Buchgesellschaft, 1972. pp. 407–65.

Wolzogen, Caroline von. *Schillers Leben*. Stuttgart/Tübingen: Cotta, 1851.

Index

University of North Carolina
Studies in the Germanic Languages
and Literatures

45 PHILLIP H. RHEIN. *The Urge to Live. A Comparative Study of Franz Kafka's "Der Prozeß" and Albert Camus' "L'Etranger."* 2nd printing. 1966. Pp. xii, 124.

50 RANDOLPH J. KLAWITER. *Stefan Zweig. A Bibliography.* 1965. Pp. xxxviii, 191.

52 MARIANA SCOTT. *The Heliand. Translated from the Old Saxon.* 1966. Pp. x, 206.

56 RICHARD H. ALLEN. *An Annotated Arthur Schnitzler Bibliography.* 1966. Pp. xiv, 151.

58 WALTER W. ARNDT ET AL., EDS. *Studies in Historical Linguistics in Honor of George S. Lane.* 1967. Pp. xx, 241.

60 J. W. THOMAS. *Medieval German Lyric Verse.* In English Translation. 1968. Pp. x, 252.

67 SIEGFRIED MEWS, ED. *Studies in German Literature of the Nineteenth and Twentieth Centuries. Festschrift for Frederic E. Coenen.* 1970. 2nd ed. 1972. Pp. xx, 251.

68 JOHN NEUBAUER. *Bifocal Vision. Novalis' Philosophy of Nature and Disease.* 1971. Pp. x, 196.

70 DONALD F. NELSON. *Portrait of the Artist as Hermes. A Study of Myth and Psychology in Thomas Mann's "Felix Krull."* 1971. Pp. xii, 146.

72 CHRISTINE OERTEL SJÖGREN. *The Marble Statue as Idea: Collected Essays on Adalbert Stifter's "Der Nachsommer."* 1972. Pp. xiv, 121.

73 DONALD G. DAVIAU AND JORUN B. JOHNS, EDS. *The Correspondence of Arthur Schnitzler and Raoul Auernheimer, with Raoul Auernheimer's Aphorisms.* 1972. Pp. xii, 161.

74 A. MARGARET ARENT MADELUNG. *"The Laxdoela Saga": Its Structural Patterns.* 1972. Pp. xiv, 261.

75 JEFFREY L. SAMMONS. *Six Essays on the Young German Novel.* 2nd ed. 1975. Pp. xiv, 187.

76 DONALD H. CROSBY AND GEORGE C. SCHOOLFIELD, EDS. *Studies in the German Drama. A Festschrift in Honor of Walter Silz.* 1974. Pp. xxvi, 255.

77 J. W. THOMAS. *Tannhäuser: Poet and Legend.* With Texts and Translation of His Works. 1974. Pp. x, 202.

78 OLGA MARX AND ERNST MORWITZ, TRANS. *The Works of Stefan George.* 2nd, rev. and enl. ed. 1974. Pp. xxviii, 431.

79 SIEGFRIED MEWS AND HERBERT KNUST, EDS. *Essays on Brecht: Theater and Politics.* 1974. Pp. xiv, 241.

80 DONALD G. DAVIAU AND GEORGE J. BUELOW. *The "Ariadne auf Naxos" of Hugo von Hofmannsthal and Richard Strauß.* 1975. Pp. x, 274.

81 ELAINE E. BONEY. *Rainer Maria Rilke: "Duinesian Elegies."* German Text with English Translation and Commentary. 2nd ed. 1977. Pp. xii, 153.

82 JANE K. BROWN. *Goethe's Cyclical Narratives: "Die Unterhaltungen deutscher Ausgewanderten" and "Wilhelm Meisters Wanderjahre."* 1975. Pp. x, 144.

83 FLORA KIMMICH. *Sonnets of Catharina von Greiffenberg: Methods of Composition.* 1975. Pp. x, 132.

84 HERBERT W. REICHERT. *Friedrich Nietzsche's Impact on Modern German Literature.* 1975. Pp. xxii, 129.

85 JAMES C. O'FLAHERTY, TIMOTHY F. SELLNER, ROBERT M. HELMS, EDS. *Studies in Nietzsche and the Classical Tradition.* 2nd ed. 1979. Pp. xviii, 278.

86 ALAN P. COTTRELL. *Goethe's "Faust." Seven Essays.* 1976. Pp. xvi, 143.

87 HUGO BEKKER. *Friedrich von Hausen: Inquiries into His Poetry.* 1977. Pp. x, 159.

88 H. G. HUETTICH. *Theater in the Planned Society: Contemporary Drama in the German Democratic Republic in Its Historical, Political, and Cultural Context.* 1978. Pp. xvi, 174.

89 DONALD G. DAVIAU, ED. *The Letters of Arthur Schnitzler to Hermann Bahr.* 1978. Pp. xii, 183.

For other volumes in the "Studies" see preceding page and p. ii.

Send orders to:
The University of North Carolina Press, P.O. Box 2288
Chapel Hill, N.C. 27514

Volumes 1–44 and 46–49 of the "Studies" have been reprinted.
They may be ordered from:
AMS Press, Inc., 56 E. 13th Street, New York, N.Y. 10003
For a complete list of reprinted titles write to:
Editor, UNCSGL&L, 441 Dey Hall 014A, UNC, Chapel Hill, N.C. 27514